The Weed, the Corn Flakes
&
The Coincidences

Bob Bennett

Clink
Street

Published by Clink Street Publishing 2023

Copyright © 2023

First edition.

The author asserts the moral right under the Copyright, Designs and Patents Act 1988 to be identified as the author of this work.

ISBN: 978-1-915785-13-8 Paperback
ISBN: 978-1-915785-14-5 Ebook

This is a novel. Any errors of fact, geography, procedures or protocols and anachronistic detail are purely the fault of the author. Some of the places and locations are real but the characters are imaginary personations. Any resemblance or similarity to actual persons living or dead is purely coincidental and my grateful thanks to those whose names I've borrowed.

Also by Bob Bennett

Easier Than it Seems
Retribution
The Gun in the Golf Bag

To Dudley
with best wishes

'The long arm of coincidence'

Chapter 1 **Friday**

England, a country synonymous with stability and predictability, had descended into chaos resulting from the National Union of Miners' industrial action which had gathered momentum and developed into one of the biggest collective strikes there had ever been. The resulting political and economic carnage was affecting millions of people. Did Prime Minister Heath grasp the seriousness of the situation?

Not 100 miles to the east in the Netherlands, the European Coal and Steel Community, founded by the Benelux countries, West Germany, France and Italy, pooled coal resources to support the economies of the member countries. Not only that, the ECSC helped to diffuse any residual tensions between countries that had been fighting each other during WWII. The benefits of the economic mergers grew, other members were added and the scope was broadened. He might have done precious little else but even Prime Minister Macmillan had recognised the advantages of the rapid economic advances and was keen to join.

Detective Chief Inspector Cartwright had always had an interest in European history. He'd lived through the war as a small boy. He'd witnessed death and destruction and now after 30 years he was beginning to understand and envy the manner in which Europe and the Dutch in particular had rebuilt themselves and continued to do so. Especially fascinating was the masterstroke in which the Netherlands had managed to annex German territory from the defeated nation and then sell it back to them to help fund the rebuilding of the country they had destroyed. Then there was the establishment of the Welfare State, international integration and cooperation, the formation of Benelux, NATO, ECSC and the European Economic Community. At least Heath had taken the country into the EEC after De Gaul had thwarted the Wilson government's attempts.

'Small consolation. Doubtful! Here we are,' Cartwright thought, 'not even halfway through the decade and Heath's government is now fudging and muddling its way through a slanging match with the trade unions whilst privateering pirates are smuggling contraband, drugs and even immigrants into the country expecting simple coppers like me to deal with them.' And then voicing his thoughts out loud in a spleen-venting sort of way to no one in particular, given that he was one of the last people on the floor anyway, 'Why don't you bugger off on your yacht, Heath? You'll have more success running cheap booze and fags across the bloody channel than you're having running the country.' He continued ranting to himself, 'Your government hasn't got a bloody clue. It takes more than a stiff upper lip. All you've managed so far is to demonstrate how not to deal with anything. You're not the man with what it takes to rise to the political and economic challenges the country's facing. You're not the man with what it takes to deal with the smuggling and people trafficking crises. At least you've had the sense to call a general election. Gawd help us! It's desperate and desperate situations call for desperate measures.' Amused by his inadvertent repetition he poured a desperate measure into his whisky glass. Desperate because it emptied the bottle.

It was Friday afternoon. DCI Cartwright sat at his desk

looking at the now empty Laphroaig bottle. Since the introduction of the three-day week and regular power cuts police work had become more difficult than normal exacerbated by the shortage of uniformed officers. At least, unlike many of the uniformed ranks, CID had been spared the temporary detachment to the coal fields of South Yorkshire where police forces from all over were mobilised in the ongoing pitched battles with striking and picketing miners. Compounding his gloom was the latest thorn in his backside delivered in the form of a memorandum from the chief constable detailing the proposals for a training course with Customs and Excise to better prepare police forces especially in coastal counties to wage war on the increase in smuggling. He studied the empty single malt bottle in an introspective manner and reflected on the fact that this very bottle was more than likely acquired illegally. And what of the state of the nation as a whole and how, or was that if, or even where, he fitted in? Was it down to him to put the world right? 'Bugger!' he exclaimed at the top of his voice.

'Did you call me, boss? What's up?' It was Doug Armstrong who had responded to the DCI's outburst and stuck his head around the door. 'C'mon, it's Friday – pub time!' he announced with a flourish. Clearly the DS hadn't picked up on the subliminal *stay away* signals that Cartwright was radiating.

'I'll get 'em in – see you there – say ten minutes?' And Armstrong was gone before Cartwright could utter 'not tonight'. The CID room was now deserted. It had long been a Friday night tradition. Officers from police headquarters in Kesgrave got together to socialise. *The Maybush* down by the River Deben was only a few minutes' drive away.

'C'mon, Cartwright' he told himself. 'Life's too short to waste it on something as destructive as anger and self-pity. Sitting here moping and getting annoyed about situations beyond my control will get me nowhere – besides which, the bottle's empty!' He tidied his desk and made a quick call to Helen, his wife. He hadn't been married for more than a few months, but Helen had already become accustomed to both the irregularity and the routines of a policeman's lot. Coming home on a Friday slightly the worse for wear through drink was par for the course. He gathered up his coat and briefcase and, doing his bit to save electricity, turned out the lights and made his way to the car park. He took an unmarked Austin Vanden Plas from the car-pool.

When he got to the pub, it was in semi-darkness and illuminated only by the flickering light being given off by the candles strategically placed around the bar. The power was off again.

'Got you a pint of Adnams, boss.'

'Thanks, Doug. I need it. I don't know why but this blasted three-day week is getting me down. Damn petty crime, burglaries, thieving and the like. I know folks are on short wages but that doesn't give 'em licence to go nicking stuff. I'm getting sick and tired of having to make excuses to the gentrified population of the county as well. It's hardly our fault we can't trace their precious antiques after they've been nicked. We just haven't got the manpower. We had a call from The Old Rectory in Tostock again this week. Some fancy sideboard and its contents had gone walkabout. I always supposed that after I transferred from Thames to the glorious Suffolk countryside my life would be a little easier. Not a bit of it! I never thought for one minute that I'd be dealing with organised crime. Then there's this bloody training course we've got to fit in. I didn't join the force to go chasing folks bringing in a bit more than their duty-free allowance. Give me some proper policing to do; life was simpler solving a murder. Give me some real blaggers any time!' Doug laughed, hoping his boss was joking.

According to the government the short-time working had been introduced as a direct result of the striking miners in order to save electricity, the shortage of which was caused by coal-starved power stations. The resulting energy crisis had led to the declaration of a state of emergency. In turn, this had decimated the labour market, shattered the economy and was ruining lives and livelihoods. The lights were going out all over the country. People were pondering when there might be a return to normal after the anxiety and uncertainty of recent months. But what would the *new normal* be? The shape of politics could change but did the government have an escape route mapped out to eventually deliver the country out of recession? Too many rhetorical questions. However, neither Cartwright nor Armstrong were particularly preoccupied with predicting the future. They hadn't been prepared for the petty crime wave and the additional legwork and door-knocking they were currently lumbered with. Was this the shape of what was to come?

The rise of the drug trade was a global phenomenon, and the UK was a big part of it. Even in Holland, and possibly to an even greater extent, it was a time of widespread social and cultural change. The old divisions of class and religion were being eroded. Teenage rebellion, informality, sexual freedom, informal clothes, strange new hairstyles, protest music, drugs – especially cannabis – and idealism were all part of a new liberalism. Traditional values were giving way to women's rights, sexuality, disarmament, and environmental issues. With groups like The Beatles and other pop stars openly talking about their cannabis experiences the appeal to youth culture was enhanced and the euphoria of getting stoned was an excuse for many to escape the reality of the mess the country was in. And with more immigration from the Caribbean and other places where the stuff was grown it was inevitable that the cannabis supply would always be sufficient to meet the increase in demand. Ten years previously when Customs and Excise officers discovered cannabis being brought into the country through the ports it was merely confiscated and thrown away – very often into whichever harbour the ship had arrived at. Importation through airports was much less common. But after the recent seizure of an enormous haul at Heathrow Airport, the authorities had begun to realise that drug smuggling wasn't just within the province of hippies and their *bit of weed*, it was big business organised by syndicates of organised crime networks across continents.

With the majority of shipments arriving by sea to ports across the entire country, those on the east coast were proving to be particularly popular with smuggling gangs since Amsterdam seemed to have become a hub where most European deals were being brokered. From the Dutch capital, scheduled ferry services and freight-carrying ships carried consignments to English ports: Dover, Ramsgate, Harwich, Felixstowe and Hull being some of the closest. Corruption amongst importers and exporters of otherwise legitimate cargoes, shipping company agents and seamen, dock workers, and even Customs officials and the police was rife, but the authorities were beginning to wise up and clamp down. The drug barons were therefore outsourcing, doing deals with local contractors: the owners of small ships and even yachts which could enter any number of the rivers and secondary harbours on the North Sea coast and remain largely undetected and therefore unchallenged.

***

Pieter Hendriks, a single man, never married, lived in a seventeenth century building which occupied the whole corner plot on *Keisersgracht* and *Reguliersgracht*, a beautiful location in Amsterdam with amazing views of the canals but yet only a few minutes' walk from all the central attractions of such a wonderful city. For all that the house had four floors, there were only two bedrooms, but four bathrooms. Hendriks was a highly qualified and skilled lapidary and a recognised expert in the art of precision with a rare ability to detect quality. Right from the early days when he was studying in Paris he was passionate about the craft and remained so even now in his retirement. Cutting, polishing and dealing in diamonds had made him a fortune, able to afford pretty much anything he wanted, and what he wanted more than anything in his retirement was excitement and antiques. He still dabbled in diamonds, but furniture had become an all-consuming passion.

Just around the corner on *Nieuwe Spiegelstraat* was *Binenbaum Antiques and Jewellery*. Hendriks was a regular patron. It was through the proprietor, Jan de Klerk, that Pieter had been introduced to Francis Forsyth who was in Amsterdam attempting to fence some precious stones that had fallen into his possession from a spurious source. Pieter, being a gregarious person, expressed his interest in English antiques and a connection was made. Frankie became a frequent visitor to Amsterdam after that, always with a few small pieces he could sell, more as an excuse for his visit than anything else. If truth be told it had been his discovery of the *De Wallen* neighbourhood, and *Kurfurstendamm* in particular which was the main attraction. It was in the *Red Light District* where he made the acquaintance of Chantal, a young lady with whom his carnal knowledge flourished. So much more exciting than Anna Cohen, a divorcee of his acquaintance. Chantal also initiated him in the psychoactive experience of marijuana, and the manner in which the sensualism of his time spent with her was enhanced. It was inevitable that he became hooked, both on Chantal and the weed.

Being something of an entrepreneur Francis could see how

a successful and profitable business could be established were he to import cannabis into the UK. He had a shrewd idea, based on his own experience, that an acquaintance known locally by his rhyming slang handle as *Berkshire* would be interested. Gerry Hunt, to give him his correct name, was aware of Frankie's Dutch connections and had previously requested details of how to make contact with working girls of the *Kurfurstendamm*. Always happy to oblige, if there was something in it for him, Frankie felt sure Berkshire would also want to be part of a weed business. Frankie's quest for a cannabis supplier led him to an address on *Keisersgracht* and a fellow known only as Jimmy. He was dumbfounded when Pieter Hendriks opened the door. Each was as surprised as the other, never expecting that they had common hobbies on the wrong side of the periphery of the underworld. The realisation only served to cement their friendship which became firm and lasting, and serving their mutual interests. It wasn't many months after that visit that Frankie had received a call from Pieter.

'I need to find an alternative means of import and export. I thought you might have some ideas or friends. Maybe you would like to be my agent in England, *misschien*?'

Frankie was highly tempted by Pieter's proposition but knew that it was a big deal, certainly out of his league so far, unless... he wondered. Maybe time to step up.

A day or so later, having been in touch with has associates, Frankie convened a meeting in a pub in Bethnal Green, in London's East End. A group of local *characters* were listening intently to Frankie's proposal and their enthusiasm was gaining momentum exponentially with every round of drinks. Frankie reluctantly outlined the manner in which he had built contacts in Amsterdam which were now well-established, reluctant as he didn't want others cashing in. His reputation for buying and selling preceded him and the meeting had absolutely no reason to doubt the voraciousness of the Dutchman's offer.

'What are we importing? People, jewellery, illegal drugs? Are you talking weed?' enquired the big ex-Navy bloke. 'I don't want anything to do with weed or drugs.'

'I'm sure you will when you 'ear my plan. I'll be perfectly frank with you gentlemen.'

'Well, you ain't earnest are you?' came an interruption.

'Kindly afford him the courtesy of allowing him to finish!' said the man called Gerry Hunt.

'My only reservation is in selling it on. That's why I've invited you blokes, knowing your wide circle of dodgy acquaintances. Seeing how I'd 'ave your varying degrees of notoriety to 'elp me, we'd 'ave a conspiracy which could result in a "nice little earner" for us all. What's more, if we can manage to successfully pull this initial deal off, there could be more opportunities in the future. Listen, mates, we can succeed where many others 'ave failed 'cos I knows a man who knows a man who owns a boat.' The boat factor was greeted with murmurings of approval. Frankie continued.

'I've 'ad many a sleepless night.'

'We know you 'ave an' we know who with.' This remark generated a few sniggers but it was Gerry Hunt who brought the meeting back to order again.

'Gentlemen please, decorum!'

'What's that then, decorum?' asked Matt, one of the local lads.

'It means order, order!'

'OK, I'll 'ave another pint in a minute when I've finished this one.'

Frankie continued once the laughter had died down, 'I've lain awake at night considering as many of the problems, let's say "difficulties" that such a big consignment would represent as I could think of, and to start with I thought "when in doubt, leave it out". Still, if you don't shoot you don't score an' with your 'elp I reckon we can get a 'at-trick. Now, who's up for it?' Everyone's hand went up. Gerry had a question.

'Francis, dear boy, I note your reservation, and might I make so bold as to suggest it would be prudent in the extreme to make contact with Mr Khan's organisation before we commit ourselves? After all, the last thing any of us would wish for is to encounter the wrath of Mr Khan.' There were nods of agreement and a general consensus that Berkshire had made a good suggestion.

***

Since the River Deben had recently been designated an area of outstanding natural beauty it had become increasingly popular with birdwatchers, walkers, and those in pursuit of many forms of waterborne leisure activities. There were many weekend sailors who chose to stay in the river between Woodbridge and the North Sea estuary at Felixstowe Ferry since the shingle banks at the mouth of the river were constantly on the move: the navigation over which was notorious for the not so intrepid voyager. But there were many sailors, sea-anglers and commercial fishermen who were familiar with the river entrance and for the few hours either side of high tide there would often be a variety of craft entering or leaving the river. What few navigation buoys there were were unlit and passage upriver at night was certainly not for the faint-hearted – which was not a description applicable to Liam O'Reilly, a wily old salt from the Irish port of Cobh. Liam was proud of his new boat, *The Michael Collins* which had only recently been recommissioned as a freight carrier after a major refit. Registered in the *Little Boat Harbour* of Skibbereen in West Cork the vessel of almost 60 feet long was renamed after the owner's hero, the revolutionary soldier and politician who became director of intelligence for the Irish Republican Army during the Irish war of independence in the early twentieth century. Liam O'Reilly had absolutely no qualms about his boat being privately chartered for the shipment of any manner of cargo and as a result of the miners' strike in Britain there was a huge demand for coal. This demand proved to be a splendid opportunity for O'Reilly, and in recent weeks he had been loading anthracite brought by lorry to Skibbereen from the Ballingary Mine in County Tipperary and running the comparatively short distance across the Irish Sea to Fishguard. The striking miners of the South Wales Coalfield didn't take too kindly to O'Reilly's enterprise which they considered to be strike breaking to the extent that, for his trouble, Liam received such a beating from a flying picket he required A&E treatment. During his recovery he thought it expedient to seek an alternative but hopefully equally lucrative cargo from and to somewhere else and back. So it was that *The Michael Collins* accepted the commission to deliver a cargo for the East End syndicate, some of the members of which he had met. Although he had his reservations initially, it didn't take too many drams of Jameson's before he agreed and set a course for the *Jan van Riebeeckhaven*, a dock in Amsterdam, to take on a cargo for delivery to a deserted spot on a river in Suffolk.

***

At first, she was certain of absolutely nothing apart from the terror she felt. The darkness compounded her fear. She was in a van. On the floor. Had she been drugged? What had happened? Oh no! Had she been...? She could hear voices but couldn't make out what was being said or even what language was being spoken. Where was she? Wherever it was, there was very little space, severely restricting any movement. She reached between her legs. Pain. Where were her panties? It was too dark to tell. All she could be sure of was that she was petrified and freezing cold. Where was her coat? Where was she now? She seemed to remember a boat. Was she on a boat? When was that? And then, above the sound of the pounding in her head, there came the noise of an engine, then another engine, people shouting, a rolling motion. Where had she heard these voices before? The sound and movement brought with them the realisation that she was in fact on a boat of some kind – a ship perhaps. She tried screaming. Had she made any sound? If so she hadn't heard it above the sound of the engines. She tried knocking on the walls of the enclosed space until her knuckles were sore. Why could no one hear? Was this really happening? Was it all some kind of nightmare? She tried again to think back over what had happened before waking up in this cold, dark place. And then there was nothing. She passed out.

Chapter 2 **Later on Friday**

Although it was his first time crossing the Deben bar, Liam hadn't encountered any difficulty in picking up the Woodbridge Haven Buoy and, in the moonlit February night, he could just make out the metes on the shore: the triangular marks a transit through which would keep *The Michael Collins* in the deeper water over the shingle. Once into the river the chart delineated the fairway. His instructions were to pass *The Ramsholt Arms* on his starboard side and make for the headlights on the opposite side where he would run onto the mud close enough to the bank to unload a part of his cargo. Sure enough, the headlights were there, confirmed by two flashes.

'There they are to be sure.' Liam gestured to his brother-in-law and crewmate, Fergal Flaherty. 'Make ready with a bowline and hold on tight when we take the mud. I don't want you going arse over tit!' Fergal made his way forward from the wheelhouse but almost immediately made his way back again, a concerned expression on his face.

'There are bloody lights all over the place, skip – it don't look right to me – look, over there, more activity than the craic in Kelly's on a Saturday night – look there they go again.' Liam throttled right back to tick-over and stuck his head out of the wheelhouse window. The decrescendo of the gentle rumble of the twin Lister ESSL8 800 horsepower engines faded to being barely audible. 'Quieter than an angel's fart' was the description applied by the engineer who had fitted them at the refit and, sure enough, over the whispering angel's bodily function, the racket from the distant field could be clearly heard.

'Well spotted, Fergal!' Liam said as he powered up again and turned to starboard to find the deep water in the fairway. 'No way we're stopping here, we'd be busted for sure! Have a look at the chart, Fergal. Accessible but remote's what we want, accessible but remote.' Fergal switched on the safe-light over the chart table and unrolled the East Coast Rivers chart. After a while he spoke, 'Here looks good – remote but accessible – Methersgate Quay. Middle of nowhere.' Liam took a quick look.

'OK, around the bend at Waldringfield and on the starboard side – yes,' he mused, 'that'll have to do then. We better let Mr McLevy know where we're going. He'll be anxious to get his merchandise and, more important, he's got the rest of our money.' Liam reached into the pocket of his oilskin trousers and fished out an envelope on which were scribbled several telephone numbers. 'I think it's this one.' He indicated the number opposite the code FBI. Fergal turned up the gain on the Sailor RT144 VHF marine band radio.

'Thames Coastguard, Thames Coastguard, this is *Ballingary, Ballingary*. Link call please.' Using his initiative Fergal had seen fit to use the boat's previous name in order to protect their anonymity. After a few seconds of white noise and crackle Thames responded.

'*Ballingary*, this is Thames. Pass your number.'

Fergal recited the number from the envelope and after a few seconds he heard the familiar tone of a telephone ringing and passed the handset to Liam. He then disappeared below again to maintain his watch over the cargo.

***

Sgt Andy Lewis and DC Ray Davies burst into the bar laughing and joking with John Randall. PC Randall was one of the few uniformed constables not dispatched to South Yorkshire. Seeing Cartwright and Armstrong at a table a little decorum was restored, and Davies walked over and proudly announced to everyone and anyone within earshot, 'We got 'im!'

'Who?'

'The sheep shagger of course,' Davies answered with a certain incredulity, since neither of the senior detectives seemed to know what they'd been up to. 'Although to be perfectly honest, it was John here and the sheep that did most of the work.'

Randall took up the story, 'Seems our rustler thought he could just stroll into the field and waltz off with Sunday dinner for the next few weeks, but the sheep had other ideas. The bloke was hanging on for dear life as the sheep dragged him round the field and when he did let go he rolled into a barbed-wire fence where he got well and truly tangled! Took us a while to extricate him. The sheep didn't seem to be too bothered though. Sorry about the state of me trousers!' The bar erupted into laughter at the sight of the rip in the backside of Randall's uniform pants. Immediately Cartwright's dark mood evaporated.

'Do we know who it was?' chuckled Armstrong.

'Oh yes! It was that daft sod from the Roughs Estate in Felixstowe, Alan Higginson. Remember, his brother, Ronnie, got sent down for life a while back?' Lewis took over the narrative. 'What's been bothering me though is a van we spotted on the track between the field and the river. At first we took it to be waiting there for Alan and his sheep. But the more I think about it I'm not so sure it was, especially with that boat which looked as if it was about to pull into the bank.

There were a few blokes, couldn't be sure how many, looked like they were waiting to start loading stuff from or into the boat. It was coming in right close to the bank. I reckon the boat crew must have seen us 'cos it changed course and took off up the river.' By way of an excuse, he continued, 'We were hardly on a covert op and being discreet. In fact, it was a bit of a laugh watching one of our local hooligans getting stitched up by a sheep. The van took off before we could investigate.' Cartwright's interest became a little keener at the mention of a boat and a van.

'Did you get the registration of the van?'

'Sorry, guv, by the time we'd got Higginson in the car, the van – a light coloured Transit, I think, – was long gone.'

'How about the boat? What sort of boat? a motorboat? Trawler? A yacht, a bloody pedalo? The QE2, perhaps?' Davies was flummoxed. 'C'mon, Ray, this is important. Seems you might have interrupted a smuggling operation. Get yourself a pint and let me have the details. I'll want a full written report. Still, well done lads, I'm glad you've got the rustling problem cleared up.' As an aside he leaned over and whispered to Armstrong, 'I daresay if we get Higginson in court the magistrates will just slap his wrist and tell him not to do it again.' Then, in the form of a general announcement to yet more off-duty policemen who had arrived, 'Listen, everyone! We've been told to expect an increase in certain illicit import undertakings, that's smuggling to you, and I suspect that this is what Lewis, Davies and company might have just witnessed tonight. So, let vigilance be our watchword! Hey, but let's not worry about that too much for now. Whose round is it?' The mood returned to one of light-hearted frivolity with banter abounding.

As per the usual Friday night routine most of the local force of law and order gathered in *The Maybush* apart from those rostered on duty. They were becoming more raucous as the evening wore on and by closing time pretty well-oiled. None of them would even have noticed if *The Ark Royal* had picked up a mooring right outside the pub. So much for vigilance!

***

In another dimly candle-lit riverside pub a few miles down-river from Kirton Creek where *The Michael Collins* had been scheduled to make the drop, a solitary customer wearing the uniform of a chief petty officer in the Royal Navy sat staring into his untouched pint in *The Ferryboat Inn*, the FBI, as it was known locally, anxiously looking at his watch every few minutes. Patrick McLevy had recently been recruited by a notorious drug dealership: an international firm, headed by and known only as Mr Khan. He was expecting a delivery.

'Are you going to drink that pint, Pat, or just sit and look at it?' Kevin Dalton the landlord was always keen to close when business was slow, when takings barely covered the cost of the candles never mind the rent or electricity when there was any available.

'OK, Kev, sorry. Can you give us half an hour? I've arranged to meet...' And before he could continue and explain who he'd arranged to meet, the door burst open and a black man wearing the kind of suit a bloke might wear to his brother-in-law's second wedding came in, closely followed by two women, dressed for a night on the town.

'Sorry, Chief McLevy, sir, we almost blew it,' the man announced with a laugh. He clearly didn't understand the seriousness of the situation or the ramifications of the job he'd taken on.

Patrick McLevy was a giant of a man at six foot six inches tall and weighing in at eighteen stone. He'd been nursing his lager for quite a while. He was fit – although maybe not quite as fit since his dishonourable discharge from the Royal Navy. His promising career as a petty officer aboard *HMS Norfolk*, a county class guided missile destroyer was cut short when a court martial deemed that he'd been drunk and a little over-enthusiastic, to say the least, when disciplining an ordinary seaman. Patrick wasn't a thug – except when he was drunk. Bar-room brawling though was his speciality and since he had compromised his entitlement to a pension from the Senior Service, he was open to any suggestion whereby there was a means to earn easy money. Patrick did not subscribe to one's fortune being preordained by fate. Luck, whether good or bad, was something you made for yourself, and he had placed himself in the right place at the right time to pick up a lucrative position overseeing the logistics of moving stuff. Transportation was such a means to easy money especially when whatever was being transported was of doubtful provenance, knocked off or just downright illegal. Mr McLevy was becoming known in certain quarters of the underworld and earning both respect and a reputation. No one argued with Mr McLevy and, like his boss Mr Khan, he was not a man to be crossed.

'What d'you mean, blew it? Shat it more like!' Patrick bawled, rising from his chair, and almost cracking his head on the low-beamed ceiling. The recent arrival apologised again and offered an explanation, his South African accent readily discernible.

'I had the van there waiting, just like I'd been told, past Lodge Farm and across Kirton Marshes to the track by the creek. I could see the boat approaching and I flashed him twice as I'd been told to. But then there were other flashing lights in a field, a lot of shouting and right old ruckus going down. I'm sure I saw a police car. I reckoned it spelled trouble because I knew the pick-up was a bit suspect. The boat must've seen it too. It didn't even stop – kept on going. So we shoved off quicker than a 'bock into a thicket and laid low in some woods until the coast was clear didn't we girls?'

The girls giggled and nodded their agreement. Stellen and Kirsten were the twenty-something-year-old, strikingly attractive twin daughters of Bandile Bosch. Bosch had fled from his native Cape Town when he lost his wife, Mandisa, who died after being beaten up by a group of white Afrikaans. His daughters were all he had now, and he was a most dutiful and attentive father. There had been occasions when he regretted the names he and Mandisa had given their twins but at least now he could smile as they reminded him of his homeland.

Bosch ordered drinks for himself and his daughters and sat at the table with Patrick. Kevin brought the drinks to the table.

'Thirty minutes then, Pat.'

'Cheers, Kev. Right, sounds like it's not you that's made a bosch of it.' Bandile rolled his eyes and shook his head.

'Still, mission aborted. Sounds like you had no alternative. But, it's not the end of the world. Better to live and fight another day.' The group sat in silence until it was broken by the trill of the telephone behind the bar. Kevin picked up the receiver.

'FBI,' he answered then listened as four sets of eyes turned to stare in Kevin's direction.

'Yes, he's here, hold on a second. Pat, it's for you.'

Patrick went over to the bar and took the receiver from Kevin. Everyone strained to eavesdrop one side of the conversation.

'Yes, they're here ... OK, you reckon that'll be safe? ... How about the cargo? ... and she's OK? ... not too serious? ... well if you're sure ... OK, see you in a while.' In a fairly ungracious manner Patrick handed the receiver back to Kevin and returned to the table.

'Well?' Bandile asked, as his daughters looked on in anticipation.

'That was Liam, the boat skipper. He's taken the last of the flood tide and making for the quay at Methersgate. Drink up. We've got to go now to get there before the ebb tide sets in. Cheers, Kev.' They left unfinished drinks on the table and piled out of the pub and into a white Ford Transit van.

'Bugger me, Bosch, a white van? I know they're inconspicuous during the day, but at night?'

'Sorry, the colour's not to your liking, sir.' He laughed. 'At least it's got seats for my girls. The bloke at the Arches, Tommy, well he gave me the keys and told me where I was to pick it up.' Bandile fired up the van and, with McLevy not in the best of humour, they shot off to liaise with Liam and *The Michael Collins* at Methersgate. Stellen and Kirsten were huddled up on the back seat busy chattering excitedly. It was all a great adventure as far as they were concerned.

***

Although the straight-line distance between the FBI and Methersgate is only a few miles, the distance by road is considerably longer since the two locations are on opposing sides of the river with the only vehicular crossing via the Wilford Bridge in Woodbridge. Traffic was light and Bandile had his foot down. Once over the bridge, Patrick issued directions onto the B1083. He was familiar with the area since he'd lived locally before joining the Navy. After about two miles the van turned right onto a rough track across farmland towards Methersgate Hall and the private quay beyond. Bandile turned the headlights off. Thick cloud had now obscured the moon and the night was black. More than once he almost came to grief. Even on the track, the girls were being thrown around on the rear seat of the passenger compartment and whilst they found it amusing to begin with they were now starting to complain. As the van slowly crept past the Hall the shape of the boat could just be determined on the quay. Bandile parked alongside and McLevy greeted Liam and Fergal and introduced Bosch and his daughters. Over the next twenty minutes, a dozen or more large carboard cartons purporting to contain packets of *Connolly's Corn Flakes* were transferred from *The Michael Collins* to the Transit with Bandile and his daughters doing the humping.

'Where's the other bloke off the boat, couldn't he help?' complained Stellen.

'He could at least give us a hand,' agreed Kirsten.

McLevy was deep in discussion with O'Reilly checking his calculations and reckoning. O'Reilly had researched current market prices and, on a total of 500lbs of herbal cannabis, he'd reckoned on the cargo, with a potential street value of something in the region of £3 an ounce being, worth £24000 according to his arithmetic, which never had been his strong suit. O'Reilly had paid for the consignment from Pieter Hendriks, Jimmy as he was generally known, the Dutch dealer, for just 30000 guilders. The Dutch currency had been entrusted to him by Frankie Forsyth. He had amassed quite a significant number of guilders from his last success-ful trade with a dealer on *Prinsengracht*. Even at the rate of two guilders to the pound this purchase was a steal. McLevy on the other hand was bankrolled to the tune of £20000 by Mr Khan and according to the briefing he had received from Rashid, Mr Khan's right-hand man, he was under instruction to pay up to £18000 for the load. The balance of £2000 from the wedge he was carrying would be his commission. McLevy wasn't much of a negotiator and went straight in at £18000 which Liam accepted like a shot. He was half expecting to be beaten down by at least a grand. His brain went into cal-culator mode. He'd bought the shipment for 18000 guilders less than the true value: about £9000 which was around 8100 Irish punts. He had been anticipating a significant return on

Frankie's investment, and so it had proved to be so far. Then there was the double-deal that McLevy knew nothing of. When that double-cross was factored in, the cash on delivery to other organisations rather than Mr Khan's would multiply the return by a factor of ten at least, or so he hoped. This sum exceeded even his wildest expectations. Then, on top of all of that, there would be the extra payments from Frankie and Gerry for the special delivery. She, the Dutch girl, would be loaded as soon as McLevy's team were out of the way. This payment alone would more than cover the cost of the diesel and Fergal's wages.

When the unloading and loading was complete O'Reilly invited everyone aboard to drink a toast to the success of the venture and the smooth transaction. They sat around the saloon table where a bottle of *Zuidam Zeer Oude Jenever* and five glasses had been set out. Liam poured stiff measures all round.

'Maybe a drop of water in the girls' glasses,' he suggested and added a liberal amount from a jug. Fergal was nowhere to be seen. McLevy handed O'Reilly a wedge of £18000 in bundles of used small denomination notes which O'Reilly insisted on slowly counting out loud. A second round was poured, and a third while the counting continued. They all shook hands and McLevy's team stepped from the boat back onto the quay. Fergal reappeared from the van at the same time.

'Just making sure everything's shipshape and Bristol fashion in your van now, we wouldn't want your goods spilling all over the place, now would we?'

It was a rhetorical question. Fergal climbed aboard the boat and let go the mooring lines and *The Michael Collins* got underway heading south back down the river.

'I hope you didn't give them those two special packets.'

'I'm not completely stupid, Liam,' Fergal replied.

'And the girl?'

'Completely out of it.'

'The other two should be as well before they get very far.'

McLevy's plan now was to make the delivery to London: a railway arch in Pedley Street, Bethnal Green, *The Acme Discount Stores*. He hoped to arrive in time for an early celebration champagne breakfast once the goods had been handed over to Mr Khan's organisation. The van pulled away from the quay on its journey, retracing its route across the track towards the B1083 and Woodbridge. Mr McLevy sat smiling, completely oblivious to the dupery he was now a part of. Inside his coat pocket were the four bundles of £500. What deceptive diddle could he now devise to ensure that those bundles remained intact. He had no intention of paying Bosch the fee he'd promised. Who said there was honour among thieves?

Chapter 3 **Saturday, Early Hours**

'I wonder where he's going at this time of night,' slurred Doug Armstrong as he lurched out of the pub.

'Who?' enquired Cartwright in a considerably less inebriated state.

'There look – that boat,' he hiccupped whilst waving his arm through an arc of 180 degrees but in the general direction of the river.

'Hey, Andy,' Cartwright called Lewis over from where he sat with his head between his knees. 'That look anything like the boat you saw earlier?'

'What boat, where? Sorry, guv, shouldn't have had those shots.'

Cartwright realised he wasn't going to get much sense out of any of them and at the same time was thankful he'd laid off the shots and remained just the wrong side of completely sober. He went back into the pub to use the telephone.

'Have you got the number for the harbourmaster at Felixstowe Ferry?' He asked Sheila, the landlady. She put down her tea-towel and drying her hands on her apron referred to a list of local phone numbers which was kept on the back-bar.

'There you are love – Charlie Brinkley.' She handed him the list.

Cartwright dialled the number. 'Hello, is that Charlie? ... Sorry to bother you at this time of night ... Morning? Is it? ... Yes I know ... It's Detective Chief Inspector Cartwright here, Suffolk Constabulary ... Yes, it is important. Look, Charlie, if you wouldn't mind, there's a commercial boat of some sort heading down the river in your direction, quite a big one, it's not showing any navigation lights ... Could you see if you can identify it for me please? ... Really, oh even better. Great ... Thanks, Charlie, very much appreciated.' Cartwright replaced the receiver on its cradle. 'Charlie Brinkley's going to call the boat on the marine VHF radio.' None of the DCI's colleagues seemed remotely interested.

Cartwright strode off to the car park with Armstrong and Lewis tacking along behind with DCs Davies and Rudd staggering uncertainly after them. A few minutes passed whilst Armstrong stopped to urinate against the wall of an outbuilding and eventually they'd all managed to get themselves into the car. Cartwright carefully manoeuvred the vehicle through the narrow lanes which ultimately led to the A1093 at Martlesham. He knew that in the state they were in discretion rather than bravado would be wise. 'Avoid the main road until it can no longer be avoided,' he told himself.

Meanwhile, the Transit had reached the main A12 trunk road to the north of Woodbridge and was proceeding south. McLevy was dozing, no doubt dreaming of the great wealth coming his way. The *Jenever* had hit the spot too.

'Can you hear that?' asked Bandile.

'What?' McLevy was less than thrilled to be disturbed from his reverie.

'That sort of rhythmic thrum-thrum-thrum noise.' McLevy cocked an ear to one side.

'You mean that sort of thrumming noise?'

'That's what I said.'

'I can hear it,' giggled Kirsten. 'There's a sort of tapping and scratching sound as well. Been coming and going since we left the quay. Sounds like it's coming from behind.' She began clapping along in time to the beat of the thrumming and accentuating the knocking.

'I can hear it too,' added Stellen. 'There, listen, can't you hear it? Didn't think it worth a mention before.' She joined in with her sister's slurred singing and clap-along punctuated now by some foot stamping. Turning towards the rear seat, McLevy raised his voice.

'Hard to hear anything with you girls making all that blasted noise, clapping and whooping and banging and going ahead. You're both pissed,' complained McLevy. 'Anyway, what about it? Be quiet, girls, enough, bloody racket!'

'But it's not us banging,' they insisted in unison.

'Ssh,' urged Bandile. Four pairs of ears concentrated on the thrumming sound which continued. If there had been any tapping or banging it had stopped.

'I reckon we might have a problem – could be a flat tyre,' suggested Bandile.

'That's all we bloody well need. Well, best we pull over and have a look then!'

The van was approaching the junction with the A1093 where ordinarily they would have turned left but Bandile continued a little further straight on towards Kesgrave since the minor road looked likely to be much quieter. He pulled partly onto the verge and stopped the engine. They all piled out. Bandile walked around the van and, sure enough, the rear near side tyre was flat.

'We must have got a puncture on that bloody track.'

'No need to state the obvious. Have we got a spare?'

'I think I saw a spare in the back,' said Kirsten.

Bandile unlocked the rear doors, put the keys in his pocket and started removing the cartons, piling them on the verge, and revealing the spare wheel and tool kit right up against a bulkhead which divided the cargo space from the front seats.

'Are you going to help?'

'The van is your responsibility,' was McLevy's barbed acidic response. He lit a cigarette and stomped up and down.

'I need a tinkle.' Stellen teetered off behind a hedge. Her dad began huffing and puffing, in between cursing and swearing at McLevy as much as at the flat tyre, as he attempted to loosen the nuts on the offending wheel.

***

Cartwright and his semi-sozzled passengers were now on the A1093 approaching the junction with the A12 where he would turn left towards Kesgrave and Police HQ. It wouldn't be the first time on a Friday they'd slept it off in the cells. The streetlights at the junction were out due to the nightly power cuts, but as he made the turn the car's headlights illuminated a scene he wasn't expecting: a scene totally out of context even before he knew what the context was.

'C'mon, chaps – wakey wakey,' he urged. 'Look what we've got here.' Cartwright drew up behind the van, got out of the car, but left the engine running with the headlights shining on what might otherwise have been a comedy sketch on TV. Here was a white Transit van, a black bloke in a made-to-measure suit, but not for him sadly. He was struggling to change a wheel while a second fellow, dressed in a Royal Navy Uniform with the insignia of crossed anchors beneath a crown and two stripes, stood smoking. On the back seat of the van was a woman who seemed to be barely conscious and what was this? An almost identical woman, with her knickers round her ankles, emerging from behind the hedge, unwell by the look of her. And at the side of the road, a pile of cardboard cartons marked *Connolly's Corn Flakes*.

Cartwright tried to supress the urge to laugh and announced his presence in his best *Dixon of Dock Green* voice, 'Evening all.'

By now the rest of Kesgrave's finest had variously fallen and fumbled their way out of the car and stood grinning at the farcical goings on which were now in *freeze frame* mode. Stellen quickly retreated behind the hedge and re-emerged a few moments later, with her underwear back where one might have expected to find it.

'Having a bit of a problem are we?' Cartwright was not normally given to sarcasm but somehow the situation demanded it. The Transit team could not have appeared more like rabbits caught in the headlights than, well, rabbits caught in the headlights.

Doug had pulled himself together sufficiently to slur, 'We' – he paused for effect as he waved his arm indicating his colleagues in an overly amateur dramatical gesture – 'are the polithe.'

'That'll do, Doug!' Cartwright took over.

'Kindly line up against the van and keep your hands where we can see them.' Addressing the uniform, 'Perhaps you could tell me who you all are and exactly what's going on here.'

'I'm Chief Petty Officer Patrick McLevy serving on the county class destroyer *HMS Norfolk*. The man changing the wheel is Bandile Bosch, an ordinary seaman who'd gone AWOL and is now in my custody.' Patrick quite often used his former rank in an attempt to bluff his way out of tricky situations. He thought this would be a good enough story for a bunch of half-cut coppers to extricate them from what otherwise would be extremely serious bother.

'And the corn flakes?'

'They're Bosch's daughters who helped me to find him. I sort of used them as bait...' This response provided the best laugh of the night with Davies and Rudd almost collapsing into paroxysms.

'No, Chief, the *Connolly's Corn Flakes*.' Cartwright indicated the cartons.

'Ah those...'

'Mind if we have a look?' And before McLevy or anyone else could object, Lewis had slit open the top of one of the boxes with his pocket-knife. He folded the lid of the carton back and there for all to see was the familiar packaging of *Connolly's Corn Flakes*. He then opened the packet and poured the contents onto the verge – corn flakes. Cartwright stood back slightly and observed the anxious glances being exchanged between Bosch and McLevy the pressure of whose ire and irk were rising quite visibly.

'And I suppose, your captain had asked you to pick up something for breakfast for the entire crew whilst you were out?' Armstrong intervened. Lewis slit open another packet from another carton and poured some of the cereal onto the ground. McLevy exploded.

'The rotten, lousy, crooked Irish bastards...!' he yelled like some wounded wild animal, unable to control himself. And before he could be restrained he'd forced his way over to the pile of cartons and with his bare hands was tearing open cartons and packets. The verge was becoming covered with corn flakes. Davies and Rudd wrestled him to the ground. Cartwright decided it was time to exert his authority. He removed his warrant card from his wallet and waved it in McLevy's direction.

'I am Detective Chief Inspector Cartwright and I'm placing you under arrest on suspicion of...' He faltered. Suspicion of what? Carrying corn flakes was hardly the crime of the century. '...On suspicion of carrying stolen goods.' McLevy was duly cautioned.

'Put him in the car, Ray.' Now galvanised into action, Davies had snapped on a pair of handcuffs and with Vaughan Rudd's assistance McLevy was bundled into the car.

'Ray, you and Vaughan take him around the corner to HQ and lock him up. Wake up whoever's on duty round there and get another car and a tow-truck here quick as!' All at once what had been the shambles of a group of Friday night revellers had become an alert and responsive unit of policemen. The cartons of the remaining packets of the breakfast cereal were reloaded into the van along with the jack, brace and spare wheel. Bosch, who hadn't managed even to loosen the wheel nuts, and his daughters remained lined up against the van under the very close attention of the DCI and DS – especially the daughters who were now both looking either very intoxicated or ill or both.

Although the wait wasn't that long, Cartwright deemed it too long. It certainly wasn't the sort of night to be standing about. A fresh breeze had sprung up and the air temperature had plummeted with the wind-chill. A Triumph 2500S patrol car eventually arrived followed by the police tow-truck, more frequently used for removing illegally parked vehicles. The Bosch family were ushered into the car and the mechanic with the tow-truck was left to deal with the Transit.

In the concealed compartment, the Dutch girl was aware that the van had stopped. She had heard voices, but she hadn't been able to discern what was said. She opened her eyes. It was still pitch black. The bindings on her wrists were cutting into her flesh. Her body ached. She tried to stretch out but no matter in which direction she tried her attempts were impeded by the restrictive capacity of the compartment. Her head began to spin again. Her mouth was dry, and she couldn't produce sufficient saliva to begin to swallow. Her eyes closed again, and she screwed them up tightly. Maybe the next time she opened them she would see something. Her mind went drifting back to her flat, the two rooms that she shared with a friend, Linde. They were on the same course at university:

History and Philosophy. Linde had lost her virginity in the flat at the end of the Christmas term. She thought she'd be the one, not Linde. There had been plenty of opportunity, but she hadn't fancied any of the boys who had made advances. They'd talked about it. What was it like? Had it hurt? Now, that special occasion, that precious moment, the first time, had been taken from her, by force. And yes it hurt. She wept but there were no tears. She screamed but there was no sound. Then the van was moving again but now the motion was different. She passed out again.

After a few minutes the Vanden Plas and the Triumph were back at Police HQ with their occupants warming up in the station. Cartwright instructed PC Randall to get a hot drink for each of the Bosch family and then keep an eye on them until he'd conducted a preliminary interview with McLevy.

'But sir, my trousers...' Obviously embarrassed by flashing his Y fronts with ladies present he was attempting to excuse himself.

'I'm sure the girls have seen it all before.' Cartwright reaffirmed the order.

'Doug, can you organise getting the Transit into the garage workshop as soon as it arrives? I want you to give it a careful once-over. I've got a feeling there's more to this than breakfast cereal.'

'Aaw c'mon, guvnor it's nearly 1.30am. Can't it wait 'til tomorrow?'

'No it can't!' My gut tells me there's something going on here, something big.'

In the interview room McLevy sat opposite DC Ray Davies waiting for the DCI. Cartwright eventually bustled into the room.

'So, Chief Petty Officer, if in fact you are, I must offer you my congratulations. In all my years as a policeman I have never heard such an unlikely story. Bizarre doesn't even begin to describe it. Just run it past me again if you wouldn't mind. It's such a fascinating fabrication. I want to make sure I've got all the detail and I could do with another good laugh. Remember you're still under caution.'

'It's as I've told you already, I've been to apprehend the man Bosch, an ordinary seaman serving on the county class destroyer *HMS Norfolk*. Bosch went AWOL after he struck a Sub-Lieutenant for calling him a "black bastard". I took his daughters with me to help me bring him back, to persuade him like.' McLevy's body language was doing absolutely nothing to convince Cartwright of the veracity of his story.

'OK, if I accept what you're telling me, and I don't, how do you explain the corn flakes?' Davies's attempt to supress laughter failed. Cartwright gave him an admonishing glare, but then he too couldn't help himself and joined in. 'And while you're inventing that part of the story, who are the rotten, lousy, crooked Irish bastards that you seem to have taken a dislike to? I'm sorry, Chief but what you're telling me is beyond my capacity for belief to accept that this is nothing but a fairy story.'

'No comment.'

'Your reaction to the corn flakes at the side of the road seemed to have upset you. Perhaps you hadn't been expecting corn flakes, or maybe you're a muesli man, or expecting to get your oats?'

'No comment.'

Davies just couldn't control himself. He'd hardly stopped falling about right from the start. The DCI's derisive wit was beyond amusing, it was hilarious.

'OK, Chief. We'll give you some time to think about it for a while. We'll go and have a word with Ordinary Seaman Bosch.' He then sent DC Davies off to get PC Randall to escort Bosch up to the interview room whilst he took McLevy to a cell. Despite the lateness of the hour Cartwright was anxious to press on with the interviews, but only after he'd put in a call to Helen, his wife, to let her know that he was at work and not drunk in a ditch somewhere.

'I'm Detective Chief Inspector Cartwright. Who are you?'

Bosch responded with his name.

'How long have you been in the Royal Navy, Brandile – may I call you Brandile?'

'No, my name is not Brandile it's Bandile and I'm not in the Navy.'

'So, you're not an ordinary seaman absent from *HMS Norfolk*.'

'No sir, I'm Bandile Bosch. I'm not nor have I ever been in any navy.'

'So how come you know Chief McLevy...?'

Bosch interrupted. 'Look, sir, I don't really know McLevy and I've no idea what he's told you, but I don't want any part of this. I'm not involved. I'm from Cape Town. I virtually had to move Table Mountain itself to get a visa to come here. I had to get away. I came to England to escape the harsh institutionalised system of racial segregation that exists in my country. I thought England would be the place I could settle down, the place where things are stable and predictable. I thought I would be able to find work, for me and for my daughters. A land of milk and honey. London, a place where my beautiful girls could maybe become fashion models. I've never been in trouble with the police. Look, I'll tell you everything I know.'

'Now there's a refreshing turn up, Ray – someone willing to help us with our enquiries and articulate with it.'

'Certainly is, guvnor,' acknowledged the DC, sobering up almost by the minute.

'I met a bloke in a pub in London and he asked if I was looking for work. He somehow seemed to know that I was.

Maybe the colour of my skin. Well, I am broke. It cost me all my savings to get here. This bloke said all I had to do was collect a van, and drive to a farm near a place called Felixstowe, pick up some parcels and stuff from a boat and drive back picking up the bloke McLevy from a pub on the way. He said I could take my girls for the ride as well. I thought the job sounded a bit too good to be true, but £100 is £100 especially when you don't have any money. The boat didn't stop where I was told to go. So, I went and told Mr McLevy, and he said we had to go somewhere else – middle of nowhere. I've never even met McLevy before today and I don't think I like him. We picked up a load of boxes of *Connolly's* and I was driving back when the van got a puncture and...'

Cartwright interrupted, 'And that's where we came in. OK, Bandile. Thank you. What was the name of the bloke in the pub in London?'

'I'm not sure, Tommy I think I heard someone call him.'

'No surname?'

'No, sir.'

'How about the pub?'

'Oh yes, it was *The Carpenter's Arms* in Cheshire Street, Bethnal Green, quite close to where I have my rooms in Bacon Street. Am I under arrest?' enquired Bosch anxiously.

'Not at the moment, but for starters you may be charged with handling stolen goods if it turns out the corn flakes were stolen, and then there's the matter of the van which may or may not have been stolen. Given the hour we'll continue this interview in the morning. I'll need to talk to your daughters as well. You're free to go for now, although I'm not sure where to at this time of night.'

Cartwright and Davies returned to the CID room where Vaughan was sleeping at his desk. Lewis was draped over a chair reading a book on philosophy.

'I think we've had enough excitement for tonight, Ray. Let's call it a day for now, back here at nine in the morning. I hope there's a cell free; I don't fancy driving home now.' As the DCI was about to leave, Armstrong came bursting into the room in a state of agitation.

'Thank goodness you're still here,' he panted. He'd obviously run up from the garage. 'You'd better come and see this.' Such panic-induced urgency left Cartwright and Davies in no doubt that they indeed ought to see whatever it was that had stirred up the DS. Armstrong was not normally renowned for getting quite so animated. The three detectives hurried down to the garage. In common with other similar establishments, police stations had special dispensation within the energy crisis state of emergency and the fluorescent lights in the workshop burned brighter than daylight. It wasn't the Transit with its innards removed that drew the detectives' attention, but the body of a young woman laid out on a makeshift mattress on the floor.

'What the...? I bloody well knew it! I just knew there was something big going on here. Is she...?' Cartwright thumped the palm of his hand with the fist of the other.

'No, boss, she's still with us but only just I reckon. Her pulse is very weak and her breathing's very shallow. I've called for an ambulance.'

'Any ID?'

'Yes, sir.' The response came from one of the mechanics who had been involved in stripping out the van's interior. 'We found this.' The mechanic held up a small leather purse on a strap. The strap was broken. 'It was with her in the concealed compartment behind what had been disguised to look like the bulkhead separating the back of the van from the front.' The purse was handed to Cartwright who opened the zip fastener. 'There are a few guilders in here, a couple of tampons, not much else except this student rail card. She's Dutch according to this: Lotte van Dijkstra.'

'So, a concealed compartment, Ray. What do you make of that?' Davies peered into the back of the van, took out his notebook and made a note of the registration: FBA643M.

'Hang on there, young lady. Ambulance'll be here any minute.' Armstrong was pacing up and down the workshop. Cartwright knelt by Lotte's side, stroked a strand of her hair from her face and gently felt for a pulse. 'It's very weak and intermittent. Whatever could she have done to deserve having been beaten up like this?' he whispered compassionately. It was evident from the severity of the abrasions and bruising that Lotte had taken a violent beating. There were possible broken bones too. What clothing she was wearing was torn and dirty and more suitable for midsummer than February. Armstrong was visibly shaken.

'Has she been...' He hesitated. 'Has she been raped?' There were fearful looks of apprehension all round. 'Did the poor lass not have a coat?' He continued his impatient pacing. 'If the ambulance doesn't arrive within the next couple of minutes I'll take her to A&E myself in Andy's Jag.'

'No you most certainly will not – the amount you've been drinking.' No sooner had his commanding officer laid the law down than a siren could be heard in the distance.

'Is there a WPC on duty here tonight?' Cartwright asked.

'I'll go and check, guv.' Davies took off in response to the DCI's question.

The comatose figure of Lotte van Dijkstra was carefully laid on a stretcher and loaded into the ambulance. Davies returned with WPC Annie McKay just in time for her to accompany the casualty in the ambulance, which duly departed in great haste.

'OK,' said Cartwright, 'this workshop is now completely off-limits to everyone until Forensics have been over this van. Doug, you're with me, Ray get McLevy back to the interview room. Now! If the bastard's asleep wake him up.' There was no doubting Cartwright's rancour and rising anger. Davies and Armstrong scurried off. With everyone gone, the mechanic lowered the workshop shutters and turned off the lights.

Bosch and his daughters were loitering in the reception area of the station as the detectives returned. Cartwright paused, and then, having clearly come to a decision, he spoke directly to the duty desk sergeant, and as he turned to leave he nodded in the direction of the Bosch family and said, 'I want these three detained in custody. Helping the police with their enquiries.'

***

'Vessel showing no navigation lights underway downstream on the River Deben, this is Felixstowe Ferry Harbourmaster, over.' Charlie Brinkley was on the VHF radio, channel sixteen. No response. 'Vessel underway down river on the Deben, this is Felixstowe Ferry Harbourmaster, over.' No response. Charlie put his hat and coat on, picked up his binoculars and walked the short distance from his house down to the jetty. The night was as dark as pitch and even the determination of where the river met the foreshore was a strain on the eyes. Charlie peered upriver beyond the Horse Sand buoy. He could see nothing. Adjusting the focus of his binoculars he riveted his gaze for several more minutes. Nothing. Then, was that the merest murmur, a tremble in the air, the faintest hum of a Lister? Charlie's sense of hearing was as sharp as a razor. Years of experience with boats and their engines and he could detect the subtle sonorities and discreet differences in engine noises. The pitch, vibration and cadence of a Lister compared to a Cummins or a Gardner, subtle as such a comparison might be, was as pronounced to Charlie as the difference in tone and timbre between a Stradivarius, an Amati, or a Guarneri to a concert violinist. He lowered the binoculars and closed his eyes, all the better for concentrating his audibility receptors. 'Yes, no doubt about it – twin Listers.' He refocused his stare as he detected a very gradual crescendo in the purr of the Listers. From his vantage point he could just make out the faintest of outlines of a small freighter, with a dim red tint glowing from the aft wheelhouse. The vessel glided past on the opposite side of the river, onwards towards the estuary. As hard as he tried, Charlie couldn't make out any detail that would assist in identifying the ship. He returned home and telephoned Police HQ to report what he had heard but barely seen.

***

With the cargo of corn flakes and two of the three *special delivery packages* safely unloaded and reloaded aboard the Transit, *The Michael Collins* had left Methersgate Quay on the ebb tide about half an hour before midnight. Liam O'Reilly was happy with the way everything had gone and couldn't stop laughing when he imagined the look on Patrick's face. His reaction when he opened the boxes would be a joy to behold. But, even so, he was slightly annoyed since he was now behind schedule having been forced to steam much further upriver than had been previously arranged. This meant that getting out of the river would be *touch and go*. The problem, however, was that if he did *touch*, the chances of *go* were slim. The depth of water across the Deben bar was absolutely critical. Sure, he had made £2000 profit from the delivery but going aground would take the shine off the result.

As the Deben buoy came into view the VHF radio crackled into life. *Vessel showing no navigation lights underway downstream on the River Deben, this is Felixstowe Ferry Harbourmaster, over.* Fergal turned the radio off.

'Now then, what would he be wanting to interfere for?' Liam wondered. 'Do you suppose we've been spotted?'

'Let's hope we can get out of this river!' Fergal was staring intently at the echo-sounder and calling out the depth of water calibrated from under the keel.

'One foot eight inches.'

'Steady at one foot eight.' A few minutes and a few yards passed.

'One foot four, one foot two inches. One foot.' The adrenalin began to course and the heart rate increase.

'Ten inches. Eight inches.' Liam could almost visualise the mud and shingle beneath the bottom of the boat. 'I hope there are no sudden humps or ridges. Please let it be flat!'

'Six inches!' Liam could now make out the Bar buoy and started whispering Hail Marys to himself.

'Two inches!' *The Michael Collins* shuddered as it grounded. Liam pushed the throttles forward in an attempt to plough a furrow over the shingle. The extra drive would either clear the hump or dig the boat further in. The boat responded to the additional power and surged forward into slightly deeper water.

'Six inches. Steady on six inches.' The sweat was beading on Liam's forehead.

'One foot increasing,' announced Fergal. The Woodbridge Haven buoy and safe water which it marked was getting ever closer. Fergal put his hands together, raised his head, looked towards the stars and mouthed 'thank you'.

'Four feet!' he announced with a huge sigh of relief. 'Well done, Skipper. That was close.'

'And that's a fact to be sure,' concurred Liam. 'Had we dried out there we'd have aroused a great deal of interest with too many curious folks wanting to poke their noses into our business. Is there any of that *Jenever* left? No water in mine!'

The Michael Collins now safely at sea steamed on towards HM Fort Roughs, known as the Roughs Tower, and at six miles off the coast, in international waters, the WWII instal-lation was one of the Maunsell Sea Forts built to protect the ports of Harwich and Felixstowe from invasion. The fort was decommissioned in 1967 since when it had been occupied by Major Paddy Bates from where he broadcast his pirate radio station, Radio Essex. The predetermined plan was to have the cannabis unloaded using the Tower's derrick. Major Paddy would pay handsomely for the drugs and sell it on with a huge mark-up or smoke himself silly. Liam didn't really mind which. It would be a tricky manoeuvre, stemming the tide and keeping it steady whilst the basket was lowered by crane down onto the deck of the ship.

Holding position in the swell just a few yards from the legs of the tower, he could make out the figure of Major Paddy on the platform above as he lowered not the large basket but a fishing weight to which was attached a plastic bag. In the bag were a bottle of Jameson's and an envelope. Fergal retrieved the envelope and handed it to Liam who tore it open and read the message.

Abort the mission. The Ballingary has been identified by HM Coastguard and it can only be a matter of time before the identity of The Michael Collins is discovered. Suggest you find somewhere discreet and adopt a new name and registration for the ship before you are discovered and arrested. Good luck and sorry. Maybe next time. Major Paddy Bates.

'Ah well, I suppose we'll have to revert to Pieter's original plan.'

'I guess so,' agreed Fergal, 'but not with *The Michael Collins* painted all over the hull. We can't use *Ballingary* again either.'

'You're right to be sure. Still, always look on the bright side, it was good of the Major to let us know, and we've got a bottle of Jameson's.'

'Aye we have that now. That's as well – because we've fin-ished the *Jenever*.'

'So, here's the plan...' The boat was now on a course towards the North East Gunfleet buoy from where they would change course slightly and come south-westerly down the east side of the Gunfleet Sand through the East Swin Channel to the Whitaker Spit and into the River Crouch. Once in the Crouch they would turn to port past Foulness Sands with a wide west sweep under the Brankfleet Spit into the River Roach. The navigation would be tricky, due to the varying depths of water which were always going to be shallow. With the luck of the Irish, they would make it to Paglesham Reach, Shuttlewood's Yard, and commission a signwriter.

Chapter 4 **Saturday, Early Hours**

On his way to the interview room Cartwright took a detour to the gents to relieve himself and try to freshen up. He was splashing water on his face when Lewis came in.

'Been looking for you, sir, there's a message from Charlie Brinkley, the harbourmaster at Felixstowe Ferry.'

'Go on, Andy, what's he say?'

'A boat left the river sometime after midnight. As you suggested, he confirms it didn't have any navigation lights lit. He couldn't be sure, but he reckons it was a small freighter – not the sort of boat that uses the Deben very often. There was no response when he tried to call on VHF. He couldn't make out a name or any identifying marks or numbers, but he was certain that it was powered by twin Lister engines.'

'Well, that's not much help is it? I know it's a long shot, but do you think someone will have seen it coming into the river... what about the coastguard... somebody will have seen it surely? Can you get onto it, Andy?'

'Will do, guv.'

When Cartwright got to the interview room, McLevy was already there, sitting at the table opposite DS Armstrong. A uniformed PC from the custody suite stood by the door. Cartwright took several deep breaths as he sat down next to his DS. He needed to maintain composure and an even-tempered state of mind.

'Who's the girl, Patrick?' Cartwright asked as he proffered a packet of cigarettes in McLevy's direction.

'You know already, Kirsten and Stellen I think they're called, Bosch's daughters.'

'No, the other girl.'

'What other girl? There is no other girl.'

'The girl in the concealed compartment in the van Lotte van Dijkstra.'

'What concealed compartment?'

McLevy's body language wasn't giving even the slightest hint of any knowledge of the hidden compartment or Lotte van Dijkstra. Either he genuinely didn't know or he was a very good actor. He took a cigarette and, in relaxed fashion, lit it, blowing smoke towards the ceiling.

'The concealed compartment in the van, that is to say the van we believe to have been stolen in London before it was driven here by Bosch. The concealed compartment you contend you know nothing about.'

'On my honour, Chief Inspector, for Queen and Country, *Si vis pacem, para bellum.*'

Cartwright gave a quizzical look at Armstrong as if to ask, 'what's he on about?'

Armstrong recalled a few words from his schoolboy Latin. 'Something to do with peace and war, I think, guv, yeah, that's it *if you want peace prepare for war.*'

McLevy continued. 'Honest, sir, I know nothing about any of this and Lotte van whatsit – well, I've never heard of her. The only van I know about is that fucking Transit.'

'Well, Patrick, let me put you in the picture. A van, closely resembling the one we now have downstairs, will have our forensic chaps all over it first thing in the morning' – he looked at his watch – 'in a couple of hours' time,' he corrected himself. 'We believe this van was involved in an illegal activity we have yet to get to the bottom of and now we have discovered a young Dutch woman, badly beaten up, a rape victim in all probability for all we know at the moment, barely alive, hidden in a concealed compartment in the van. You know, the van with the puncture, the van that you, Bosch and his daughters were riding in a few hours ago. You know, Ordinary Seaman Bosch, the man gone AWOL that you arrested.'

There was something about the manner in which McLevy reacted that suggested to Cartwright that whoever he was, he knew much more than he was letting on.

'OK, Patrick, that's all for now.' The PC escorted him back to his cell.

'What do you make of it, Doug?'

'He's up to something, smuggling perhaps, but he says he knows nothing about our Lotte.'

'Yes I agree. There's something not right. Let's have a go at Bosch.'

Bosch was brought into the room escorted by the custody PC.

'Now let me get it right, Bandile, is that correct?'

'Yes, sir, and I've already told you everything I know. Why am I now in a cell? Am I under arrest now?'

'Is there something we should be arresting you for then, Bandile?' Cartwright asked with a smile. Bosch remained silent.

'*Ik weet dat het vroeg is, maar goedemorgen.*' Armstrong and Bosch looked at Cartwright in complete surprise. 'I know it's early, but good morning. Have you ever been to the Netherlands, Holland, Bandile?'

'No, sir.'

'But I thought your country, South Africa, has a special relationship with the Netherlands, you know, a long history of cooperation built on mutually beneficial economics and a similarity of language, you know, Dutch and Afrikaans. Do you speak Dutch, Bandile?'

'I've never been to the Netherlands and I don't speak Dutch or Afrikaans. I only speak English.'

'*Is jy seker?*'

'Yes I'm sure.' No sooner had he answered, than Bosch reddened and began to perspire as he realised he'd fallen for Cartwright's ruse.

'A-ha so you do know some Afrikaans.' Cartwright was not only delighted that his ploy had worked but that he had pronounced the question sufficiently accurately to be understood.

'Well of course, but only a little. We did it in school for a while. I am South African after all but I'm certainly not fluent in the language by any manner of means. Afrikaans has become the hateful tongue of apartheid.' Armstrong merely looked on with an expression of incredulity at his boss's linguistic prowess. Cartwright was now in full flow. He felt sure that Bosch was hiding something and with the adrenalin coursing through his veins he was determined to discover whatever it was.

'Why'd you come to England?'

'I told you, to escape apartheid.'

'Where'd you steal the van from?'

'I didn't steal it. The bloke that hired me told me where to collect it from. Grimsby Street, just by Shoreditch Station. Near where I live.'

'What was in the hidden compartment in the van?'

'I didn't know there was a hidden compartment.'

'Who arranged for you to meet up with a boat last night?'

'The bloke in the pub I guess. I told you.'

'Do you know a young Dutch woman, Lotte van Dijkstra?'

'No.'

'When did you last visit Holland?'

'I've never visited Holland.'

'What were you expecting to pick up last night?'

'I don't know.'

'Connolly's Corn Flakes?'

'No. I don't know. Maybe.'

'Ever been to Amsterdam?'

'Er, no.'

'Is jy seker?'

'Yes I'm sure.'

'Who is Lotte van Dijkstra? A friend of your daughters perhaps?'

The questions were coming thick and fast, and Bosch was becoming flustered and plainly feeling intimidated. With his head in his hands, he began to cry. It was clear he was almost exhausted and that he'd had enough.

'I don't know anything more than I've told you.'

'Where are the precious stones?'

'What precious stones?'

'Perhaps it was cannabis?'

'No, please stop. On the lives of my daughters, I swear I know nothing.'

'OK, Bandile. Take him back to his cell, Constable.'

'I need to see my girls,' he pleaded, drying his eyes. 'They're not well. Maybe it was the drink. I think the drinks on the boat were drugged.'

'You were drinking on the boat?'

'Yes, the captain proposed a toast to a successful venture. We all drank some sort of gin I think. He poured water into my daughters' glasses.'

'I see,' said Cartwright, not in the manner of any great revelation but as one would when two plus two are getting closer to making four.

'Let him see his daughters, oh and, Constable, leave the cell door unlocked.'

Bosch was escorted back to his cell, leaving Cartwright and Armstrong in the interview room. Cartwright clasped his hands behind his head, tilted his chair back, put his feet up on the table and yawned.

'Never had you down as a linguist, guv,' commented Armstrong.

'I'm not.'

'But... the Dutch and the Afrikaans... how come...?'

Cartwright was amused. 'Didn't you see me talking to the desk sergeant? Sergeant Khumalo, he's from Johannesburg!'

'Oh, I get it, he gave you the heads-up on a couple of phrases.'

'Steady on, Doug, you might make a detective yet.' They both laughed.

'Let's try and grab a few hours' shut-eye before we pick up where we left off.'

Chapter 5 **Saturday Early Hours**

Andy Lewis had always been one of the DCI's blue-eyed boys ever since as a PC he'd been co-opted as his driver. Now Sgt Lewis, he was being mentored by Cartwright and it was only a question of time before Sgt Lewis joined CID. Conscientious as ever, Lewis had been at it all night in an attempt to identify and locate the small ship from the Deben, which was without doubt, in his mind, at least implicated in what was now being referred to as the *Corn Flakes Caper*. He'd directed his first enquiry to Thames Coastguard.

'Coastguard. Chief Officer Chris Barnard speaking.'

'Good morning, sir, I am Sergeant Lewis, Suffolk Police. Sorry to bother you at this hour.'

'That's OK, Sergeant, nothing much happening tonight. What can I do for you?'

'We're anxious to trace and make contact with a ship, a small freighter we think, which left the Deben around midnight.'

'Do you know the name?'

'No, 'fraid not. According to Felixstowe Ferry Harbourmaster, it left the river without its navigation lights on, and he couldn't identify it.'

'Oh that doesn't surprise me,' the coastguard officer laughed. 'Old Charlie's eyesight has been failing for years.

He's got ears like Jodrell Bank though! I did hear Charlie trying to call a vessel on VHF but getting no response. Apart from that, VHF traffic has been quiet.' He continued laughing to himself. 'Haven't seen Charlie in quite a while. Must pay him a visit. Anyway, Sergeant Lewis, apart from the regular Townsend Thoresen ferry and a couple of small trawlers out of Harwich, I've had nothing on the radar all night although I did get a blip from the *Ballingary*. She called me up for a link call 2130 hours last night. I reckon that could have been her that left the Deben sometime after midnight. I saw her on the radar and, as you say, no nav lights so I couldn't pick her up with my binoculars.'

'Do we know anything about the *Ballingary* – where'd she been, where was she going?'

'No sorry, Sergeant, small freighters like that just carry on with their business, here and there, carrying whatever load they can get. We used to call them tramp steamers back in the day. You might try Lloyds Register, they might know, but then with a name like *Ballingary*, well sounds Irish to me. Try the Mercantile Marine Office in Dublin.'

'I'll do that. Thank you, sir you've been most helpful.'

'You're most welcome. I hope you manage to trace her.'

Lewis's next call wasn't answered. The Mercantile Marine Office in Dublin wasn't open. He'd forgotten it was still very early and a Saturday after all. Using his initiative, he decided on another approach. From the cabinet where all manner of reference materials were kept he found an old road atlas which contained a map of Ireland. After a few minutes careful study, he'd located the town of Ballingary and using his powers of reasoning, he surmised that a ship with this name would have connections with a local port – and there it was, the port, Skibbereen. A call to International Directory Enquiries eventually found him the number for Baltimore and Skibbereen

Harbour Commissioners. Given that one could now call the Republic of Ireland direct from the UK Lewis dialled the number. Thus it was that he ultimately discovered that the *Ballingary* was indeed a small freighter but no longer named the *Ballingary*. She had undergone a complete refit and was now *The Michael Collins* and owned by a Liam O'Reilly. Lewis's informant at the Harbour Commissioners office could not have been more helpful.

'Ah well now, you'll be needing his address although he's never home, always at sea now, but then he needs to be working, picking up whatever cargo he can to be in a position to pay for that refit. Those Listers must have cost a fortune.'

Lewis terminated the call and jubilantly thumped the desk. 'Listers! Good old Charlie.'

***

It was 9.00am when Cartwright finally felt sufficiently human to heave himself from the bunk in the cell he'd adopted for the night. He needed a shower, a shave and a change of clothes, all of which would have to wait until he'd briefed the team.

Given that it was a Saturday, with a considerable detachment of the uniformed compliment of the Kesgrave headquarters in South Yorkshire, the briefing room was still busy. The general hubbub died down as the DCI and Chief Superintendent Nigel Gibbons entered the room.

'Right, quiet please, ladies and gentlemen, and thank you for giving up your weekend. It seems that even before we've had the benefit of the training course with HM Customs we're in the midst of a smuggling operation or some form of people trafficking, organised major crime in any event. Cartwright, if you will, please.'

The DCI, for all that he felt and looked terrible, knew that he had to be at his assertive best for the next few minutes.

Gibbons was not his greatest fan and was always on his back or looking for an excuse to make adverse criticism.

'Last night, we believe a boat made a rendezvous with a Transit van somewhere on the Deben between Waldringfield and Woodbridge. We have the van in our workshop and I hope to have Forensics' report later today. We have the occupants of the van in custody.

The van was loaded with...' He paused knowing that the room was about to erupt. 'With *Connolly's Corn Flakes...*' And yes, the room erupted. Even Gibbons managed a smile. 'But seriously, quiet please, seriously, a concealed compartment was discovered in the van. In this compartment we found a young Dutch woman, Lotte van Dijkstra, barely alive, having been beaten almost to death, and almost certainly sexually assaulted. She is in the Ipswich Hospital at present. I expect a report on her condition later this morning. We have four suspects in custody...' And Cartwright's synopsis continued.

'It is essential, ladies and gentlemen, that vigilance is our watchword. Any form of smuggling racket is likely to be on the increase and our part of the coastline is prime territory for landing illegal cargo, human or otherwise.' He went on to instruct specific officers to specific tasks. 'Amy, get straight to the hospital now and relieve Annie Mackay. She's been there with our Dutch girl all night. Let me know as soon as there's something to report. Doug, you and your team, I want everything we can discover about the suspect Bandile Bosch and his daughters, Stellen and Kirsten.' Gibbons gave Cartwright a sideways look which seemed to say, 'are you serious? Kirsten Bosch and Stellen Bosch'.

'Ray, you and Vaughan, you're on McLevy. I want his life history, his Naval record, everything. Bruno, I want you to find out who our mystery visitor from the Netherlands is.' DC Bruno Mennens, an ex-patriot Dutchman, was the obvious choice for this part of the investigation. 'Andy, let me know after this briefing how we're getting on with the ship. Remember, boys and girls, vigilance. We're going to send a message, loud and clear, to smugglers, whether it be drugs, diamonds, booze, fags, antiques, works of art, or even people; you land on our patch and you'll be nicked!' The round of applause this last statement received was a clear indication of the manner in which Cartwright had motivated the force. Motivational encouragement was a gift Gibbons had never been endowed with nor had he ever acquired but despite his resentment of Cartwright's skill, even he put his hands together, albeit briefly.

Chapter 6 **Saturday About Midday**

In Pedley Street, a sign featuring a personified characterisation of Warner Brothers' Wile E Coyote who in the *Road Runner* Looney Tunes cartoons was always attempting to blow up some form of wayward bantam cock, the Road Runner, with sticks of dynamite from the Acme Discount Stores. The partners and proprietors of the business under one of the Pedley Street railway arches had agreed that this was a great name for their enterprise *Acme* – the achievement of excellence.

Matt Taylor had just finished unloading a pallet of stolen television sets.

'So, where the bleedin' 'ell is 'e?'

'Don't sweat, 'e'll be 'ere.' Tommy Martin was singing to himself, a tuneless version of Lulu's 'Man who Sold the World' as he went about stacking some cases of illegally obtained vodka of doubtful provenance.

'Well, I've done, Tom, 'ow 'bout you?'

'Yeah, I'm there. C'mon let's go.' Tom flicked the switch and the electric motor whirred into life lowering the metal roller-shutter. They locked it in place and secured the door, top and bottom, with bolt-cropper-proof padlocks.

The Carpenter's Arms in Cheshire Street is just a stone's throw from Bethnal Green Station to the east and Shoreditch to the

west and just a few minutes' walk from the Acme Discount
Stores. The pub hadn't been open but a few minutes, when the
two regular customers arrived. They ordered and took their
drinks to a table by the window. Tommy looked at his watch.

'Yeah, Matt, you're right. Where the bleedin' 'ell is 'e?
Surely, 'e should'er bin 'ere by nah. I 'ope naht's gone wrong.'

Matt was Tommy's number two, so to speak, his sidekick,
but no less a petty villain. They'd met during the 50s whilst
in the army doing their National Service. They became best of
friends through a common interest – easy money, maximum
reward, minimum effort.

'I told you so, din't I? Bloody Sarf Africans – 'es wot's gone
wrong if anyfing 'as. Yer can't trust 'em.'

''E's bin 'eld up or summat, broke darn mebbe. 'E wouldn't
cross us not wi' McLevy riding shotgun.'

'Well, I 'ope you're right, Tom. Who is this McLevy bloke
anyway? Sounds a bit like a Scotch Yid to me.'

'Big fella, remember? 'E was at that meet we 'ad in 'ere wiv
Frankie, Berkshire. According to Frankie, Liam says if 'e was
in the Navy 'e's an OK geezer. Anyway don't forget, we're all
in on the scam.' Tom reminded his partner of how the current, cunning conspiracy was supposed to work. The double
switch.

'Remember it's Irish Liam wot was layin' out Frankie's
funny money up front to Jimmy the Dutchman. It's Liam
what's pulling the double shufty. Mr Khan don't know that.
Rancid don't know that an' McLevy don't know that. Then
McLevy pays back Liam who then squares up Frankie, using
the twenty-grand wedge that Mr Khan put up in the first
place. They're all taking a slice off the top and at the end of
the day everybody wins 'cept Mr Khan. We's well darn the
pecking order but we get summat for nowt. We'll stitch
McLevy up a few quid fer late deliv'ry as well. You can bet
that 'e's creamed off at least a couple a monkeys of Mr Khan's

money anyway an' Mr Khan's not goin' to be best pleased wiv McLevy for losing the gear. All we 'ave to do is store the gear for Frankie. We might get a bung from Berkshire for introducing the girls. Owt else an' we expresses our surprise an' ignorance to any other bugger.'

'Can we get away with stitching up Mr Khan, Tom? Why've we never met 'im? Why is it 'e always sends 'is flunky? 'E worries me!' Mere mention of the name was enough to make even a hardened villain go weak at the knees. Mr Khan's operation was thought to stretch from Pakistan to London and it was probably an irrational fear of the unknown, maybe of hordes of marauding *katana*-wielding Pakistanis, the Northwest Frontier revisited that caused unrest in the underworld. Yet, apart from his closest lieutenants, no one had ever knowingly met him in person.

'Mr high and bloody mighty Khan can shove it right up 'is Khyber. If we's careful, there shouldn't be a problem. Say nowt, stay shtum.'

'So, if we ain't storin' anyfing for the time being, then our bung is just from supplying the prossies. But that's gone tits up as well. We better find somefin' else, eh, Tom, 'cos I'm about b'rasic?'

'Summat'll turn up, it alus does. Our ship'll come in. You wait an' see,' Tom prophesised.

'You know 'ow 'im next door is alus on about 'ow some of the girls 'ave passed their best before date and some are no longer on the game? *It is imperative that I update my catalogue.* That's wot' 'e says, ole Berkshire... *demand is exceeding supply.'* Matt often mimicked their neighbour with a very passable imitation of his aristocratically cultured accent.

''An' you know 'ow 'e goes walkabout and rounds a few up off the street. P'raps we can round a few extras up for 'im as well, what d'you reckon?'

'I reckon!'

Gerry Hunt, or *Berkshire* as he had become known locally, was the tenant of the next arch. That he should have been dubbed *Berkshire* was entirely appropriate according to the clientele of *The Carpenter's Arms* and the compendium of Cockney Rhyming Slang, given his failings as an antique dealer and the nature of his subsidiary business. It was common knowledge throughout the Metropolitan District and within the range of Bow bells that Gerry's antiques enterprise was a front, and he was always the first to admit to anyone that whilst antique dealing was not necessarily his primary enterprise he did manage a side-line. Tommy and Matt were Gerry's *aides-de-camp*, his right-hand men when it came to the recruitment of personnel though neither had been anywhere near a camp since their time at Catterick.

'Well, there's the Dutch bird, s'posed to be coming in the van. Bit a 'igh class, 'ighly educated university crumpet. Apparently Liam's bloke, Fergal, was going to scrobble 'er and try a sample. Then there's them Sarf African dusky maidens – you know the daughters of wo's'is name, the bloke McLevy got to drive the van. Remember we did a deal wiv Liam as far as the Dutch girl were concerned. She might not be on the game yet, but I wouldn't mind breakin' 'er in, give 'er a bit a coachin' like, if Fergal ain't already. I reckon she'll soon get used to 'er new job.'

'Oh yeah, really nice-lookin' girls those sisters. Weren't Liam going to slip 'em a Mickey? Get them away from their ol' man? Tasty Twins innit? Should be good earners, them, goin' out as a twosome. I 'ope the Scotch Yid's behavin' 'imself, we don't want shop-soiled do we nah? Best you don't do any coaching then innit?' They laughed and Matt ordered another Scotch for them both as they continued with their banter whilst waiting.

Another hour passed.

'Look' 'ere, Tom, I don't reckon 'e's comin'. I'm s'posed

to be darn *The Beggar* by one. I'm meetin' Frankie afore we go to the Park. 'E might 'ave summat for us, summat casual. Anyway, 'ow much longer we goin' to sit in 'ere wi our thumbs up our arses?' Matt was a keen West Ham United supporter, and he always met his mate Frankie *the Fence* Forsyth in *The Blind Beggar* on home game match days before getting a lift to Upton Park. Frankie was a dark horse, a fanatical West Ham fan, always liked to be accepted as *one of the lads* but there was much more to him and his activities than anyone realised. In general, he kept himself to himself and as far as he was concerned, the less people knew, the better. He was content to be thought of as the local small-time crook who bought and sold stuff.

'You an' yer bleedin footie! Who yer got today then?' Tom asked.

'West Brom bloody Albion, mate. Should be a good 'un, but you never know. It's like that Brian Clough bloke said, "we got a good team on paper, shame we was playing on grass!"'

'Yer don't mind if I come do yer?'

'Course not, pal. Better than wastin' our time 'ere.' They drank up and sauntered off down Vallance Road to Whitechapel.

At *The Blind Beggar* Frankie was at the bar studying the football pages in the *Mirror*.

'Eh up, Matt, Tom. 'As your ship come in yet? Know what I mean?' Tom gestured to the barman. 'No, Tom, no drinks 'ere now. We ain't got time for a drink 'cos we 'ave to get the bus. Me van got nicked on Tuesday,' said Frankie relieving the itch on the side of his nose by a couple of taps of the finger.

Chapter 7 **Monday**

Cartwright was in his office early on Monday morning, thinking positively and determined to embrace the day whatever it threw up. *Carpe diem!* He was somewhat taken aback when his phone rang.

'Cartwright.'

'Sorry to call so early, sir, it's Amy, WPC Amy Reynolds, sir. I'm at the hospi...'

'Amy, yes of course. What news?'

'Well, sir, good news. Lotte's conscious and wide awake. She's just eaten a bowl of porridge and two rounds of toast. She still looks a bit of a mess but she's feeling much better. The doctor says she's well enough to answer questions and I thought you'd...'

'I'm on my way, Amy. Well done.' He grabbed his coat from the hook and was on his way downstairs and encountered Armstrong on his way up.

'Our Dutch girl, Lotte, is up to answering questions. I'm on my way there now. Could you chase up Davies and Vaughan make sure they're doing something useful, and you take over researching McLevy? Start with...' He paused and scratched his head. 'Well, I'm not sure. The Admiralty? Whoever it is deals with Navy personnel. If McLevy is a Navy man we should be able to get some background.'

'OK, boss, I'm on it! Oh, and good luck with Lotte.'

When he arrived at the hospital he was directed to the Brantham Ward where Lotte had been admitted for emergency assessment. She had now been moved to a side room. WPC Amy Reynolds was sitting outside, nursing a cup of hospital tea or coffee, she wasn't sure which it was.

'Well done, Amy, no don't get up – no on second thoughts you'd better come in with me. I don't want to intimidate the poor girl, and perhaps best if there's a chaperone in the room anyway. I assume you've struck up a relationship with her already?'

'Yes, sir, she's a very friendly girl, her English is very good and she's coping really well under the circumstances although I think she may be at that controlled state of rape trauma syndrome.'

'Excuse me?'

'It's when a victim acts without emotion as if nothing has happened and everything is fine, unlike the hysterical open emotion, shock and disbelief, floods of tears and the like.'

'Hmm, thanks, Amy. I'm glad you're here.' Why is it, Cartwright wondered, that training for male police officers never covered any of that kind of thing?

'Hello, Lotte, this is Detective Chief Inspector Cartwright. He's a very, very nice man!' Cartwright could feel himself blushing. Lotte was in a semi-reclined, not quite a sitting position in bed, wearing a hospital issue robe, a very pretty girl despite the extensive bruising to her face.

'Hallo, goedemorgen. Hoe vel je je nu? Spreekt u Engels?'

'Ja natuurlijk. Veel beter bedankt. Your Dutch is very good, Inspector.'

'Oh, I don't think so. Certainly not as good as your English. If you don't mind we'll continue in English.'

'Helemaal niet.'

Cartwright and Amy had just positioned themselves sitting either side of the bed when a doctor came in.

'Good morning, I'm Mr Morrison. I repaired Lotte's ruptured spleen yesterday.' Just like that, abrupt and as matter of fact as if announcing he'd just finished doing the washing up. 'She'll be fine now.' His assured prognostication was delivered with what could have been interpreted as a cast-iron guarantee. 'The broken ribs will be sore for a while and she'll need to avoid heavy lifting, but the periorbital hematomas, lacerations and contusions will heal quite readily. I don't think there's any risk of an unwanted pregnancy given the amount of vaginal bleeding there was after the rape. Good morning.' And he was gone.

'Well, whatever happened to good old fashioned bedside manner, hey, Lotte? Had I been in your situation I would have expected a little more in the way of sympathy or compassion. Perhaps a "how are you feeling?" What say you, Amy?'

'Yes, sir.'

'I hope you heard that, Lotte. No lifting heavy weights. What on earth does the man think you do?' Even if he made allowances for the fact that NHS staff were over pressed, Cartwright was appalled by the manner of Morrison's stilted remarks and the downright rudeness of the man. He tried not to dwell on it and redoubled his condolent and tender pity.

'You've had a very nasty and life-threatening experience. It was purely by luck that we found you. If we hadn't you'd almost certainly be dead. I hope you feel up to talking about it. You see, the sooner we know what happened, the sooner we can get after the culprits.'

'I understand, Inspector. I am a bit sore, but I'll try to tell you everything I can remember.'

'Were you bought here against your will?'

'*Wat bedoel je?* How do you mean?'

'Were you forced to come to England?'

'Yes.' Hesitation.

'Look, Lotte, if this all gets too distressing for you, do please let me know and we can continue another time.' Lotte swallowed and took a deep breath.

'It was Tuesday night. I was walking home, late. I'd been out with some friends to a coffee shop, where many students go. I thought I was being followed. I ignored it at first but got scared so started to run. Suddenly a van pulled up just in front of me and a man got out. He was walking towards me. The man who had been following me had caught up.' She stopped, her eyes closed, almost as if she were reliving the moment.

'A hand came from behind, pulled the hood of my parka down, around my neck and a rag over my nose and mouth. I remember the smell on the cloth, and then I saw the syringe. *Ik probeerde te schreeuwen.* I tried to scream... The next thing I remember was being on the floor of a van. A man was on top of me, and I couldn't fight him off. It was like I had no strength, like I was numb. He was forcing my head onto the floor. I thought my skull would burst with the pain. I was shivering with cold, and my nose was bleeding. I tried to scream again but no sound would come... After he had finished he tied my hands behind my back and my feet were also tied together. I was so cold, so cold and shivering. My coat was gone, my panties and tights were lying on the floor and my skirt was torn. I was very frightened. I thought I would die. They left me in the van for a long time. *Ik weet niet hoe lang.* I don't know how long.'

'Did you get a look at either of the men who did this to you? Could you describe either of them? Would you recognise either of them if you saw them again?'

'One of them. The man that raped me was average height and build with fair red coloured hair – do you say ginger? He had a tattoo on the side of his neck. I remember, I saw it quite clearly when he... It was in a foreign language I didn't understand. It could have been in the same language I heard spoken when they pulled me out of the van and pushed me onto the boat.'

'A boat? You came to England by boat?'

'Yes.'

'Do you know what time it was or which day this was?'

'No, it was dark. It must have been very early morning I think. Maybe Friday? I did recognise the place – *Jan van Riebeeckhaven*.'

'Did you recognise anything else?'

'Part of the boat's name... *Michael* I think. I couldn't see all of it. I was pushed down some stairs, I fell. I think that's when I hurt my ribs. I was locked in a cabin with no windows. It was full of big cardboard boxes.' She stopped again and screwed her eyes tightly closed. After a few seconds she continued.

'It was the man who raped me. He gave me some water.'

'Well done, Lotte, You're very brave. Can you carry on?' Amy leaned forward and held Lotte's hand.

'There was a lot of shouting in a foreign language, not Dutch, not English, the same as before. Then the boat's engine started, and we began to move. Nothing happened for a few hours. I was sick. Then the man came in, the same man. With a syringe. He injected my arm. I remember worrying about my purse and my coat. I really wanted my coat. I was cold. Then I was here in this hospital.'

'So, you remember nothing between being put on a boat and waking up here?'

'No, sir, but I can't be sure. I was a virgin, me and Linde... No it doesn't matter, it's nothing at all.' Silent tears began to run down her cheeks.

'Thank you, Lotte, *heel veel dank. Je bent erg behulpzaam geweest*. Get some rest now and we'll come and see you again tomorrow.'

'Inspector, *zou je het mijn vader kunnen laten weten alsjeblieft?*'

Outside in the corridor, Cartwright told Amy that he would send Annie Mackay to relieve her as soon as he got back to the station. 'I think she wants me to contact her father. I'd better get DC Mennens here as well, Lotte must think I can speak Dutch!'

'Sounds double Dutch to me, sir,' said Amy.

'Never mind the double Dutch, make mine a double Scotch, Laphroaig!'

Chapter 8 **Monday**

In Pedley Street Tom and Matt were quizzing their neighbour whilst taking a speculative walk around his *showroom*.

'Anybody come looking fer us on Sat'd'y or yes'd'y, Gerry?'

'I didn't encounter a single soul all weekend, gentlemen. Were you anticipating the arrival of someone perchance?'

'You knows full well we was, you ole faggot.'

'No, Matthew, I'm as straight as... well you know. Matthew please! Remove your posterior from that chair immediately!' Matt had sat down in one of the more legitimate pieces Gerry had for sale.

'What this old chair?'

'My dear boy, that old chair as you call it is an eighteenth-century French Louis XV carved gilt wood Fauteil armchair – worth around £1500.'

'So that's a no is it?' Matt asked for confirmation of the answer to the original question as he arose from the chair.

'We was expecting a d'livery, as you know, Gerry, including some fresh meat,' said Tommy.

'Ah well, bugger it eh, Tom? No skin off our arses is it?' stated Matt as he was about to open a door on a mid-seventeenth-century Swedish Rococo cabinet.

'Now that's a very pragmatic, philanthropic and conceptive

attitude you're adopting there, Matthew, and leave that cabinet alone if you don't mind.'

'If you say so, Gerald old bean.' Whilst Tommy found Matt's response amusing he was disappointed rather more by the non-arrival of the weed than fresh female flesh. New girls could be listed in Gerry's alternative catalogue at any time. It was the missing consignment of cannabis which concerned him, particularly given the double-cross they were hoping to pull off. Not that he was a misogynist; on the contrary, he fancied himself as a ladies' man and was always willing to test-drive new models. Noticing a framed picture on the wall above the Louis XV chair, Matt was curious.

'I 'ope she ain't one of the latest in our catalogue sitting there drying her fanny off.'

'No, Matthew, she isn't. That picture was painted in about 1858 by an American artist called Whistler, James Abbott McNeil Whistler, and the young lady is merely enjoying the open air. The picture is entitled *En Plein Soleil* and it's probably priceless. Now, if we've no further business to conduct I'd appreciate it, gentlemen, if you'd very kindly fuck off.'

'I think he wants us leave, Matt.'

***

'OK, I'm off. I promised Helen I'd get home tonight at a reasonable time,' Cartwright shouted to Armstrong as he was tidying his desk as he habitually did before leaving.

'You got time for a swift one, boss, there's something I want to run past you while its fresh in my mind.'

'Well, OK, if it's pertinent to the case.'

Some ten minutes later they were in *The Maybush*.

'I've been thinking, guv. Try this for size. There's a shipment of weed in Amsterdam destined for Bethnal Green. The skipper of the vessel commissioned to carry the shipment, what's his name? The Irishman, O'Reilly, decides he'll try a bit of private enterprise by pulling a fast one, so he knocks off the weed, leaves it stashed away safely on the ship and gives McLevy a load of corn flakes instead. The girl is somehow part of the original deal, recruited from one of Amsterdam's brothels in *De Rosse Buurt* about to start a new career in London's East End perhaps. She's been kidnapped and is also on the ship having been drugged, with the delivery boy getting his leg over and sampling, not to mention damaging, the goods on the way.'

Cartwright revealed that he had led a sheltered existence away from the realities of such things. 'Aren't those Amsterdam brothels illegal?' Cartwright's naivety surprised Armstrong.

'C'mon, guv, seriously? Prostitution has been going on in the old part of the harbour since the fifteenth century. The police have got the girls off the street, and they're now allowed to solicit through windows provided the curtains are almost fully closed. The houses where girls are working are identified by red lights – *De Rosse Buurt*, the Red Light District.'

'How do you know all this?'

'Can't say without incriminating myself,' Armstrong joked before continuing with his theory. 'While the corn flakes, which McLevy thinks is the weed, are being transferred from the ship to the van, Lotte is bundled into a hidden compartment in the van. McLevy, who's the middleman, wants to keep it a secret from Bosch because Bosch is a bit of a Puritan, besides which O'Reilly and McLevy have got designs on Stellen and Kirsten joining Lotte in a Bethnal Green brothel.' Cartwright sat nodding his head. He could see where his colleague was coming from.

'So, O'Reilly, or his crew, slips Bosch's girls a Mickey while neither Bosch nor McLevy are looking. But what about the van?' Cartwright asked.

'That's been nicked somewhere in London, it's a London registration at least. And it's been modified with the addition of a concealed compartment built in by the villain who's presumably waiting for his stash of cannabis and three girls for his brothel to arrive.'

'OK, I hear you. But didn't Lotte say she was a student, snatched off the street walking home from a cafe. I wouldn't have thought for one minute she was a member of the profession.'

'Makes no difference to my scenario whether she was or not, does it though?'

'No, I suppose not. We really must find Liam bloody O'Reilly. He holds the key to the entire mess. And who is Mr Big in this whole operation? Is it O'Reilly? I don't think McLevy's behind it. He's only a middleman. Perhaps the whole deal is orchestrated by some London villain we're not aware of yet? Come on, Doug, we're going to London as soon as we can get away in the morning. I'll get Gibbo to give Bethnal Green nick a call. We don't want to upset the local plod and go stepping on anybody's toes. Tell Andy.'

Chapter 9 **Tuesday**

It was two days after the event that DC Mennens of the Suffolk Police managed to make contact with Willem van Dijkstra to inform him what had befallen his daughter. His initial reaction was one of unbridled rage, not only with the perpetrator but with the English police for the delay in getting in touch with him. He resolved there and then that he would do whatever it took to find whoever and exact retribution. Ordinarily he was a mild-mannered, non-violent person, a curator at the *Rijksmuseum* in Amsterdam, who doted on his daughter, but now he was angry, full of hate and revengeful. His initial response to the call took the form of a rant.

'Een vader hoort zijn kind niet te beschermen? Isn't a father supposed to protect his child, to keep her safe and see her grow into adulthood?' Lotte was still very much *his little girl*. He felt absolutely powerless and was blaming himself. After an hour of pacing up and down, breathing fire and brimstone, pausing only to pour and swallow measure after measure of Vieux, he broke down and slumped into his favourite armchair sitting with his head in his hands sobbing until he fell asleep. When he woke up he telephoned the hospital in Ipswich and was able to actually speak to Lotte. It was small comfort to learn that she was recovering from the physical injuries. Willem was concerned that the mental trauma would come

later. He made a second call, this time to the police, and was told that a suspect had been identified and that it would only be a matter of days before he would be arrested. He wanted to protest when he was told that Lotte could be required to pick him out at an identity parade and, if necessary, to give evidence in court. But he knew that the due rule of law had to be followed.

***

By the time Cartwright arrived in his office at Kesgrave HQ, Chief Superintendent Gibbons, early for once, had declared the *Corn Flakes Caper* a major incident and was busy rounding up everyone involved so far in the briefing room.

'Ah, Cartwright there you are.'

'Yes here I am.' Cartwright's response conveyed a smouldering resentment at Gibbons' interference. Most if not everyone in the room was aware of the animosity with which HQ's two senior officers regarded each other. Most if not everyone in the room were in the DCI's camp. Notwithstanding the invidious relationship between them, exchanges between Cartwright and Gibbons in public always stopped short of snapping and snarling at each other – much to the dismay of those listening.

'So, are we any further forward?' There was scant courtesy in Gibbons' enquiry.

'Yes, sir. Quite significant developments in fact.'

'Do please be so kind as to share them with us then,' came the parsimonious sneer.

Ignoring the sarcasm which Cartwright knew only too well was intended to inflame his indignation, he proceeded to give chapter and verse of the chronology of intelligence which had been gathered thus far.

'So, we know almost for certain that Lotte van Dijkstra was

abducted in Amsterdam, raped, and beaten up, and brought to Felixstowe on a small ship, *The Michael Collins*, owned and skippered by an Irish National, Liam O'Reilly. While the ship was berthed on Methersgate Quay, on the River Deben, we can surmise that Lotte, drugged, bound hand and foot and unconscious, was hidden in a concealed compartment our mechanics found in the van we have in our workshop. We can also gather that the van, probably stolen in London, was there to collect an as yet unknown illegal cargo. From what we have gathered from Patrick McLevy, currently under arrest on a charge which won't stick, the cargo he was expecting was not *Connolly's Corn Flakes*.' There was a rumble of amusement around the room but the expression on Gibbons' face was sufficient to sour the brief moment of levity. Cartwright continued, 'I'm prepared, however, to accept McLevy's contention that he knew nothing of the girl – for the time being at least. The other people involved, Bandile Bosch, a recent arrival in the UK from South Africa, who has been 100% co-operative, and his two daughters, I believe are innocent although Bandile has admitted that he thought there was something, and I quote, "a bit too good to be true", about the driving job. Now has anyone got anything to add?' He and Gibbons scoured the room, possibly more in hope than expectation that someone would have a snippet or two of additional information. Cartwright raised his eyebrows in Lewis's direction. He felt certain Andy would have something.

'Andy?'

'Sir, we can be certain that the ship involved was *The Michael Collins*, formerly known as *Ballingary*.'

'How can we be certain?'

'The engines, Listers, and by the evidence of Charlie Brinkley's ears, substantiated by Chief Officer Chris Barnard of Thames Coastguard with further confirmation from the Mercantile Marine Office in Dublin and the Baltimore and Skibbereen Harbour commissioners.'

'Thank you, Sergeant Lewis.' At the mention of Charlie Brinkley's ears, Gibbons had initially appeared highly sceptical, but even he had found the substantive evidence compelling.

'Doug, anything further on the Bosch connection?'

'Not much that we don't know already, guv. The family lived on a settlement twenty miles outside Cape Town, Mitchell's Plain, on the Cape Flats which are on the False Bay Coast...'

Gibbons interrupted, 'Spare us the bloody travelogue, Armstrong!'

The DS, unperturbed, continued, 'The Mitchell's Plain settlement is an ANC, that's the African National Congress for you ignorant foot-soldiers, an ANC stronghold of the anti-apartheid movement. Apparently Mrs Bosch, Mandisa, died after she was mugged and beaten by white Afrikaan thugs for straying into a whites only area. As we know there are twin daughters aged 24. Bosch has no criminal record, and the family is here legally with all the correct visas.'

'Thank you, Doug. Seems like an OK family to me. I don't know which racist it was that suggested Blacks have a lower IQ than Whites. Certainly isn't the case with Bandile Bosch. Do we know how the daughters are?'

'We had the doctor examine them. He reckons they had almost certainly been drugged – possibly Rohypnol. They're recovered now, sir.'

'Thank you, Doug. Now, Ray, Vaughan, how'd you get on with McLevy's background?'

It was Vaughan that answered. 'We contacted the Ministry of Defence and they put us in touch with "The Navy List" – that's a public record of ships and personnel and stuff like that. From there we got in touch with *HMS Norfolk's* Commander...'

Gibbons interrupted again, 'Why not the captain? Always pays to go to the top I find.'

Ray Davies responded, 'With respect, sir, on a destroyer the Commander is the captain, so to speak.' Cartwright smiled. *That told him, well done lads*! he thought. Davies continued, 'McLevy did serve on *HMS Norfolk*, as petty officer, not the chief petty officer as he has been claiming. He was dishonourably discharged. He has a record, causing an affray, two counts of GBH. Apparently a bit too handy with his fists especially after he's had a few. Interesting fact as well, sir, Prince Charles served on the *Norfolk* for a while in 1971.' A broad grin spread across the face of Gibbons who everyone knew was very much a Royalist sycophant.

'Well done, Detectives!' One might have thought he'd just had a personal introduction!

'Excellent work, everybody. Now, we need to press on. Bruno I want you and WPC Reynolds or WPC McKay to go and visit Lotte. See if she's remembered anything else which might help and get the contact details for her father.'

Annie McKay spoke up, 'Already done, sir, and we've spoken to him. He's a curator at the big museum in Amsterdam, seemed like a nice fellow once he'd calmed down.'

'Begrijpelijk zeker!' added DC Mennens.

'What's that he said?' Gibbons wanted to know.

'Understandable for sure!' answered Cartwright.

'Not understandable to me, what did he say?'

'Understandable, for sure!' Gibbons was totally bamboozled!

Cartwright smiled as he continued, 'As soon as we've determined what we're going to do with McLevy and Bosch, DS Armstrong and I will be taking a trip to East London and having a discreet sniff around in Bethnal Green. Somebody there will have been expecting a load of something and, I suspect, not corn flakes. They'll be wondering where it is. OK that's it. Vigilance, remember!'

'And one other thing.' Gibbons always liked the last word.

'You'll be pleased to hear, I'm sure, that I've spoken to the Assistant Commissioner. He has agreed to put your training course with HM Customs in abeyance for the time being. And with Prime Minister Heath having called a general election I'm sure we can look forward to these idle commie miners ending their strike, meaning of course that we'll get our uniforms back.'

Given the absence of any doubt as to the Chief Super's political leaning there was an ironic cheer.

Chapter 10 **Later on Tuesday**

Armstrong and Cartwright sat in the DCI's office.

'Have you contacted the media yet?' Armstrong asked.

'Oh yes, there's an appeal for witnesses gone out and all coastguard stations have been put on alert. That ship holds most if not all of the answers.' They sat in silence for a while, deep in thought. The appearance of Ray Davies brought them both back to the real world.

'What is it, Ray?'

'Well, technically, it's a form of fraud, is what it is.'

'What is?'

'Impersonating a military officer. McLevy was claiming to be something which he most certainly was not. He'd never made it to chief petty officer, and he'd been dishonourably discharged. Yet he would have had us believe that he was still on active service and at CPO rank.'

'Good point well made, Ray.'

'At least that's a charge which will stick but is it enough to hold him any longer?' asked Armstrong.

'It's a new one on me. I guess I'd better ask Gibbons.'

'How about Bosch?'

'That's another tricky one. We don't know for certain whether or not the van he was driving was stolen and until we know for sure that it was... I suppose we can let him go.'

'But what about aiding and abetting fraud and kidnapping? And theft. Where did all those corn flakes come from?'

'You can bet they were knocked off from somewhere, but where? Remember they were being loaded into the van from a ship we know had arrived from Amsterdam. Lotte told us she recognised the harbour. I wonder, do the Dutch eat corn flakes?'

'Buggered if I know!' exclaimed Davies.

'Me neither, but assuming they were stolen he is guilty of handling, more importantly, there's the abduction. To what extent if any was our man McLevy involved? My initial inclination at least is to believe that he was ignorant of what was going on, although I'm prepared to be convinced otherwise if we come up with any compelling evidence.'

'I'm pretty sure that somewhere at the bottom of this there are drugs involved. It's a fine complicated mess especially when we factor in Lotte: raped and beaten up. Who was responsible for that? And then there're Bosch's daughters: drugged, possibly for the same purpose. Have a think about it while I go and have a word with Gibbo.'

After half an hour, Cartwright returned to his office.

'Well?' asked Armstrong.

'Gibbo says we have to release McLevy. Handling stolen corn flakes and impersonating a Naval Officer are insufficient grounds for holding him any longer. Gibbo's also of the opinion that, on the balance of probabilities at the moment, he wasn't involved in any kidnapping conspiracy. But he will ultimately have to answer the impersonating and handling charges in court when we've concluded our investigation. We may find some answers in Bethnal Green. We also need to find that ship.'

DC Mennens knocked on the open door and entered.

'Excuse me, sir.'

'Ah, Bruno, what news?'

'Well, I've been speaking with Commandant Gerritsen of the *Korps Nationale Politie* in Amsterdam. Apparently, Willem van Dijkstra, Lotte's father, wasn't very happy with us and went to see Gerritsen. I think they must be friends from what I can gather. The Dutch police wasted no time in finding a witness who actually saw Lotte being bundled into a van. Not only that, but he wrote down the registration of the van. The owner was traced and arrested, given a grilling Dutch style and confessed. Seems that someone, speaking in English but in a dialect he didn't recognise, offered the van owner a sum of money just to drive, stop to pick up a girl then drive to the *Jan van Riebeeckhaven*.'

'Good work, Bruno. I think this more or less confirms what Lotte has told us. We need to find that ship!' Cartwright emphasised the need with a thump on his desk.

Chapter 11 **Tuesday**

The Sexual Offences Act of 1956 made keeping a brothel an offence. The Street Offences Act of 1959 stated that it shall be an offence for a common prostitute to loiter or solicit in a street or public place for the purpose of prostitution. A prostitute convicted under the Act could be fined £80 so many of them were leaving the pavements and becoming *call-girls*. For a one-off advertising fee, girls in the Metropolitan Borough of Bethnal Green, Shoreditch and Whitechapel districts could have a listing in Gerry Hunt's *alternative* catalogue: one of a series of London-wide local directories of prostitutes. These *contact magazines* as they were known were widely and not too discreetly available and provided details of the services offered, descriptions of the ladies and their various tariffs. Such directories were, in certain quarters, deemed to amount to a conspiracy to corrupt public morals, but Gerry, for one, didn't seem to be unduly concerned even after the penalty for living off immoral earnings was increased to seven years' imprisonment. And for their part, as far as Tom and Matt were concerned, it would be their contention that any commission they received was in respect of putting girls in touch with a modelling agency.

Gerry was struggling with an old Olivetti typewriter preparing a revision to his contact magazine. He thought the amended front cover exemplified the touch of class he'd been searching for: *Bethnal Green International Escort Services* and then on a lower line in small type, *and so much more!* With a Dutch girl and two South Africans potentially on the books Gerry felt quite justified in the *international* description.

'I wonder if my neighbouring Cockney fellows are any closer to getting details of my new girls?' he asked himself. And, having posed the question to himself, he popped around to the next-door arch hoping that Tommy or Matt would be in a position to provide the answer.

'I say, Thomas, Matthew, when might I anticipate the arrival of my new ladies? I really must get my revised maga- zine to the printer. Surely you realise that it is to the detri- ment of our standard of living so many of the current entries are no longer operational, in short, shagged out, dear boys.'

'Allo, Berkshire ole' cock. Good day to you too! I'm sorry, but gawd knows. Like I said at the weekend, we was expecting a shipment on Sat'd'y mornin' but it never come did it? As you know, our man McLevy was s'posed to be bringin' the van darn from the east coast wiv' a load a gear which 'e thought we'd be storin' for Mr Khan. Plan was that the African, you know the geezer what was drivin', 'e would 'ave bin bumped off somewhere on the way, whilst his daughters were coma- tose. Your three fresh tarts would 'ave bin on the van and 'ere now if all 'ad gone to plan, but it bleedin' well din't, did it? 'Ere, you wanna fag?' Tommy proffered a packet of *Benson & Hedges* in Gerry's direction.

'Kindly refrain from referring to my operatives as tarts. Ladies, if you don't mind, Thomas, please. You think my enterprise is so common as to have tarts? Please! – and no thank you.' He held up the flat of his palm towards the ciga- rette packet. 'You're only tempting me because you know I'm trying to give up.' Gerry flounced out and returned to his own empire.

'Wot's ole Berkshire want then, Tom – as if I can't guess, comin' in 'ere wi' a face like a smacked arse?' Matt appeared from the back of the arch with several cases of Bulmers cider on a sack barrow.

'We've got a contact number for McLevy ain't we? Time we bent 'is ear I reckon, find out where it all went down the lavvy.'

'I agree. 'E's in some poncy guesthouse innit, in F'lixtowe wherever that is?'

'D' yo' think we should 'ave a word wiv Mr Khan's bloke first?'

'You mean Rancid? Yeah, Rancid, a word, better 'ad.' They both laughed.

***

McLevy had been released on bail with a court hearing date due to be set within 28 days. Since his discharge from the Navy, he'd been renting a room in the Grafton Guesthouse on Felixstowe's sea front. A Temperance establishment – clean, comfortable, basic, reasonably priced but above all, anonymous.

There was a knock on his door, it was Mrs Arnold, the landlady. 'Patrick, are you in?'

McLevy opened the door. 'What's up, Eleanor?'

'There have been two men, telephoned you twice now, in fact one of them has rung three times. Both say it's very important that you call them. Look I've written the names and numbers on this piece of paper. You can use the phone in my sitting room if you like.' Patrick retreated into his room and closed the door. He stared at the names and numbers on the paper. He'd known that he'd have to answer to Mr Khan sooner or later and it was only to be expected that the other members of the syndicate would want a progress report. He lit a cigarette despite Mrs Arnold's house rules and her insistence that there was to be no smoking in the room. He needed to think.

***

As for Bosch, well he'd been released without charge, and with his daughters had returned to Shoreditch and their tiny flat on the first floor of a terraced house in Bacon Street. The area was pretty grim, and the accommodation was far from commensurate with the kind of dwelling suitable for two attractive, aspiring fashion models and their father. It just wasn't big enough for the three people, with only two damp rooms and a small kitchenette alive with specimens that would have been less out of place in a laboratory. But it was all Bosch could afford until he found work. He was really looking forward to sleeping in a bed rather than on the couch in the flat which was at least a foot too short. Perhaps, all things considered, it was a slight improvement on the settlement in Mitchell's Plain – or was it? Bosch sometimes wondered. At least in South Africa one could sit in warm sunshine most of the time. It was a pity the Luftwaffe had missed Bacon Street and other less than salubrious areas during the Blitz. So far, the *land of milk and honey* had proved to be nothing of the kind. He was desperate to find somewhere better and optimistic that, once he'd received payment for the recent abortive driving job, he would be able to afford to do just that.

Chapter 12 **Wednesday**

Gerry Hunt's passion for antiques and fine art was the slippery slope that had led to his downfall. One could almost say he was becoming obsessive. Not that there's anything wrong with being passionate or fanatical about anything but in Gerry's case his passion, in common with his knowledge, exceeded his self-expressed expertise. He had an enormously inflated estimation of his erudition particularly when it came to bidding at an auction. He was always immaculately turned out and looked the part in his *country gent* outfit whether he was at Sotheby's or a local house clearance sale. He had become a frequent patron of a few auction houses and a favourite with auctioneers who knew that he would allow the bidding to run away with him. On one infamous occasion he got completely carried away when a particular lot, a George III Mahogany bow-fronted chest of drawers, took his fancy. The adrenalin rush during the bidding was such that when the hammer came down he had paid way over the odds and it wasn't until he came to sell it, when he hoped to make a handsome profit, that he discovered it was a reproduction with the net result, a huge loss. Then there was the set of six William and Mary dining chairs. It wasn't until it was too late that a real expert pointed out to poor old Gerry that they had been reupholstered in a not particularly expert fashion with a cheap anachronistic Mary Quant chintzy style imitation fabric. And so it continued over a period of years until inevitably he was facing bankruptcy. The pinnacle of his disastrous effectuation took the form of the seventeenth-century oak Wainscot chair, for which he paid a small fortune that he didn't have. The chair had been stolen from St Leonard's Parish church in Shoreditch. He was convicted of receiving stolen goods and it was whilst serving time in Pentonville that he discovered that St Leonard was the Patron Saint of Prisoners. How appropriate! During those three months he resolved never to bid at an auction again but to open his own antiques saleroom stocked with genuine, not quite so genuine, and downright ersatz antiques, bric-a-brac and high-class junk.

One day it was suggested to him by a less than shy but nevertheless retiring *madam* he met in *The Carpenter's Arms* that his *bona fide* antique business presented an ideal opportunity for diversification. She advised him that the nature of her business had been far more lucrative than his second-hand furniture sales would ever be. That was good enough for Gerry. He parted with another small fortune which he didn't have for the acquisition of her contact magazine and personal introductions to her working girls. Whilst he was diligent and conscientious in promoting his auxiliary pursuit his first love remained with antiques even if his main source of income became derived from pimping.

At least once a week Gerry would take a walk around his *manor* just for the sake of keeping in touch with anything which might be going on that he could turn to his advantage. Quite frequently, and with no regard for the 1959 Act, he came across girls loitering with intent on street corners near to Spitalfields Market. By apprising them of the law, using his charm, his powers of persuasion and offering a discounted rate he was generally successful in recruiting them into his directory. Admittedly this class of working girl was at the lower end of the market, but Gerry was keen to develop his contact magazine into as comprehensive a reference directory as possible and cater for the needs of the extremely wealthy requiring high-class escorts to those who could barely afford a quick hand-job in a back-alley. His walk would generally take him along Whitechapel Road to *The Blind Beggar* and today was no exception.

'Berkshire – me ole mate. 'Ow's it 'anging?' It was Frankie *the Fence* who greeted Gerry as he stepped into the gloomy, but nonetheless welcoming, establishment, the watering hole formerly made notorious by Ronnie Kray after the fatal shooting of Georgie Cornell in 1965.

'I woz 'oping you'd pop in today, wot you 'avin'?'

'Why, thank you kindly, Francis dear boy. A modest libation, a gin and tonic would be most welcome. Now, what have you got for me?'

'Well, we ain't exactly got it yet but we should 'ave it tomorra.'

'What precisely? Do tell please.'

In hushed conspiratorial tones Frankie whispered, 'I knows a foreign bloke, a very, very wealthy bloke from a diff'rent country, what 'as tipped me off about a couple a pieces 'e really wants. 'E's prepared to pay whatever we ask. As it 'appens, I knows 'ow we can get 'old of 'em.' Gerry was licking his lips and salivating almost as much as a Kennel Club Labrador.

'What are these pieces, Francis?'

'Well, there's a rare Jules Leleu Art Deco palisander an' mother-a-pearl marquetry sideboard thingy and 'e also wants also a Pugin table what was commissioned by King George IV, 'e, King George, that is, not the foreign fella, wanted it for Windsor Castle. My man, the Dutchman, was biddin' on these pieces in an auction somewhere in 'olland but 'e got out-bidded by some English toff. Since then, it 'as come to my knowledge who this English toff is and where these pieces are now residin'. Now I ain't got much of a clue with antiques but you 'ave. If we were to go an' nick this gear can we stick it in your shop and get my rich Dutch geezer to deal with you direct? Remember, price is no object an' I'd only want a modest cut. Would you be int'rested?'

'I most certainly would be, dear boy. When you say you haven't got them, where exactly are these items at present?'

'Ah well, they're in a stately 'ome in Suffolk, a gaff called Melton 'all. But I'm plannin' to 'ave 'em away tonight.' Frankie smiled and looked Gerry right in the eye and tapped the side of his nose with his forefinger: that itch again.

'We'll drop 'em off at the Arches tomorra early doors.'

At the Acme Discount Stores the telephone was ringing, and ringing, and ringing.

'Are you goin' to answer that, Tom? I'm bloody knee deep in these soddin' dodgy car-radios. Even the bloody labels are wrong. *Blaupunkt* is what them are s'posed to be. The label says *Bruinpunkt*. Don't know about punkt, more like funkt.' The incessant ringing stopped when Tom, who hadn't heard a word of Matt's gripe, picked up.

'Acme!' Matt stopped what he was doing and strained to hear who was on the phone.

'Patrick! Well, I'll be buggered! Finally! Where the fuck have you been?' Now Tommy, being party to the scam, knew very well that the weed was still on the boat, but in the interests of keeping Patrick in the dark he had to ask, 'Where's Mr Khan's weed? And, where are the African girls?' During the protracted silence which followed, Matt assumed from the fact that Tom was saying nothing apart from making the occasional grunting noise, that McLevy was answering Tom's compound question. Eventually, Tom, clearly less than happy with Patrick's responses, had a word or two...

'Well, it's not our bleedin' fault either.' Tom's blood pressure was rising in equal measure with his volume. He decided to put the frighteners on.

'You'd better get your arse down here. Mr Khan wants to see you in person ... *Carpenter's Arms*. Friday! Midday! Don't be late, McLevy or you will be the late McLevy.' Tom replaced the receiver and Matt applauded.

'Eh, Tommy, I liked that, the late McLevy. Very good, pal. I take it 'e's not caught on then? You reckon mentioning of Mr Khan will scare 'im into turning up?' Tom smiled but the smile was soon wiped from his face as the phone started ringing again.

'Give me a bleedin' break – Hello, what!' he shouted down the mouthpiece. 'Acme!' Then after a pause,

'Oh, sorry, Frankie, I wouldn't 'ave bawled if I'd 'ave knowd it were you. What can we do for you? ... What tonight? ... Where's that you say, Suffolk? ... Straight in, straight out, no bother? ... Are you sure? ... You're certain they're away? ... What's that, back tomorrow? ... I see. 'As to be tonight then ... No I don't think so.... 'Ow much? ... OK then, you should 'ave said so. That's different. See you about 9.00.

'Matt, we're working tonight, a little removals job for Frankie *the Fence*.'

Then, for a third time, the phone began to ring. 'Now what? Bloody 'ell. Matt! Matt! Your turn.' After a crash and a few expletives Matt appeared.

'Hello, Acme! ... Sorry you'll need to speak to my partner about that ... Yeah, 'e's right 'ere.' Matt offered the receiver to Tom and mouthed the words, 'Liam O'Reilly.' Tom immediately grabbed the receiver.

'Liam! ... Yeah, this is Tom ... You couldn't, ... Who, Major Bates? ... You 'ave? ... Well, Liam, that's bloody brilliant ... You crafty ole bastard, Liam ... Where? ... When's that, Liam? ... Right you are, Liam. I'll let 'em know, Liam ... It's a coincidence, Liam, but we've just 'ad McLevy on the blower ... Is he?' Tom began laughing. 'Stupid git! ... Yeah, we will, Liam. Bloody brilliant! Cheers, Liam. He replaced the receiver and turned to his partner. 'That was Liam.'

'Was it really? Well, I'll be fucked!'

***

It was around 8.15 when the burgundy-coloured Commer Space Van pulled up outside *The Carpenter's Arms*. Frankie switched off the lights and carefully locked the van's doors and went into the public bar. Matt and Tom were already there, and had been for some time judging by the state they were in.

'Time fer a quickie then afore the off, Frankie?' Matt offered.

'Ah, go on then – I'll just 'ave 'alf a mild.'

''Ow 'bout you, Tom?'

'Nah, best not otherwise we'll be stoppin' for a gypsy's kiss every ten bloody minutes.'

The three of them climbed into the front of the van and motored off towards Stratford, with Frankie driving, heading for East Anglia. When they got to *The Green Man* round-about at Wanstead, Tom ventured to suggest that perhaps Frankie's sense of direction was just a little misguided.

'Look, Frankie, you silly ole fart, we're goin' the wrong bleedin' way. Still since we're 'ere, can we stop? I'm bustin' for a gypsy's.' Frankie pulled in and parked. Tom disappeared into the pub and the gents' toilet. Matt found an AA Book of the Road in the glove box and was familiarising himself with the route they should have been on.

'Right then, smart-arse Mr Navigator, which way?'

'Follow the signs to Romford and we should pick up the A12 from there,' instructed Matt.

'I was goin' that way, anyway, save goin' through bleedin'

Manor Park and Ilford.' muttered Frankie. 'Since I met Anna, I bin drivin' this way quite often. I bet you've never bin further east than Upton Park. It's a good road now, the A12 'specially since they've built bypasses 'round Brentford and Mountnessing. There's three lanes at Ingatestone up to the Boreham interchange you know, then when we get on to the Witham bypass, I bet we can get this van up to 70, I reckon.'

'You're kiddin'. Engine sounds like a bag a chisels.'

'That's 'cos it's a diesel, they're s'posed to make that noise.'

'What like a London cab, belching and farting fumes out the exhaust?'

'No not like that at all. This 'ere's got a Perkins. It's only a bloody Perkins 4108 no less,' said Frankie with a degree of pride.

'Where d'you nick it from?' enquired Tom.

'Never you mind. We'll be back an' unloaded before the owner knows it's bin gone.' After a period of silence apart from the bag of chisels, it was Matt who picked up on something Frankie had said earlier.

''Oo's this Anna then, you sly ol' git? You 'avin' a bit on the side?'

'Never you mind. Just a lady friend o' mine. She used to live in Spitalfields but got wed an' moved up East Anglia. I does 'er a good turn now an' again, an' she does me one in return.'

'You mean she gives you one in return?' Laughter.

The journey past Chelmsford and Colchester proceeded through light traffic in silence until, on the approach to Ipswich, Matt asked, 'Where d'we go here then?'

'We 'as to go through Ipswich, but it's no problem. We've come from London, so we goes in on the London Road. We're goin' to Woodbridge, so we goes out on the Woodbridge Road. Easy peasy.'

And it was. Just as Frankie had suggested. Out on

Woodbridge Road, through Kesgrave, and, totally oblivious to the fact, they drove right past the Suffolk Constabulary HQ.

'Right, lads, we're getting near now, another fifteen or twenty minutes. It's a big country 'ouse. Stands in over seven acres a' parkland wot stretches down to the river. It's built with what they calls Suffolk white bricks 'cept they ain't.'

'Ain't what?'

'White.'

Before Matt or Tom were able to ask for a determination of the definitive shade of brick, Frankie continued, 'Don't forget to wipe yer feet, an' wear yer gloves. King George's table's in the main central reception room. Make sure you get the right room, 'cos there's four other reception rooms. The one you want is central,' he emphasised in a manner one would explain something simple to an imbecile. 'The posh mother-o'-pearl sideboard's in the dinin' room – not the breakfast room, the dinin' room. There's other stuff, but we ain't got much time to go searching on spec though nine bedrooms and four bathrooms. Might be worth a quick shufty in the wine cellar though. Don't bother with the coach-house next door, 'e's 'ad that converted to a swimmin' pool.'

'You're 100% bang on that there's nobody in?'

'Certain! 'E's gone abroad for some winter sunshine.'

''Ow d'you know that?'

'I knows the woman wot's the housekeeper. 'S my Anna innit?'

'Ah, your bit on the side. All makes sense now!'

'Broke it off wi 'er 'usband after about twelve month. I get her a bit of weed every now an' again.'

'It might be a stupid question, Frankie, but 'ow d'we get in?' asked Tom, practical as always.

'Leave that to me. I got a key to the French windows.'

''Ow d'you manage that then?'

'I told you. Anna Cohen, the woman wot does the judge's housekeepin'.'

'What judge? Nobody said anything about no judge.'

'Didn't I mention it? The judge wot owns the 'ouse. Richard Bertrand 'is name is. 'Spect they calls him Dick, 'is mates. Justice Dick, get it? 'E's a judge at the 'igh court in Ipswich.' Matt and Tom looked at each other, wearing facial expressions which read 'what's 'e on about?' then 'bloody hell', or 'bugger me', or words to that effect. Frankie had to explain. ''Cos 'e's got no balls! Justice Dick.' The penny dropped and everyone fell about laughing.

It was almost 2.00am by the time the Commer was loaded and underway, southbound. The burglary had gone without a hitch. In addition to the named pieces of antique furniture as ordered, Tom had picked up a Persian Heriz carpet while Matt had made a selection from the wine cellar.

After stopping for diesel at an all-night filling station on the A12 at Woodbridge, the drive back to London was sedate, Frankie not wanting to attract any unwanted attention from night-time police patrols. At 5.00am the Commer was parked outside the Pedley Street arch bearing the sign *Berkshire Antiques*. A light was on, and Gerry greeted his partners in crime at the door.

'I trust the mission was immaculately executed?'

'According to plan, Berkshire, according to plan.'

'Absolutely splendid. My felicitations, you fellows, good eggs all! Now may we get our opulent acquisitions into the showroom before we attract the unwanted attention of any early birds and then, round to Sid's. I think I owe you breakfast.'

Chapter 13 **Later on Wednesday**

The police station in Victoria Park Square served the Metropolitan Borough of Bethnal Green where Superintendent Robin Tickner was taking a call from his opposite number in Kesgrave, Chief Superintendent Gibbons.

'He's not a bad copper really. In fact, he's rather good, but I get the impression he resents my input into whatever case he's on: an attitude which I find infuriating and frustrating in equal measure. Consequently, we don't get on terribly well I'm afraid. But if you could tolerate putting up with him for a couple of days, it would be hugely appreciated and a great help. DCI Cartwright is sure he'll find the answers to some of the questions in your locality. He's been tipped off about a local pub, *The Carpenter's Arms.*'

'*The Carpenter's Arms* eh? Oh yes. We know it, and the characters that use it are known to us. You'll find answers to questions which haven't been asked yet in there, as well as the meaning of life, and beyond.' Superintendent Tickner had no qualms about affording a professional courtesy to Cartwright.

'We'll keep an eye on him.' In just a brief conversation Tickner had recognised the cause of the animosity. 'Pompous arse,' he thought.

***

Back at Kesgrave Cartwright and Armstrong were preparing to leave.

'Where's Lewis?' asked Cartwright.

'Probably got his head in that book again,' suggested Armstrong.

'I applaud the man that wants to better himself and get on in life through the acquisition of knowledge, but he really should be doing it on his own time though.'

'Doing what, sir?' At that very moment Lewis walked into Cartwright's office carrying an open book.

'Guv, you'll appreciate this, knowing how you and the Chief Super get on so well: "Before arguing with anyone ask yourself, will whoever I'm arguing with have the mental capacity or maturity to grasp the concept of a different perspective – if not the argument is pointless."'

'Thank you, Andy I'll bear that in mind. Now are we ready? I don't want to spend any more time than we have to in London, so the sooner we leave the sooner we can be back.'

The telephone rang. Cartwright thought twice before picking up the receiver. The other two looked on wondering whether or not he would. He did!

'Cartwright.' The DCI listened intently for a few moments making occasional notes on his pad. Eventually, he replaced the receiver and uttered a response, from which his colleagues knew in a second that something was up.

'Shit!'

'What's up then, guv?'

'Andy ring Superintendent – what's his name? At Bethnal Green.'

'Tickner, guv.'

'That's it, Robin Tickner. We'll need to let him know we won't be there today. Something's come up, something with "top priority" stamped all over it.'

'Whatever's that then?' asked Armstrong.

'His Honour Judge Richard Bertrand.'

'What, not the judge at the High Court?'

'The very same. He's been burgled.'

'Can't we send Ray and Vaughan, it's not like he's that important is it?'

'As far as we're concerned, he is. Just remember he's appointed by the Queen on a recommendation from the Lord Chancellor and he's insisting that the most senior detective investigates immediately. Andy you can drive me. Doug you press on with the *Corn Flakes Caper*.'

Lewis felt the urge to comment as they walked down to the garage.

'Can't argue with the mental capacity or maturity with this one, guvnor.'

'Oh, I'm not so sure,' countered Cartwright who was all too familiar with His Honour's misanthropic temperament. He was not relishing the encounter.

As the Jaguar XJ12 pulled up in front of Melton Hall the door opened, and the imposing figure of His Honour appeared on the threshold. Cartwright and Lewis waved their warrant cards in the Judge's direction.

'Come in please, gentlemen.'

They were ushered into a reception room and invited to sit on a Thomas Lloyd brown leather Chesterfield sofa. The Judge explained how he had returned from ten days in the Cayman Islands early that morning and discovered his palisander sideboard and Pugin table missing. Lewis, who was taking notes, looked quizzically at his guvnor. Cartwright nodded.

'Forgive my ignorance, Your Honour, a palisander?'

'In short, it's a rare Brazilian rosewood. Beautiful. Mine is inlaid with mother of pearl.'

'And a Pugin?'

'Augustus Pugin was a nineteenth century architect who

was revolutionary in promoting the Gothic style. He also designed furniture. The missing table was commissioned by George IV, so clearly a very individual item and very probably priceless. My insurance company has photographs.'

'Is there anything else missing, sir?'

'Yes. A Persian Heriz carpet, and several bottles of vintage wine have been taken from the cellar. I have prepared a list for you, although I daresay the burglars have quaffed it by now, like a cheap plonk! They wouldn't know any better.'

The Judge handed the list to Cartwright who took a cursory glance at it before putting it into his jacket pocket.

'Have you detected any sign of a forced entry?' Cartwright asked.

'No, but then I'm not a detective, you are, or supposed to be. The Chief Super has his doubts.' Cartwright and Lewis were both feeling uncomfortable.

'Do you mind if we take a look around then?'

'Isn't that what detectives are supposed to do?'

The Judge guided the policemen through the ground floor reception rooms and pointed out where the missing pieces had previously stood. When they came to the sitting room with the French windows, Cartwright paused.

'All the doors and windows were locked while you were away of course?' The question was rhetorical, but even so the Judge gave him a look which said, 'Do you think I'm stupid?'

'Does anyone else have keys?'

'Yes, Mrs Cohen, my housekeeper.' Lewis wrote the name down.

'Mm,' Cartwright pondered. 'May I use your telephone please?'

After he'd made the call, he explained to the Judge that a forensic team would be calling to dust for fingerprints and make casts of tyre tracks in the drive. He'd had enough of feeling intimidated and decided it was time to go.

'I'm very sorry about the theft of your furniture, Your Honour, and obviously we'll do all we can to try and recover it and bring the culprits to justice.'

'I hope you will, in fact you better had if you value your careers. And when you have apprehended these criminals I hope they come up before me!' The malevolence in the Judge's response almost made Lewis shiver.

'It would help if you would ask your insurance company to send me copies of the photographs. As it is, it seems to me that the thieves knew exactly what they were after, and I imagine there would have been two or three of them, with a van. I'm guessing the items were heavy. As for the wine, I think that would have been an opportunistic theft and as you suggest may be unrecoverable by now.' The Judge led the way to the front door.

In the car, Lewis loosened his tie. 'What a horrible man, vindictive bastard. God help any criminal who ends up in his court. It's like I've been reading, guv. The dignified and the efficient. I'm sure he has influence and that's the efficient element; his business is in getting results. Let the punishment fit the crime so to speak, the efficient. But has he gained that prerogative through the confidence of the people? The population needs to have trust in the judicial system, the dignified element, so to speak. Efficiency won't work if it's not dignified.'

'Bloody hell, Lewis, whatever have you been reading? That's all above my head.'

'Some bloke called Bagehot, very interesting but I'm not sure I understand it myself!'

He put the car into gear, and they cruised back to Kesgrave with Cartwright metaphorically scratching his head.

Back at HQ Cartwright sat at his desk and went to the bottom drawer of his desk and then remembered that he finished the Laphroaig the previous Friday. He made a mental note to get a new bottle.

'How'd it go with Bertrand?' Doug Armstrong had crept in.

'No better or worse than you might have expected. You know what he's like.'

'As good as that eh? Well, I've had a result of sorts. Apparently FBA 643M is a 1973 model white Ford Transit stolen in Whitechapel sometime just over a week ago. That's the van we've got downstairs. Apparently the concealed compartment was fitted by the registered owner, a Francis Forsyth, known to the police, has a record, mainly for receiving.

'Ah well, that's something at least. If the tax and insurance are in order maybe we can get it back to him. We'll bring Bosch in again. If he didn't steal the van himself, he might know who did. We know he was the driver.'

'Be easier to get the Met to arrest him. He lives on their patch according to the address he gave. We can interview him when we go down there.'

'Good call, Doug. Right, get Davies and Rudd on the case of the Judge's missing furniture. Tell them to start with Mrs what's her name, the housekeeper. Cohen, that's it, Mrs Cohen.'

Chapter 14 **Thursday**

The Michael Collins lay in Paglesham Reach having arrived on the Monday. At low water the vessel settled quite comfortably in the mud and happily refloated a few hours into each new floodtide. Harry Lindley, one of the hands at Shuttlewood's Yard, had been given the job of preparing the hull, erasing the proud name of the former director of intelligence for the IRA, rubbing down the paintwork, and providing a freshly primed, undercoated and overcoated surface in readiness for the signwriter. Early March was hardly the right time of year for such a job, with the boat afloat, on the mud or somewhere in between, and Harry was perhaps not at his most conscientious. However, the paint job was a good colour match and it just needed to harden before the new name could be applied.

O'Reilly had been in touch with the Mercantile Marine in Dublin where he had spoken to Aoife O'Donnell, 'a most obliging young woman by the sound of her voice at least' Liam thought at the time. The reregistration and renaming proved to be a fairly painless and easy process thanks to Aoife, who had succumbed to Liam's offer of a bribe, and was short-circuiting the procedures and formalities that he would otherwise have been obliged to undergo. The nightmare of changing *The Ballingary* to *The Michael Collins* was still a vivid memory.

The new name and registration number and the

accompanying documentation had arrived at the yard by post, and in the workshop, one of Shuttlewood's shipwrights was carving the new registration number onto a plaque of oak. This would be affixed to a bulkhead on the ship. The signwriter was precariously seated on a plank suspended over the gunwale at the bow, skilfully engaged in his commission.

Just before the high spring tide the following morning *The Eamon de Valera* slipped quietly away scouring a passage through the creeks around Potton Island towards the Havengore Bridge which by previous arrangement opened obligingly to allow the boat through, then across the Maplin Sands and into the open water of the Thames Estuary at the South Shoebury buoy. Rather than force the ebb tide up the Thames, Liam opted for a few hours at Queenborough, at the mouth of the Medway River. It would then be plain sailing up the London River to Limehouse Basin.

***

In his room at the Grafton Guesthouse, Pat McLevy had spent a couple of days in a tortuous wrestling match with his conscience. He'd only stepped out once, and that was just to buy cigarettes. Since his dishonourable discharge McLevy had been living on his wits, ducking and diving, bobbing and weaving, earning a shilling or two wherever he could or otherwise existing on the £9.20p unemployment benefit. Up until the most recent incident, he had had dealings with the police, usually when they were called to restore order after a pub fight had broken out, but he'd always got away with either a caution, a night in the cells to sober up and cool off or a fine in a magistrates' court. He had no option other than to respond to the summons to answer to Mr Khan.

He and Mr Khan had never previously met. All his dealings

with Mr Khan had been through a third party, Rashid. At six foot six inches tall Rashid saw eye to eye with McLevy, in the physical sense only. His physique in general was something else though, formidable. With his long black hair and unkempt beard, he resembled Khan Baba the legendary 70 stone Pakistani giant.

McLevy had often wondered how or why it should have been that Mr Khan should have put his trust in a total stranger and to the tune of £20k. It might not have been a household name in East Anglia but everyone in the Metropolitan Borough of Bethnal Green had heard of Mr Khan. Very few had met him. Well, nobody would admit to having met him, or met him and lived to tell the tale. Even in his anonymity he commanded respect and seemingly everyone was wary of him, especially McLevy under the present circumstances. He had been given a large sum of money to buy a shipment of cannabis. He had failed to deliver. The money was gone, apart from his commission, and there was nothing to show for it. But that wasn't his fault. Or was it? Maybe he should have checked the boxes as they were transhipped from the boat to the van. Mr Khan had a reputation as an anonymous drug baron. Despite his incognito status, his inglorious, obscure notoriety as a smuggler was manifest throughout the underworld. Mr Khan was interconnected with drug cartels on a worldwide scale but continued to outwit the police and other enforcement agencies, possibly as a result of his guile and ingenuity, the police being under-resourced, but more likely down to remaining off the grid.

Most of McLevy's £2000 commission had been used for paying off debts, bar bills, and sundry expenses. But there would still be sufficient to meet the costs of day to day living until something else turned up. Patrick McLevy knew the trip to London had to be made. Out of the Navy, out of work, out of luck, and, if you didn't count his bedsit in Felixstowe, with no fixed abode. He was attempting to locate his sister at an address in Spitalfields before his appointment with Mr Khan at *The Carpenter's Arms.* He and his sister hadn't spoken or seen each other for several years since she had married, but Patrick thought it was worth taking a chance on re-establishing contact in the hope that Anna might help him out in one way or another, even if only in the short term. It proved to be a wasted visit. The diminutive figure that answered the door appeared to be quite frail, in his sixties. He was wearing a Fair Isle cardigan over his grandad shirt and maroon corduroy trousers. McLevy looked him up and down from his skull cap to his moccasin slippers. The man peered at McLevy over his half-moon glasses and introduced himself as Jacob Kahn. McLevy spluttered involuntarily at the name. 'No, it can't be!' he thought.

'But, but...' he stammered, 'you're, you are, are you...?'

'Jewish, yes. My parents were Polish Jews from Wlodowa. Is that a problem?'

'No, no not at all. I too am Jewish,' McLevy answered with relief. 'It's just that I'm obliged to meet another Mr Khan later this morning, but I believe he's from Pakistan. The coincidence threw me there for a moment.' They laughed politely.

'I was hoping to catch up with my sister, she lives here, or she certainly used to. Anna McLevy, sorry Anna Cohen. She got married you see,' he explained.

'Ah, I see, Anna Cohen is your sister. Well, I'm afraid Anna and her husband moved away almost two years ago.' Patrick's disappointment was obvious. Jacob Kahn continued, 'Look I was about to go to the synagogue. Would you like to join me? Maybe, no surely, someone there will know where your sister and her husband moved to.'

'I'd like that,' Patrick lied, 'but I haven't got my yarmulke with me I'm afraid.'

'I'm sure we can find you one.'

And so it was that Patrick McLevy became a member of the community at the United Working Men's Synagogue in Cheshire Street, Bethnal Green, where, over a period of weeks, Jacob and his temporary lodger Patrick became firm friends.

***

As the end of the month approached the media was full of politics. Prime Minister Heath was in trouble. It looked highly likely that his government would be deposed and there were all manner of issues, many divisive, which were creating something of a political storm. However, there was optimism in certain quarters. If the Tories failed to win the general election outright, would the Liberals be prepared to form a coalition government? It was doubtful. That would put the Labour party with Harold Wilson in charge for a second time. 'Surely,' thought Cartwright, 'a Labour Government will bring the miners' strike to an end?'

They, that is to say Cartwright, Armstrong and Lewis, were on their way to London and the police station in Victoria Park Square where it had been arranged for them to liaise with Superintendent Tickner. After the initial formalities, they were introduced to DS Michael Willett who Tickner had assigned to assist *our colleagues from the country*.

'As it's getting on for opening time, why don't I take you to *The Carpenter's Arms*, the hotbed of crime and culture in this parish,' Willett suggested. 'I'm sure you'd like some refreshment a little better than coffee after your journey and you'll get to meet some of our local celebrities.' The DCI and DS were both agreeable to the suggestion. Lewis was noncommittal; he was the driver. The visitors were taking in the amenable surroundings of the pub when Cartwright noticed a familiar form at the bar.

'Well, well, well! If it isn't Chief Petty Officer McLevy, or is just Petty Officer McLevy, or shouldn't it be plain old Mr McLevy now?' McLevy had been leaning on the bar deep in conversation with another man.

'Oh, it's you, Mr Cartwright sir, oh and Sergeant Armstrong too. Fancy seeing you here!'

'That's Detective Chief Inspector Cartwright to you, McLevy, and I was just thinking exactly the same thing,' stated Cartwright.

'I'd love to stay and chat, Chief Inspector, but I've got a train to catch.' McLevy swallowed the best part of a whole pint in one, and without so much as a *by your leave* he left in a hurry. Armstrong brought Willett up to speed on the story so far and Willett reciprocated with character analyses of the local suspects.

'Well, for what it's worth, the guy he was talking to is Thomas "Tommy" Martin, a local entrepreneur and minor villain. He's well connected with most of the scams going on around here, if not the instigator. Tommy and his mate Matthew Taylor, joined at the hip, run a very dubious "discount" store from one of the railway arches: discount's about right! First thing you have to do is discount where the stock might have come from. Say one thing for him though, Tommy's quite an affable chap really, and he's thorough. Always covers his back though, dodgy receipts, invoices and the like. Oh look, here's the other one, not quite such a shining light. Hello Matt.' Cartwright turned towards the door to see Matt Taylor do a double take and think twice about coming in.

'You got a minute or two, Matt? Hey, Tommy, come and join us for a sec please.'

'Hello, Mr Willett. Didn't realise you liked a lunchtime snifter.'

'Well, you know, Tom, I like to keep my finger on the pulse of what's happening in the underworld. Let me introduce a couple of colleagues from the country. DCI Cartwright and DS Armstrong are investigating a possible smuggling racket and what's worse, it's connected to a kidnapping, assault and rape and their enquiries have led them here. Now you wouldn't know anything about any of that would you?'

'No, Mr Willett. We ain't 'eard nowt about owt like that, 'ave we, Matt?'

'No, Tommy. Nowt. Out of our league.'

'Well, how about a stolen Transit then, more in your style?'

'Aw, come on, Mr Willett you know I'm disqualified and can't drive.'

'When has a lost licence been a problem for you, Tommy?'

'What are you insinuatin', Mr Willett. I'm not sure I like your tone.'

'Oh dear, oh dear. What'd you have for breakfast Tommy?' asked Armstrong.

'What's that got to do wi' owt?'

'Just curious.'

'Bacon sarnie, since you ask.' Tom's response was ever so slightly indignant.

'How do you know Patrick McLevy?' asked Cartwright. Tommy was thinking fast.

'We was in the Navy together.'

'Now don't give me all that old pony,' said Willett. 'I know very well that you and Matt were both in the army and you know that I know.'

'OK, you're right, Mr Willett. 'E's just a drinkin' mate. Lives up your way I think, Mr Cartwright.'

'Oh yes, we know. He's due in court in a couple of weeks.'

Before the banter progressed any further the bar door opened again and in walked Bandile Bosch. Tommy panicked. ''Scuse me, gents I 'ave to go to the gents.' Tom disappeared out of the back door in a hurry leaving Matt to retreat to the far corner of the bar looking bewildered.

'What does that tell you?' asked Willett.

'Maybe it was something we said,' jested Armstrong.

'Hello, Bandile.' Armstrong extended his hand which Bandile took. 'This your local?'

'I'm surprised to see you here, Sergeant. I'm not a big drinker but, I suppose yes, it's my local, it's the nearest pub to where I live.'

'Hello, Bandy, usual?' came a shout from behind the bar.

'Well, I must say, for someone who's not a big drinker, you seem to be a regular customer,' Cartwright observed. Bosch appeared nervous.

'I've been coming in every day in the hope that I'll see the man that gave me that driving job. I haven't been paid you see, and me and my girls getting a bit desperate.'

'Can you describe him?'

'Oh yes.' And he did, down to a tee. 'He was with another couple of chaps. I think one of them called his mate Tommy.'

All eyes turned from the bar; Matt was no longer there either.

'Have you seen McLevy in here before then, Bandile?'

'No sir, only that once. If I do I'll, I'll...'

'No you won't, Bandile. You're not that sort of man. You just missed him anyway. He was here a few minutes ago.' Bosch's frustration was obvious. 'You continue to help us with our enquiries, and we might turn a blind eye to the fact that the van you were driving was stolen and you were driving without a licence.'

'I have a South African licence, is that not good enough?' Bosch looked crestfallen as he added, 'Oh dear. I really didn't know, but thinking about it, I should have realised.'

'Andy, buy Bandile a drink. He needs a bit of a reviver.'

The policemen sat around an empty table. 'Get another round in please, Andy.' Cartwright handed him a £5 note.

'Well, I'm glad we came down here. I didn't expect to see two of the main players in our drama taking centre stage albeit briefly, or so soon. You've got it easy here, Mick, if all your suspects use this pub as their headquarters!'

'Yes, maybe. I think you can reckon on Tom and Matt having more than a bit part in this saga as well,' added Michael Willett.

Chapter 15 **Saturday**

The Eamon de Valera left Queenborough early with the Irish tricolour flying proudly from the stern with the Red Ensign courtesy flag from the mast on the wheelhouse roof. Having given the sunken munitions ship *The Richard Montgomery* a wide berth the ship was past the Nore Swatchway and into the main channel on the new flood tide with the lights of Southend visible through the mist of the dawn.

'So, Liam, why of all the names you might have gone for did you choose *Eamon de Valera*?' asked Fergal, passing up a sausage sandwich from the galley.

'Well, Fergal, the history of my country has always been something I have been profoundly interested in. You'll be remembering for sure the reasons I changed the name from *Ballingary* to *Michael Collins*. Michael was my hero. A revolutionary fighter. I am carrying on that fight in my own small way.'

'Oh I know that well enough, Liam. But Eamon, why Eamon? Didn't he abandon the IRA?'

'That he did, Fergal. Still, he was an Irish statesman, a political leader, and a prominent figure in the war of independence, and for all that he deserted the cause as some say, he recognised Michael as the greater man. Eamon has said in his own words which I have learned by heart: "It is my considered opinion that in the fullness of time history will record the greatness of Michael Collins and it will be recorded at my expense." Now it takes a great man to make such an admission don't you think? I, Fergal, am a patriot. Your tattoo says it all. *Tiocfaidh ar la*, and it will. Our day will come! – and it could be very, very soon. I'd have the tattoo meself but I never got around to it and it'll be superfluous anyway when our day has arrived. Look now, that's Canvey Island over there on the starboard bow.'

'Ah well now, that's alright then. It's where it should be.' The next few miles were covered in silence whilst breakfast was finished.

It was but a few hours with the Listers purring away that *The Eamon de Valera* was approaching the eastern limit of the Pool of London and Limehouse Basin on the northern side of the river.

'Call 'em up, Fergal. With our Irish good fortune we shouldn't have to wait too long for the lock.' Sure enough, the lock was made ready and waiting for them when they rounded the West India and Millwall Docks on the Isle of Dogs.

As soon as the ship was safely berthed alongside the quay Liam went to find a telephone call box. He wanted the cargo unloaded as soon as possible. In recent times because of the *Troubles* the police had carried out random spot checks on Irish-flagged vessels. The last thing Liam needed now was for the plan to come adrift at the last hurdle.

'If only we hadn't had to make the bloody link call. If Paddy Bates knew about it, then every ship in the South North Sea knows as well. Unloading at the Roughs would have been as easy as opening a fresh bottle of the *Jameson's*. Unloading here will be worse than not having a bottle to open.'

***

Cartwright and Armstrong were the guests of Superintendent Tickner, having been invited out for dinner in a West End restaurant, courtesy of the Met. Mick Willett made up the group. Left to his own devices Andy Lewis was having a few drinks in *The Carpenter's Arms* whilst furthering his education with some pretty heavy duty reading. He'd managed to find himself a reasonably priced room for the night in Brick Lane.

Five men entered the public bar in high spirits, laughing and joking. Two of them, Lewis thought he recognised from lunchtime. One of them was something of a cut above the rest. He was extremely well dressed by comparison. As he unbuttoned his overcoat, Lewis noticed the gold chain, presumably attached to a pocket-watch, a Hunter, in his waistcoat pocket. His bowtie and rimless spectacles gave him a distinguished, affluent appearance. The remaining two were so obviously Irish, one didn't need to be an aspiring detective to work it out. The look, the dress, the brogue, the pints of Guinness said it all. Lewis surreptitiously sidled over to the bar to order himself another drink and attempt to eavesdrop. He could understand the toff, but the Cockney and the Irish were not so easy. Perhaps more significant than what he heard was what he saw. *Tiocfaidh ar la* tattooed on the neck of the Irishman with the red hair. He made a note.

Mr Bowtie and rimless glasses only stayed for around an hour. When he left, so did Lewis. He didn't have to tail him very far before he disappeared into one of the railway arches under the sign *Berkshire Antiques*. Lewis assumed he was the owner or proprietor since he had the keys to the corrugated steel door within the roller-shutter which covered the entire frontage. The lights went on and the door closed. Lewis watched and waited. It was only a few minutes before a woman approached him.

'You looking for business, love?' she asked seductively. For all that Lewis was a country boy and such a proposition was well outside any previous experience, he was somewhat taken aback, but fully aware of what was being implied.

'Er, not tonight thank you,' he replied politely.

'OK, love, suit yourself.' She crossed the street and knocked on the door at Berkshire Antiques. The door was almost immediately opened by Mr Bowtie, now in his shirtsleeves. The woman reached into her handbag and withdrew what Lewis was as certain as he could be from a distance was a wad of banknotes. She handed them to the bowtie who proceeded to count them as they both stood in the open doorway. He was clearly satisfied with the total and counted out several and handed them back to the woman who replaced them in her handbag.

He was about to close the door when a man appeared from out of nowhere. Lewis overheard him greet Mr Bowtie, 'Goodnight, Gerry.' The woman linked arms with the man, and they disappeared down the road and into the night. Lewis was trying to relate what he had seen with what he knew with what he suspected but couldn't be sure that he was getting the correct answer.

'Well fancy that,' he thought to himself as he went back to the pub. The Cockneys and the Irish were still there although no longer in each other's company. The Irish were playing dominoes, the Cockneys, darts. Lewis ordered a pint of bitter and decided that watching the darts might prove to be more educational in terms of *intelligence*.

After another pint he felt he was brave enough to have a word.

'Excuse me, fellas, I don't want to interrupt your game but I'm looking for some female company for the evening, and you blokes look like locals and might know...'

'Yes, mate, we know. There's a knocking shop just down the road.' It was Matt being helpful. He didn't realise just how helpful he was being. 'Berkshire Antiques, knock on the door ask for Gerry – 'e'll probably open the door anyway. Tell 'im Matt sent you.'

'Thanks very much. I'm from out of town, you know how it is...'

'No, mate, I don't. Only bin out o' town once, an' didn't like it, it were closed!' He laughed. Lewis decided not to make any further comment and left. Out in the street he found himself a discreet vantage point and watched the pub door. It couldn't be too long before closing time and he'd decided to follow the Cockneys or the Irish, whichever pair left first. It was the Irish.

Lewis looked at his watch. It was almost 10.30pm. Tailing the two Irishmen was easy. They were intoxicated to the point of having no idea there was anyone behind them. Just before the turn into Brick Lane the one with the tattoo decided he needed to take a leak and urinated against the side of a parked car. Lewis crossed to the opposite side of the road and walked ahead assuming they would continue on down Brick Lane. They did and then hailed a black cab. Lewis was almost at his overnight digs and would have abandoned the tail but for the sight of a cab approaching him with its light illuminated, albeit on the wrong side of the road. It's not often one can get a taxi at the drop of a hat, so to speak, but on this occasion Lewis was lucky. He put his arm out and the cab drew up alongside him.

'Where to, guvnor?' Lewis already had his warrant card out and he thrust it through the cabbie's window.

'Can you follow that cab, the one that just left here going south please?'

'Cor blimey, guvnor, yes, sir. Jump in. Always wanted to hear a fare say, "follow that cab". Thought it only 'appened in movies.' The turning circle on an Austin FX4D was quite unlike anything Lewis had ever driven and he was impressed. It was hardly minutes before his driver had caught up. By Aldgate East Tube Station, the pursuit turned into Commercial Road and continued on to the A13 Limehouse Road. Both cabs pulled up by Limehouse Station and disgorged their respective passengers. Lewis paid off his cabbie and feigned entering the station as he watched his quarry stagger off towards the basin. Lewis followed and watched as they climbed aboard a boat, *The Eamon de Valera*.

He took another cab back to his Brick Lane bed and breakfast and during the ride did more mental arithmetic. This time he was sure he'd got the correct answer. Hadn't Lotte van Dijkstra said she'd been abducted on a boat? Didn't she say she could identify her kidnapper, the man who raped her, fair reddish hair and a tattoo on his neck? Where were Cartwright and Armstrong when you needed them?

Chapter 16 **Sunday**

Willett, Tickner, Cartwright and Armstrong were already gathered in Willett's office in the Victoria Park Square nick when Lewis turned up.

'Good of you to join us, Andy,' was Cartwright's sarcastic greeting. 'Heavy night was it?'

'You don't know the half of it, guv. Sorry I'm a bit on the drag.'

'So, what if anything did you discover last night?' asked DS Willett. Lewis went on to explain how his evening had begun in *The Carpenter's Arms* and developed thereafter.

His senior colleagues listened intently, and after a good ten minutes, during which Lewis had been the only person to speak, it was Superintendent Tickner who was the first to make a response. 'That's excellent work, Sergeant, well done.'

Then, as if by way of an excuse, Willett added, 'Of course, and as the Superintendent is aware, we've known about the secondary activities carried on at the Berkshire Antiques for some time. But, to be frank, we let them get on with it. At least that way, it keeps the working girls off the streets, isn't that right, sir?' He sought confirmation from his Superintendent. But before Tickner could answer, Lewis jumped in.

'With respect, sir, not all of them. I was propositioned last night whilst I was maintaining observation of the antiques store.' Willett wilted a little.

'Did you take advantage?' joked Armstrong.

'Excuse me, Detective Sergeant, but I shall treat that question with the contempt it deserves.' Lewis clearly didn't understand he was merely having his leg pulled.

'Now, now, chaps,' intervened Cartwright. 'It's as the Super says, Andy, bloody good work. Priority now is to keep a 24-hour watch on that ship. How are we fixed for manpower?'

'We'll put a team together, Inspector, although we are a bit short-handed at present – miners' picket you know.'

'Oh yes, we know!'

With the meeting over, Cartwright rang Kesgrave and asked for Davies or Rudd. It was Vaughan Rudd who answered the extension in the detectives' room.

'Cartwright here, Vaughan. How're we getting on with the Judge's burglary?'

'Not too well I'm afraid, sir. Forensics didn't turn up anything, no prints, no tyre tracks, nothing. We've spoken to all the neighbours, and no one saw or heard anything suspicious or otherwise.'

'How about the cleaning lady, what's her name?'

'Mrs Cohen. Anna Cohen. Yes we traced her and drew a blank there, but she's got previous for possession with intent and we charged her with possession again.'

'Oh, so Mrs Cohen likes a bit of weed eh? Do we know her supplier?'

'Says she bought £3-worth from a bloke in a pub. A likely story. Not been in the area very long. Moved to Woodbridge from London when she got married. That's as far as we got.'

'And is the Judge on your back?'

''Fraid so, sir. But we've been managing to palm him off with a "we're doing the rounds of antique dealers with the photographs we got from the insurance company" routine. I reckon the stuff's long gone, personally. Abroad I shouldn't wonder.'

'OK, Vaughan, keep at it. We won't be back for a few days yet. Things are hotting up down here. We've located the boat which we're about to stake out.'

Willett went down to the locker room, looking for volunteers for the stake-out planned for later that evening, once it had got dark. With a promise of overtime payments, he had soon recruited a force big enough for the task.

DCI Cartwright and Sergeant Andy Lewis sat in the XJ12 parked in Goodhart Place far enough away to be out of sight but near enough for Cartwright to see what was happening through his binoculars. It being a Sunday, cold and with a threat of rain, the streets were quiet. An unmarked but nevertheless conspicuous paddy wagon was parked in Northey Street on the opposite side of the lock with the two detective sergeants and a platoon of uniformed men. In Narrow Street there was a burgundy coloured Commer van the rear doors of which were open. Four men had formed a chain and packages were being passed down the line from a fifth man on the ship and loaded into the back of the van. The operation seemed to be under the supervision of a sixth man, who was pointing here and there and giving instructions. The fifth man appeared to be about to close the ship's wheelhouse door and Cartwright barked the order into the radio. Police spilled out of the paddy wagon and began running towards the Commer. Several gunshots rang out and the lenses on two paddy wagon headlights shattered onto the ground. Policemen in and out of uniform dived into whatever cover they could and the Commer sped away and was last sighted disappearing northbound up Burdett Road. By the time Lewis had turned the Jaguar round, the van was long gone. Cartwright called Victoria Park Square on the radio and requested whatever assistance in the form of vehicles could be made available. The dispatcher pledged to do what she could which to Cartwright and Lewis didn't sound optimistic. Meanwhile the Commer sped up Burdett Road, left into St Paul's Way, Ben Jonson Road and Stepney Green.

'Go on, son, drive it like you stole it,' urged Matt.

'We did steal it!' shouted Tom over the squeal of the tyres as he threw the van into a hard left at the Mile End Road junction. At Whitechapel he made a right into Vallance Road, left into Buxton Road and finally right onto Brick Lane and with the gearbox screaming in protest, into Pedley Street. Gerry had thought far enough ahead to force an entry into the vacant arch next to his and the shutter was up. Tom bounced up the kerb barely easing off the gas, into the arch, skidded to a halt, Matt jumped out and the shutter came down.

'Well, Thomas, I must say that as much as I enjoy a scenic route as much as anyone, I would have come straight up Burdett Road and into Grove Road and turned right at Roman Road, a much more direct route and smoother ride altogether. What say you dear boy?'

'That XJ12 would 'ave caught you before you'd got to Mile End Park, you silly old duffer.'

They all stood in silence straining their ears for the first hint of a siren, but none came.

'So, gentlemen, I suggest we conceal half of the shipment in my Swedish Rococo cabinet, and Thomas, Matthew, perhaps the other half in your establishment. I trust you have an appropriate and suitable place of concealment where our treasure may be camouflaged or otherwise obscured?'

'What's 'e say?'

'Can we 'ide it?'

'Oh, right.'

'Now come along let's set about it and divide the spoils. Thomas, may we leave it to you to dispose of the transport?'

'Yeah, I was thinkin' about that. In the early hours, burgundy'll look black don't you reckon? Not so conspicuous. I'll run it up to Victoria Park and dump it in one o' the lakes.'

'Splendid.'

The encounter with the police had been too close for comfort and had it not been for the quick thinking of Gerry Hunt the members of the syndicate could all now be lamenting in the cells rather than in the more hospitable surroundings of *The Carpenter's Arms*. With 250lbs of cannabis safely hidden in a seventeenth-century Swedish Rococo cabinet in Berkshire's emporium, and the other 250lbs stashed inside 56lb bags of custard powder in the Acme Discount Stores, the original plan, or plan B at least, had reached its conclusion. How were they now to deceive Mr Khan. If plan A had worked out, Major Paddy would be sitting on the drugs out of everyone's reach. Now here it was, right in their own backyard. However treacherous any deception might prove to be, their mendacity would require consistency and moreover it would need to be bulletproof – literally.

'So, where'd you get it?' asked Tom.

'To what are you referring exactly, dear boy?' responded Gerry.

'The shooter.'

'Well, I rather think that's none of your business. But since you ask, I have been a member of the Lord Roberts Centre for over twenty years.' Gerry made the announcement with a shameless if not brazen show of vanity and in the expectation that the others would understand the significance.

''Oo the fuck is Lord Roberts when 'e's at 'ome then?' asked Matt.

'It's a gun club in Surrey, dear boy. Lord Roberts was the founder. I pop down there when I can just to keep my eye in, don't you know.'

'No, we don't,' answered Tom.

'Still, your fine display of marksmanship got us all out of

trouble tonight, and that's a fact to be sure it is.' Liam was clearly grateful. 'I only hope the coppers aren't keeping my ship under surveillance. We need to get away as soon as we're loaded with that stuff for Jimmy, don't we, Fergal?' Fergal was a man of few words, particularly in company.

'Aye, that we do!'

'So, pray tell, what is our course of action from here then? There is half a hundredweight of illegal drugs sitting in my Swedish Rococo and a similar amount next door. Mr Khan was expecting such a delivery and were he to get wind of what we have here he would readily come to the conclusion, and quite reasonably so, that we had ripped him off. But our dear colleague Francis has actually paid for the whole amount. Is not that correct, Francis?' Frankie nodded and Gerry continued, 'Therefore, is it not unreasonable that Frankie should expect to take delivery of the whole amount?' The general consensus seemed to be in agreement.

'What do we give Mr Khan? Corn flakes?' asked Frankie.

'Nah, can't do that. They're still in the van and the fuzz still 'as the van.'

'Ah well now, I have an idea.'

'Oh do reveal all, Mr O'Reilly, after all, you do have Mr Khan's money.'

'As I see it, it was Patrick who was working for Mr Khan, and it was Patrick who hired me and my ship, and it was Patrick who pocketed £2000 to my certain knowledge. Therefore, should it not be down to Patrick to explain to Mr Khan that his cargo was confiscated by the police? Surely, sooner or later, Mr Khan will have heard about a shooting at Limehouse, and he can jump to whatever conclusion he likes. Is that not a good enough explanation?'

'Aye it is that,' was the extent of Fergal's contribution to the syndicate's brainstorming. If only there had been a few brains to storm.

'Well, this is indeed a conundrum and the conception of an assured and armour-plated explanation which will guarantee our joint and several preservation will require wiser heads than ours I fear.'

'What's he say, Tom?'

'Not sure, Matt.'

'I think Liam's story may just be good enough to keep Mr Khan at bay for a while, but obviously we don't want Frankie implicated in any way. We need to disperse this herbal remedy as expeditiously as possible, reimburse Frankie and then, when the boys in blue come calling, and they will, gentlemen, make no mistake, we can all plead ignorance with total impunity. Matthew, old chap, please do the honours.' Gerry proffered a £10 note in Matt's direction and made a *round* gesture.

Chapter 17 **Monday**

'Well, that was a total shambles, gentlemen.' Superintendent Tickner was passing judgement at a debriefing of those involved in the Limehouse fiasco. Cartwright was carrying the can.

'To be fair, sir, we weren't expecting firearms to be involved and by the time we had safely established that we were not the target, they were long gone. The shooting was merely a diversion.'

'Any news on the van? That shouldn't be too hard to trace, a van that colour.'

'Not yet, sir. But the entire Met knows we're looking for it. It'll turn up before long I'm sure. In the meantime, I've left two uniformed PCs, both with firearms training, guarding the ship.'

'So, what do you propose from here, Chief Inspector?'

'We're going to the dock this morning with a forensic team to see what's what. It's obvious that this vessel had brought in an illegal shipment of something although we can't be sure of what just yet. And it's almost certain that it was also the boat on which Lotte van Dijkstra was abducted.'

'I see. OK. I look forward to your report first thing tomorrow morning.'

After the forensic team had finished their work on board, they left with evidence bags containing items which required minute scrutiny in their laboratory. Armstrong and Willett went aboard to see what they could find. Apart from the sort of general provisions one would expect to find in a small ship's galley, there was little of any great significance apart from the ship's log. For some reason, this was of no interest to Forensics.

'This might prove to be an interesting read. I'll take it back to the nick. I'll take these as well.' Armstrong picked up a packet of corn flakes. Willett continued snapping with his Canon F35ML.

***

Bandile Bosch was talking to his daughters as he was washing up the coffee cups. A cup of coffee was welcome but no substitute for a proper breakfast.

'The problem is that far too many whites still believe that there are very real differences in intelligence between them and us. A man at the employment exchange told me today that my IQ was much lower than his and if I needed to claim welfare I shouldn't have children. It's as well I am not a man of violence. It's attitudes like that which we have tried to escape from.' The girls were both reading, sharing an old edition of *Vogue* magazine and not really listening.

'You just wait and see. The Bosch family is going to rise above all this. We will become respected. What I've noticed so far is that the Brits are champions at muddling and fudging their way through the middle-ground where they exist. That's not for us, girls. We can do better. We will do better. McLevy owes me and I'm going to collect.'

'Yes, Papa,' came the disinterested response in unison.

Bosch put on his coat and left the washing up. He needed to get out. Bacon Street was claustrophobic. He had been brought up in thousands of acres of space. He now needed space in which to think. He had to do something. He owed it to his daughters more than to himself. After walking for half an hour but not really knowing where he was going, he found himself at Limehouse Basin. There were several uniformed and armed policemen about and they seemed to be taking a particular interest in one boat, a boat which was vaguely familiar, but the name was different, *The Eamon de Valera*. Bosch stood and observed with interest. He knew immediately that this was an Irish registered ship. The name and the Irish tricolour were a dead giveaway. He recalled reading about troubles in Ireland – Protestants and Catholics, Loyalists and Republicans, shootings and bombings. Could this be connected in some way, he wondered? No, he knew this ship. He'd been aboard this ship. He'd helped to unload this ship. As he continued to gaze at the police activity, someone tapped him on the shoulder. He turned to face a police warrant card being waved in his face.

'I'm Detective Sergeant Armstrong of... wait a minute.' The stern expression gave way to a smile as recognition spread across Armstrong's face. 'You're Bosch. Bandile Bosch.'

'Hello, Detective Armstrong.'

'Bandile, what brings you here I wonder? You know anything about this boat or the shooting last night?'

'Not the shooting, sir, but I think I recognise the boat. It's very similar to the one we took the cargo of corn flakes from in Suffolk but I'm sure that was *The Michael Collins* not *Eamon de Valera*.'

'You really don't know do you?'

'Know what, sir?'

'Oh, never mind. Speaking of corn flakes, did you have any breakfast this morning?'

'No, Mr Armstrong. We only have money for the rent at the moment.'

'Ah well it's your lucky day. Here. This was left on the boat. You may as well have it. We've still got loads at the station in Suffolk.' Armstrong laughed as he handed Bosch the packet of corn flakes he taken from the boat.

'Thanks, Mr Armstrong. You've no idea how much this means to me and my girls.'

Bosch continued walking, past the Shadwell Docks and on to Wapping High Street. He sat on a bench and watched the river, a tug towing six lighters loaded to the gunnels with coal. 'Maybe I could get a job on the river,' he thought to himself. He dozed off.

It was the drizzle that woke him up. It was getting dark and quite a stretch of the legs to walk back but no distance at all compared to the mileages he used to cover in South Africa.

When Bosch got home Stellen and Kirsten were watching television – a small black and white set – *Rising Damp*. Highly appropriate, thought Bandile.

'Here, girls, at least we've got breakfast in the morning, *Connolly's Corn Flakes*.' He thought it prudent not to explain how he came by them.

'I've seen enough of those in the last few days thank you,' said Kirsten.

'Me too!' insisted Stellen.

'Well, I'm not too proud. I shall have corn flakes for breakfast tomorrow, you two can please yourselves.' He put the packet on the kitchenette larder cupboard and sat down to watch TV with his girls.

***

McLevy knew he was in trouble, and he was all too well aware that it would only get worse. He'd been in touch with some old shipmates from the *Norfolk*. A group of sailors could put up a good fight if, when he did finally meet Mr Khan, the situation looked like deteriorating into a scrap but none of his former Navy mates wanted anything to do with him. He was on his own, apart from his new friend Jacob who had been kind enough to let him stay for a few days 'while he sorted himself out'. Certainly, he'd been made welcome by the community at the synagogue too and that had been some comfort, but he really couldn't burden these people with his problem. It hadn't been entirely his fault, but he'd messed up. It was now down to him to clear the mess up and he'd all but decided how he was going to do it.

In *The Carpenter's Arms* it was generally quiet on a Monday. McLevy ordered a double *Captain Morgan* and a pint of lager and remained standing at the bar. After a while he attracted the landlord's attention.

'Has Mr Khan been in recently?' The landlord gave him a curious, probing stare as he stood polishing a glass.

'Who wants to know?'

'I do. I was supposed to meet him here last Friday, but something came up.'

'Nobody sees Mr Khan in public, if at all. Look, I don't want any trouble in here,' he cautioned.

'Neither do I, I can promise you.'

'I can probably get word to him. Who shall I say is asking?' Just at that moment another customer came into the bar. The landlord looked towards the door, then back at McLevy and mouthed, 'Just a minute, sorry.'

'Evening, Frankie. Usual?'

'Please, Stan, thanks.' Stan began pulling a pint and turned again towards McLevy.

'So, who is it?'

'McLevy. Patrick McLevy.' Not having recognised him when he came in Frankie cast a glance in McLevy's direction, did a double take and retreated to the furthest corner of the bar with his pint, but not before Patrick had noticed him. After a few moments he followed.

'Evening, Frankie. It is Frankie isn't it? Remember we first met when I asked if I could borrow your van and then again when we had that meet with Mr Khan's man Rancid and that Irish bastard Liam O'Reilly?'

'Oh aye. Patrick ain't it, 'ow you doin', Pat?' Frankie feigned belated recognition. 'Shame it all went tits up.'

'Tell me about it. That bloody Irish bastard. Stitched me right up, and Mr Khan. I don't suppose you've got any idea where I might find him, have you?'

'Who, Mr Khan? Sorry, Pat. I ain't never seen 'im. Always dealt wi' Rancid. 'E's Mr Khan's top bloke.'

'I'm just hoping that Mr Khan understands that it wasn't me that ripped him off, but I'm not sure he will.' Frankie made no response. 'I was supposed to meet him here last week, but I bottled out. I've asked the landlord here to get a message to him.'

'Oh, you 'ave, 'ave you? If I was you, I'd bugger off an' keep a low profile. I've 'eard 'e's goin' to get 'is £20000 back off you even if 'e 'as to take it one limb at a time. Still, it's none of my business, thank gawd!'

'Shit!'

Half an hour went by during which Patrick ordered another round. Frankie declined and made his excuses for having to leave. Eventually, Stan walked over.

'OK, Patrick, I've managed to get a message to Mr Khan and he says you're to meet him at midday Wednesday if you know what's good for you.'

'What here?'

'No. You get the tube, Central Line from 'ere, Bethnal

Green, to Blake Hall. Ongar's the last stop, Blake Hall's the last stop but one.'

When Frankie left the pub he went straight to the Acme Discount Stores. The shutter was down and he banged on the door for what seemed like ages before Tom answered.

'We're closed, come back tomorra.'

'Tom, Tom, it's me Frankie. Let me in for gawd's sake.' The door in the shutter opened.

'Where's the bloody fire? What's up, Frank?'

'Where's Liam?'

'Dunno, 'idin' up somewhere, with 'is psycho brother-in-law.'

'Shit'll 'it the fan if 'e goes to *The Carpenter's*. McLevy's in there.' Tom gave Frankie a sort of *sideways* look and began to laugh.

'Don't get yer knickers in a twist, Frank, it ain't our problem is it?'

'Well, I s'pose not. But 'e's a big bugger, McLevy. I wouldn't want to come up against 'im in a scrap. Built like a brick shithouse 'e is. 'E told me 'e's trying to get a meet wi' Mr Khan an' all.'

'Don't envy 'im that one. But like I said, we don't need to worry. As far as Mr Khan an' McLevy are concerned we're squeaky clean an' we've got the gear. Shame about the girls though. Now I was just goin' to pop to the pub meself, but I reckon I might give it a miss under the circumstances. Do you fancy a snifter 'ere?' Tom disappeared to the back of the store and returned with a bottle of *Famous Grouse* and two glasses.

Chapter 18 **Tuesday**

The telephone was ringing on the front desk at the Bethnal Green Police Station in Victoria Park Square. Duty Officer PC Alistair Nichols answered the call.

'Sorry to bother you. I'm David Groom, one of the park keepers at Victoria Park. I thought you should know that there's a van in the big lake.'

'A van, you say, in the lake?'

'Yes, a van. It's a sort of purple colour, a Commer I think. If you come into the park by the Crown Gate West, off Old Ford Road, you know, just before the roundabout, you can't miss it. It's only half submerged.'

'OK, thank you, Mr Groom. Now, this van, have you got the registration number?'

'Well no. It's half submerged!'

'Oh yes, of course. Any idea when or how it got there?'

'Must have been overnight. It wasn't there when I left yesterday afternoon, but it was there when I arrived at seven o'clock this morning.'

'How do you suppose it got there?'

'I think I'll leave you blokes to work that one out.' The line went dead.

A few minutes later DS Willett came through the front door. 'Morning, Alistair, got the early turn again.' It was a statement rather than a question.

'Morning, Mick. What do you make of this? I've just had a call from the parkie up the road. There's a van in his lake. Purple Commer...' before the PC could say anything else DS Willett had run across the front office, through the door and up to Superintendent Tickner's office.

Later that morning a break-down truck pulled into the yard behind the police station with the Commer in tow. Apart from the fact that it still had water dripping from the doors, it appeared to be otherwise undamaged if one ignored the tangle of wires pulled from beneath the dashboard. Clearly, the vehicle had been hot-wired. The number, UVY 436M was checked against the register of missing vehicles. The Commer was on the list. The registered owner was a Christopher Webb of Grassington Road in Sidcup. PC Nichols telephoned the owner who turned out to be the proprietor of a greengrocer's shop *Webb's Wonderful*. He informed PC Nichols that he had reported his van stolen to the Sidcup police on the Monday of the previous week. Meanwhile, out in the yard, Willett, Cartwright and Armstrong were examining the van: the van which had got away from them two days ago.

'Bloody awful colour!' observed Willett.

'Maybe our Mr Webb chose it because it's the same colour as an aubergine. It's a fruit and veg van after all and he has named his shop after a lettuce.'

'If that's the extent of any useful contribution you have to the case, Doug, I'll thank you to keep any more to yourself.'

A little while later, over coffee, the detectives were surmising.

'So, we reckon that this van was nicked in Sidcup over a week ago, specifically for this job? It gets loaded with what-ever from *The Eamon de Valera* in Limehouse, takes off going north, unloads somewhere and is then dumped in the lake.'

'That's about the size of it, I guess.'

'Well, that suggests to me that the driver wasn't local. Surely a local would have known that the lake wasn't deep enough to totally submerge a van?'

'Well, it suggests to me that he was local. He obviously had knowledge of side roads and short cuts to get away from us as he did.'

'Either way, maybe he wasn't that bothered? Just wanted to ditch it.'

'Now, enough suggestions, where's the evidence? There was nothing incriminating in the van was there?'

'Unless you count this. It might be something or it might be nothing.' Willett produced a scrap of paper: a till receipt from a filling station on the A12 at Woodbridge.

'From up your way isn't it?'

'Indeed it is. I wonder...'

'Anyway, all this talk of vans, one van at a time please. Doug, give Kesgrave a call and get Davies to check if Forensics have done with the Transit and whether the puncture's mended. If it is he can drive it down here and we can return it to its rightful owner. Oh yes, and get him to bring those photos, the ones of the Judge's antiques.'

'The Transit was nicked from down here then?' enquired Willett.

'Yes, the owner is a...' Armstrong referred to his notebook '...a Francis Forsyth.'

'Francis Forsyth? Frankie *the Fence* Forsyth! Well bugger me! It's a small world.'

'You know him then?' said Cartwright asking the obvious.

'Know him? I should say so. Frankie's rap sheet must be as thick as the phone book. Mainly petty stuff, receiving mostly. But I've always reckoned there's more to Frankie than meets the eye.'

'Well, I'd say it's one hell of a coincidence. We have a known criminal whose van gets stolen here, and used in whatever the crime was, plus the abduction, on our home turf. One hell of a coincidence, and you know, Doug, how I feel about coincidences.'

'Indeed I do, guv!'

'And that's one of the things that's been bugging me.'

'What's that then?'

'Unlike the Commer, there's no evidence to suggest that the Transit was hot-wired. We know the Commer was and we find a fuel receipt from a garage near Melton Hall. Does that not imply, gentlemen, that whoever stole the Transit had the keys? And, does that not imply that the Commer was used in the Melton Hall blag?' An air of near excitement pervaded the atmosphere. 'I think we might have a breakthrough in prospect. Doug, give Bosch a pull. He's living here, in Bacon Street. Let's confirm that he used the keys. If he did, that suggests that your man Francis Forsyth didn't have his van stolen at all. He lent it to someone! Pull him in, Mick. I need a word with Frankie. The Judge's antiques are not going to be too far away either.'

'Don't know about a breakthrough, guv, I reckon the water's just got muddier than that lake.'

***

Bandile Bosch had popped out early for some fresh milk. Now, seated around the table in the kitchenette, he opened the packet of *Connolly's Corn Flakes* and poured out three servings. As he filled his own bowl he detected a clinking sound. At first he thought it was one of the girls tapping her bowl with a spoon. But no. There it was again. There had been something in the packet that wasn't corn flakes. He moved the contents of the bowl around with his spoon and there it was, a ring, a gold ring, or so it appeared to be, with a setting of a large stone surrounded by smaller ones.

'Well now, there's a turn up.' He passed the ring to Stellen. She inspected it and passed it to Kirsten. She held it up the light. It sparkled. She tried it on the fourth finger of her left hand.

'Looks very much like someone's wedding ring,' she suggested. 'Or perhaps an engagement ring. It looks expensive.' She passed the ring back to Bandile.

Bandile placed the ring on the table and shook the box.

'I wonder if there are any more?' He took the tray from beside the cabinet and emptied the contents of the box onto it. Amongst the corn flakes there were other items of jewellery, several rings, a necklace, individual stones, and a small, black velvet pouch secured with a drawstring. Bosch slackened the drawstring and emptied the contents onto the tray. Surely these were diamonds? Lots of them in varying sizes, all uncut. He was lost for words. He sat staring at the jewellery with his mouth open in astonishment.

'Dad, dad! What are we going to do?'

'Eat the corn flakes. Pass the milk please.'

After they'd finished their breakfast, Bosch returned the diamonds to the pouch and gathered up the other pieces.

'Have we got something suitable to put these in? I need to think.'

Bosch always considered that he did his best thinking when he was out and about. Walking. Nowhere in particular, just walking, and thinking. Many were the occasions in the past when he would leave the settlement in Mitchell's Plain in Cape Town and go walking, walking and thinking. Sometimes he would let his mind wander and his thoughts would dwell on some random topic or other. At other times he would have a specific subject in mind, or a decision that needed to be made, just as he did now. Back in South Africa he had Mandisa to talk things over with but now she was gone, and he missed her more than he would ever admit to his daughters. The girls were now his motivation. He had to do right by them. He owed that to Mandisa. What would she tell him to do? What would his father advise?

He left Bacon Street and took the back streets towards Globe Town and the Meath Gardens. He recalled as a boy discussing things with his father. His father, the wisest man he had ever known. He was a great thinker, his father, almost a philosopher in his own right. He remembered those trips on the back of his father's *Tote Gote* the small American motorcycle that was forever breaking down. Trips to Grassy Park and the Rondevlie Nature Reserve. The Kraalfontein Public Library. Embossed in his memory were the huge leather-bound tomes his father would slide from the shelves and take to the reading room, St Thomas Aquinas, Aristotle, Descartes, Marx, Ruskin. What was it that Ruskin had written? From the deepest recesses of his memory he could hear his father's voice. 'Now here's a code by which we should all live. "Your honesty is not to be based either on religion or policy. Both your religion and policy must be based on it."' But there again, given his current situation, would honesty be the best policy? If this jewellery was genuine it could be worth a lot of money. *Lead us not into temptation.* Bosch knew that handling stolen property was a criminal offence for which he could go to prison. Surely this jewellery was stolen. Think! The jewellery was in a box of corn flakes. The boat up the river in Suffolk had come from Holland and was carrying corn flakes. Think! Maybe all the boxes contained jewellery. The jewellery was being smuggled. Think!

'That's it! That's what I'll do!' he spoke out loud, a *eureka* moment.

'Excuse me?' He hadn't noticed the woman pushing the pram passing the bench he was sitting on. 'Are you speaking to me?' She seemed somewhat affronted.

'Sorry, madam. I've been wrestling with a dilemma, but I've just reached a decision.'

'Oh, well, good, that's alright then. I hope you'll be very 'appy.' And on she went on her circumnavigation.

DS Armstrong was just on his way out of the Victoria Park Square police station as Bandile Bosch was making his way in.

'I was just coming to see you, Sergeant.' The excitement in his voice raised Armstrong's curiosity.

'Well, likewise, Bandile. How about you go first?'

'Is there somewhere private? I have to show you something, something I found in that box of corn flakes you gave me. Be better if no one else saw.' Armstrong was intrigued and led Bosch into a small interview room. Bosch removed from his pocket a large, coloured handkerchief tied by the corners. He undid the knot and spread the handkerchief on the table. Armstrong's jaw dropped and he stood gazing at the treasure-trove. Eventually he sat down.

'Wow!'

'And there's these as well,' said Bandile as he emptied the contents of the pouch onto the handkerchief.

'Wow!' repeated the Sergeant. Delicately, he picked up one of the cut diamonds and, very carefully rotating it between thumb and forefinger, he held it up to the light. 'Wow! Don't move stay right here. The chief needs to see these.' He rushed out of the room almost knocking over a chair in his haste.

Initially, Cartwright and Willett were almost as lost for words as Armstrong had been. One by one, the pieces were examined in silence.

'Bandile Bosch!' hailed Cartwright in the manner of a compere at a variety show introducing the next act. 'The first time I met you my instinct told me you were a man of integrity, an honest man. My instinct was right. The last thing 99 men out of a hundred in your parlous situation would have done is just what you have done. You are that one in a hundred, a thousand maybe. Thank you. Now, what we have here, although I'm no expert, is an extremely valuable selection of stolen jewellery and precious stones. What we must do is establish where it was stolen from, its estimated value, and who stole it. If we can return it all to its rightful owner, there may well be a reward which by rights will be yours. Doug, we know this came hidden in a cereal packet. Now, we know where there's a van load of similar packets, well I hope we do unless...'

'Don't even think it,' Armstrong interjected. 'Call Davies, get him to load all the corn flakes back in the van and drive it down here. We may find more hidden treasure!'

'Yes, guv. One slight problem, I spoke to Ray earlier and they don't have the keys.'

'Yes, Mr Cartwright, sir, I forgot to give them to you the night we were in your police station. I still have them at home.'

'Mick, can you find a local dealer that might be able to do a valuation for us?'

'Yes, guv.'

'Then get on to Interpol and let's see what they know about Bandile's find. Bandile, we're going to lock all this stuff in the safe, but we'll keep you posted when there's any news. Now, do you reckon you can pop home and bring those keys in for us please? I'd like to buy you lunch in our cafeteria when you come back.'

Chapter 19 **Wednesday**

The *M/S Basto V* had just berthed in the new terminal at Sheerness and was disgorging cars and lorries. Strictly a freight-carrying service, but occasional exceptions were made for certain passengers, individuals with influence who knew the right people in the right places and had the wherewithal to buy themselves passage. One such foot passenger was making his way to the railway terminus and the next train to London Victoria. He was Pieter Hendriks. He carried a small holdall and a briefcase. The main reasons for his visit were twofold; to collect what he was owed by Frankie Forsyth and to have a word with Liam O'Reilly. When that part of the business was done he intended to do some sightseeing and maybe take in a few antique dealerships as well. On arriving at Victoria, he caught an anti-clockwise Circle Line underground train and alighted at Temple from where he walked along the Embankment to *The Black Friar*, a pub by Blackfriars Bridge at the end of Queen Victoria Street. This was the predetermined venue where Hendriks and Frankie had arranged to meet.

'Pieter, over 'ere mate.' Hendriks, intrigued by the pub's décor, hadn't noticed Frankie when he first entered.

'Ah, there you are my dear friend Francis. How are you?' After the exchange of initial disingenuous pleasantries, Pieter got to the nitty-gritty.

'You received the shipment, *ja*?

'Oh yar, yar, mate. That bit weren't a problem at all. We've got it stashed nice an' safe for the time bein', waitin' until we's sure a certain Pakistani outfit ain't goin' to give us any angst.

'*Neem me niet kwalijk, wat is 'angst'?*'

'Grief, mate, you know, bother, trouble, angst.'

'OK I see. Quite wise. And what about the special corn flakes?'

'Ah, bad news there, Pieter. The van with the corn flakes got busted and the cops 'ave the special corn flakes packets.'

Hendriks was not a man to get excited or agitated. There were never any problems, only opportunities in Hendrik's book. 'The police have the corn flakes. I see.' He took his pipe from his jacket pocket and methodically, and with an art practised over many years, filled the bowl from a tin of *Amsterdamer Fijne Snede*. Wearing an expression which suggested irritation, he struck a match and after some preliminary smouldering the conflagration was set. His irritation metamorphosed into a relaxed and contemplative contentment and the atmosphere was pervaded by an aromatic stench – or so Frankie thought.

'Bloody 'ell, Pieter, what's that you's burning?' Hendriks wasn't inclined to furnish a response. Frankie lit a Player's Number 6 in competition. Hendriks sat puffing away considering what alternatives were open to him.

'The police have the corn flakes,' he repeated. 'Including the special delivery packets which were supposed to come directly to you?'

'I reckon they must 'ave, 'cos they ain't come my way yet.'

'Oh dear. That is most unfortunate. *Neuken!*' Frankie made an assumption on the translation of the expletive.

'But, there's a bright side, Pieter, always look on the bright side.'

'Oh I do, I do. What is your bright side?'

'We 'ave your furniture. You know, those antique bits you wanted from that country house.'

'You mean the Jules Leleu palisander sideboard and the Pugin table?'

'Yeah, that's the gear. It's up the East End safely hidden in plain sight in my mate's antiques shop. And, more good news, Liam's boat is still in Limehouse Dock, and he could ship 'em back for you.'

Pieter Hendriks' disappointment dissipated and he tapped out his pipe into an ashtray and ordered a glass of *de Kuyper's*.

'I think you should take me there, Francis. Have you decided on a price?'

'No, I'm leaving that to my mate, the bloke what runs the shop. He's an expert. Berkshire's Antiques, it's called.'

'Berkshire, like the English county, is the man's name *ja*?'

'Yar, yar, no, mate. We just calls 'im that.'

'Why?'

'Because 'e is!' Whether Hendriks had understood is doubtful, but they left *The Black Friar* together, heading for the railway arches in Pedley Street with Frankie casually regaling Pieter with tales of his nights of unbridled passion with Chantal. Nothing further about the *special* corn flakes packets was mentioned.

***

Mick Willett and Doug Armstrong boarded a Central Line tube at Bethnal Green. They were headed for Theydon Bois where they had an appointment with an Abraham Moszkowicz, a specialist jeweller at his workshop in Coppice Row. DS Willett carried Bosch's jewellery find. It was now wrapped in a silk scarf, in a leather satchel and inside a locked briefcase which was chained to his wrist. There were plenty of seats on the train and the two detectives sat side by side, by the double opening doors, and in common with all London tube travellers, they sat in silence avoiding any eye contact with others whilst staring blankly at the floor or contemplating the footwear of passengers sitting opposite who were probably doing exactly the same. At first, Armstrong didn't notice the figure of McLevy on the other side of the partition. It wasn't until the train stopped at Mile End and he turned to look at passengers getting on and off when the sight of a familiar suspect caught his eye and snapped him out of his tube-induced somnambulance. The doors closed and the train moved off.

'Sit tight, Mick, I'm just going to have a word with that fellow over there. He's a person of interest to us and if the guvnor were here he'd have a fit. He hates coincidences.'

'Hello, Patrick, fancy seeing you here.' McLevy looked distinctly uncomfortable. He didn't respond to Armstrong's greeting.

'Where you off to then? You haven't forgotten your guest appearance in Ipswich court this week have you?'

'Look, Mr Armstrong, you don't need to keep tabs on me. I'll be there don't worry.' The train emerged from the tunnel at Leyton and McLevy turned to look out of the window.

'So where are you off to this morning?'

'Not that it's any of your concern, but I'm going to see a man about a job. I've got an interview.'

'Now why don't I believe you? I ask myself. Doesn't a man going for a job interview generally have a shave and put a collar and tie on, you know, smarten himself up a bit? Job interview? Don't give me that old pony. You're no more seeing a man about a job than you're seeing a man about a dog.'

'Look, Mr Armstrong, I've told you where I'm going, what I'm doing. If you don't believe me, well, that's your problem not mine. Now if you don't mind...' Armstrong resumed his seat.

'What was all that about then? Who is that guy?'

'That is Patrick McLevy. He's involved with the corn flake caper but as yet we're not sure how. He's in court in Ipswich this week on a charge of impersonating a Royal Naval Officer and handling stolen property. Says he's on his way to a job interview, but I doubt that.'

'Is it worth you tailing him. It doesn't really need two of us to get this stuff valued. I mean, he could lead you to... well, who knows what?'

'It might have been worth a tail, but now he knows he's been spotted, he'll be wary. He might even expect me to tail him, so I won't. We'll find out what his game is sooner or later.'

'Ah right. Oh, by the way, I forgot to tell you. When Frankie *the Fence* collected his van, he admitted to me that it was your man there, McLevy, who arranged the loan of it with him.'

'Bloody hell, another coincidence. The guvnor's going to love this. The various threads in this case are a right birds' nest of mess. Have we still got that ship impounded?'

'Yes, it's still under armed guard in Limehouse. As far as we know, no one's been near it.'

***

Mr Khan had suggested Blake Hall station as the rendezvous for his meeting with McLevy for a very good reason. The station was readily accessible by tube, yet it probably handled less than two dozen passengers a day and was remote from any significant settlement. The station building itself, a substantial country house, had lost much of its former imposing grandeur from when the station, then owned by the Great Eastern Railway, served principally as a goods yard handling agricultural produce from nearby farms. Since the yard had closed eight years previously, the building had fallen into disrepair and was no longer in use. Mr Khan's man, Rashid Khan, would have no problem in gaining entry to set up a venue for his meeting with McLevy.

The train pulled into Blake Hall, the doors opened and McLevy was the only passenger to alight onto the deserted platform. Willett and Armstrong watched him get off and as the train eased its way onwards they saw the grin which accompanied the contemptuous disrespect manifest in the single middle finger held aloft. As the train disappeared into the distance McLevy checked his watch. He was a few minutes early. Then, from across the track and the old station house, appeared the monstrous form of Rashid Khan who was beckoning him over. Patrick's pulse rate quickened. He had a bad feeling about this encounter. Rashid ushered him into a room which had probably previously been used as a waiting room. Rashid placed his hands on Patrick's shoulders and bore down on him with the force of a one-ton hydraulic press until he was sitting on a stool. He stood directly behind him.

'You sit, you wait!' There was no mistaking what he had to do. Patrick took a packet of cigarettes from his pocket.

'You, no smoke!' There was no mistaking what he had not to do. He replaced the packet.

'Patrick, I am so disappointed.' The voice came from behind him. It was a voice he recognised. He tried to turn to see who had spoken but Rashid had now pinned his arms to his sides and, despite his own not inconsiderable size and strength, sitting as he was on the stool he was no match for Rashid. He couldn't move.

'Patrick, I trusted you. I trusted you with my money, I trusted you to deliver. You let me down.' He tried again to turn, to see who was speaking. Whose voice was that?

'Patrick, the people I engage only have the one chance. You have had yours and failed. And so, you must repay.'

Patrick was about to speak, to make his excuses, plead for leniency, time to pay, whatever.

'You, quiet!'

He'd had enough of this. Directing all his strength to his thighs he forced himself upright in one thrusting movement taking Rashid by surprise. As he rose, Patrick broke free from the restraining grip Rashid had on his arms and as he spun around he rammed his right elbow into Rashid's midriff. He completed the gyration and his left fist, propelled with every ounce he could muster connected with Rashid's face. He followed this immense blow in one flowing movement with a headbutt to Rashid's nose which broke and instantly started to stream blood. Then, as Rashid staggered backwards, a kick to the groin found its mark, but the impact was compromised as it was impeded somewhat by Rashid's shalwar kameez. Even so, having scored with the element of surprise, McLevy now had the upper hand and, with his blood boiling, Rashid was no match for Patrick's agility and bar-brawling skills. McLevy spun round like a shot-putter winding up before launching the shot and another elbow was propelled to Rashid Khan's face, and then, taking a grip on one of his arms, Patrick pirouetted and swung his arms as hard as he could. A lesser, lighter figure would have been whipped over and onto his back, but the audible crack suggested that the Pakistani's arm had been broken. He was now growling and wailing like a wounded bear. This bellowing coupled with the stridency of the roaring and shouting which accompanied Patrick's exertions even drowned out the rattle of a southbound tube train. Rashid, now attempting to defend himself with one arm from the fury of the barrage of battering he was receiving, was all but beaten. Then the voice pierced the air.

'Stop it! Enough!' Patrick turned to seek out the source of whoever it was that would interrupt his scrap and in doing so failed to see Rashid draw a Smith & Wesson Model 10 handgun from his shalwar. But with one eye almost fully closed and with a severe cut across the eyebrow and an inability to focus from the other as a result of a broken cheek bone the shot, when it came, missed Patrick. It didn't miss the other man in the room though. He died instantly the .38 calibre bullet hit his chest. Rashid slumped to the floor in a heap. He was unconscious and bleeding all over the well-trodden quarry tiles.

Patrick walked over to the dead man. He'd recognised the voice and now in a flash he recognised the maroon corduroy trousers, the diminutive size, the half-moon glasses. This was Mr Kahn. Jacob Kahn, the Jew, the pillar of the synagogue. Not the infamous Pakistani head of a drugs cartel Mr Khan he had been expecting. Now he was totally confused. Was Mr Kahn also Mr Khan? Were they one and the same person or were there two people? Only one thing was certain. This Mr Kahn – or was it that Mr Khan? – was dead. He rifled through the dead man's pockets and removed a wallet and bunch of keys. Anxious to flee the scene, Patrick looked over to the heap of Rashid, seemingly lifeless, the gun still in his hand. He knelt beside the obese monster and gripping his hand around Rashid's he fired a shot into the temple of his prostrate body, the blood almost instantly seeping from the wound and congealing in the mass of black hair.

Patrick McLevy left the building and secured the door behind him. He walked out onto the platform. He slowly regained control of his breathing. He looked back at the building with the scene inside etched into his retinas. He didn't have to wait too long before a southbound train pulled into the platform. The section of the train where he sat was empty apart from a young mother with a pushchair. Her toddler took a shine to Patrick and seemed particularly fasci-nated by the bloodstain on his jacket which he hadn't noticed. The young mother gathered up her offspring and positioned him, or was it her, back in the pushchair. They left the train at Woodford. Patrick opened the wallet he had lifted from the dead man. Here was the confirmation. It was Jacob Kahn. Here were his driving licence, his synagogue membership card and a Visa credit card. There was also a thick wedge of banknotes. It wouldn't do to be counting them on the train. On the keyring, there was the front door key to the house in Spitalfields, the house where he'd been made so welcome. There was also a second Yale type key, and a set of car keys. The whole situation was quite bizarre, and Patrick was having great difficulty getting his head around the simplicity yet the duplicity of it. Mr Big. Khan! The international drug baron with a fearsome reputation throughout the nether regions of the underworld across continents was none other than a little Jewish fellow Jacob Kahn, using the same name but spelled differently. Jacob Kahn must have known who he was, so why the pretence? Why this contrived confrontation at Blake Hall when the whole matter could have been settled amicably in the genteel Spitalfields sitting room? The anonymous face behind the name, hiding behind Rashid Khan, the real Mr Big in physical terms at least, all 50 stone of him. It would take a crew with block and tackle to remove that corpse when it was discovered. Patrick smiled to himself. Relief. He no longer had to worry about the stolen cannabis shipment. He now had a London address he could use and call his own, a car as well if he could find out where it was kept. He had new friends at the synagogue. And by the feel of the thickness of the wallet he wouldn't be short of cash for a while.

He thought about getting out at Bethnal Green and going to *The Carpenter's* but decided against it. He'd ride the Central Line to Liverpool Street and take the first train to Ipswich and then back to the Grafton Guesthouse in Felixstowe. His court case was tomorrow, and the dust needed to settle on the recent carnage. His one big concern, Detective Sergeant Armstrong. Would he put two and two together when the bodies at Blake Hall station were discovered? McLevy drifted into a fitful sleep and dreamt. Part of his dream kept recurring. He was back on board ship on the Beira Patrol, stood at ease on the foredeck with the rest of the crew listening to another one of the *old man*'s motivational speeches. The Navy was blockading the port of Beira since the Rhodesians were attempting to circumvent the sanctions imposed on the country by the British by importing oil through the Portuguese Mozambique port. The *old man*, Commander Matthew Reeve, regularly quoted from Nietzsche and the quotation floating back through Petty Officer McLevy's subconscious now seemed personally relevant. *He who would fight with monsters should look to it that he himself does not become a monster.* There was no doubting that Rashid Khan was a monster, not averse to violence. Patrick McLevy was mindful of Nietzsche's advice. He had fought a monster. Had he become a monster? That would be for others to decide. Either way, then so be it. He would look to it that he derived maximum benefit from the situation, starting with Jacob Kahn's credit card.

Chapter 20 **Thursday**

Superintendent Tickner had called a briefing meeting principally for an update on developments. DCI Cartwright, DSs
Armstrong and Willett and Sgt Lewis had all crammed into
a small interview room at the Victoria Park Square police station. It was DS Armstrong who reported first.

'During our examination of *The Eamon de Valera* in
Limehouse dock, we discovered a packet of corn flakes. I gave
this packet to Bandile Bosch who coincidentally was out
walking down by the dock,' Armstrong explained.

'Coincidentally? Oh dear, oh dear.' Cartwright sighed.

'Bosch is a decent bloke and fallen on hard times. I felt
sorry for him.'

'You sure you weren't trying to worm your way in with one
of his daughters?' quipped Lewis.

'Anyway, my contention that he's a decent bloke is substantiated by the fact that on discovering there was more in
the packet than corn flakes, he handed the jewellery over. We
have since tried to establish where it came from.'

Mick Willett took up the narrative. 'Our meeting with
jeweller Abe Moszkowicz in Theydon Bois has proved to be
illuminating, to say the least. He was meticulous in his examination of the jewellery which Bosch handed in to us and he
has provided us with a description and value of some of the

more valuable pieces.' Willett produced a sheet of paper from a file, and he proceeded to read out loud.

'A 2-carat diamond solitaire ring in platinum, value in the region of £1300. A 30-carat diamond choker, value in the region of £2000. A cluster of emeralds and diamonds set in a white gold ring, value in the region of £2500. An 18-carat yellow gold sapphire solitaire ring with rubies, value in the region of £8000. A selection of single gemstones including uncut diamonds...'

'Yes, OK, Mick thank you. I think we get the picture. Do we know where they were stolen from? I'm presuming they were stolen?'

'We can only presume they were stolen at present. I have had this list and some photographs sent to Interpol and we're circulating it around local pawn shops and jewellery dealers, although the evidence would seem to indicate they've arrived in the UK from the Netherlands. As we know Amsterdam is a major centre for jewellery, and diamonds in particular, and our little haul was found in a packet of corn flakes which we know arrived in London on a ship from Amsterdam.'

'There may be more in the consignment of corn flakes we have in Kesgrave, in the van we apprehended driven by Bosch.'

'The van was driven by Bosch?' queried Tickner. 'Another coincidence, Detective Inspector?'

Cartwright slowly shook his head. 'Yes, sir, it appears that way, but you know how I feel about coincidences. We now have various leads which we're following up and the pieces in this jigsaw are beginning to fit. We'll be examining the rest of the corn flake packets when the van arrives here later today.'

'Well, I'm pleased to hear it. Your Chief Superintendent Gibbons has been on the phone and wants you back in Ipswich, soonest.' This news was greeted with a collective groan.

***

Susan Robbins had been given a second chance. She was a pretty girl and when she appeared before the Bethnal Green Magistrates charged with soliciting, Robin Tickner had taken something of a shine to her and offered her a job at Victoria Park Square police station as a typist and clerk in the post room. Susan had just about come to terms with the operation of the new-fangled facsimile machine, and, after several attempts, the catalogue of jewellery had finally been transmitted to Interpol Offices in The Hague, Lyons, and Wiesbaden. Susan hadn't been working for the police for very long but already the regular hours and nature of the work were becoming tedious. She was bored with it and thinking of leaving. Her previous occupation had been far more lucrative, and it wouldn't be difficult to re-establish herself. What is more, it was all together more exciting. But, just occasionally, there would be some small nugget of information that she was certain she could turn to her advantage, like the day she gave her previous working colleagues the heads-up when she learned of extra street patrols. Looking through some of the handwritten pages waiting to be typed there was one which had really stimulated her imagination. Just now and then an item marked *confidential* passed through her hands and, as had been impressed upon her, such items were to remain strictly confidential. She knew full well that any breach of confidentiality would result in summary dismissal but having reread the material she had just faxed, she thought it might be worth the risk. Here was a catalogue of jewellery worth a fortune and not a small fortune either: more than she had earned during her entire career *on the game.* Was there someone she could talk to without arousing suspicion? Was the jewellery still on the premises? In the safe in the evidence room perhaps? Who was that PC who worked in the evidence room? The windmills of Susan's mind were turning. He looked like the type who would be unable to resist the offer of a sexual favour. And the accompanying report which she hadn't yet finished typing said there was probably more which had been smuggled into the country in boxes of corn flakes. Even the busiest of girls on Gerry Hunt's agency directory would never realise such wealth as this jewellery collection was worth. If she could get her hands on this treasure she knew a man who would buy it. 'Steady, Susan,' she thought to herself, 'one step at a time. Nicking stuff from the nick? Whoever heard of such a thing?'

***

Later that afternoon a white Transit van pulled into the yard behind Victoria Park Square Police Station with Detective Constable Ray Davies at the wheel. He parked and locked the van and, since he was unfamiliar with this particular police station, walked around to the front public entrance and ID'd himself to the desk sergeant.

'They were all in the interview room a little earlier,' was the response when Davies asked for Cartwright or Armstrong. He followed the directions he was given.

'Well done, Ray. Good journey I hope?' greeted Cartwright. 'When you've had your break, I want you to bring in all those boxes of corn flakes. We're going to go through every one, flake by bloody flake. There's treasure in them there boxes!'

'Wouldn't one of those new luggage x-ray machines they have in airports be quicker, guv?'

'Probably would but in case you hadn't noticed, we haven't got one and we're a police station not an airport. Get to it, Ray!'

The boxes were piled in the lobby by the rear door and Davies and Armstrong began the task of carefully emptying each one's contents into rubbish bags in hope rather than expectation that one of them would strike gold. They hadn't been at it for more than a few minutes when the lobby door opened, and Susan Robbins came in returning from her lunch-break. Ray Davies, ever the ladies' man, introduced himself. 'Well, hello!' he said sounding more like Leslie Phillips in a *Carry On* film than Leslie Phillips did.

'We could use some help here if you've nothing better to do.' Susan could not believe her good fortune. Only having learned about the corn flake boxes a couple of hours earlier, here they now were, and she was being asked to help search through them!

'Well, I ought to get back to the post room really.' She hesitated.

'I'm sure you won't be missed for twenty minutes. I'll explain where you've been if anybody asks. Be worth a drink after you finish work, what do you say?'

'Oh well, if you're sure.' She gave the detectives her best alluring smile and as she undid the second top button of her blouse and bent over the stack of boxes she knew exactly what she was doing.

Later, in *The Carpenter's Arms*, Ray and Susan sat in a far corner of the bar, she with her *Cinzano* and lemonade and he with his pint of lager. Always a conscientious copper in the past, Ray Davies' head had been turned. He was becoming besotted. They both understood that *shop* talk was out of order, but even so it wasn't long before Susan knew the background to the entire corn flake saga and Ray knew all about the discovery made in one packet.

'Shame we didn't find any more jewellery this afternoon,' she said. 'We could have run away together.' Ray merely sat, mouth agape, infatuated beyond reason. Amongst other things, he was now wondering whether Susan's last suggestion had any mileage. 'Still, I expect they'll turn up somewhere,' she said.

Chapter 21 **Friday**

In the dock of Ipswich Magistrates Court sat the forlorn but nevertheless imposing figure of Patrick McLevy. The stentorian tones of the court usher reverberated around the court. 'All rise!' And they did. Then, as the three magistrates took their seats on the bench, everyone sat, apart from the defendant. The Clerk of the Court read from the charge sheet. Several pairs of eyes in the public and press galleries were firmly fixed on McLevy. Would his body language reveal guilt or innocence?

'Patrick McLevy, you are charged that on Friday 15th February, having conspired with others as yet unknown, you abducted Lotte van Dijkstra causing grievous bodily harm whilst unlawfully impersonating an officer of Her Majesty's Royal Navy, namely a chief petty officer. How do you plead?' With an assuredness that belied the precariousness of the situation he knew he was in McLevy confidently entered his plea.

'Not guilty, Your Worships.'

A *sotto voce* murmur accompanied by shuffling feet and fidgeting rustled around the court.

The three magistrates stared at the defendant. The Chair, a late middle-aged woman wearing a pale green twinset and pearls beneath a pale yellow jacket peered over the top of her spectacles with an acerbic sneer. Perhaps she thought she looked like the first primrose of spring. She didn't!

'Mr McLevy, I see you are unrepresented. Are you intending to represent yourself?'

'I hadn't really thought about it, Your Worship.' More murmuring.

'Then I suggest that you do. Given the gravity of the charge, you should appoint Counsel to represent you. We note that you have previous convictions for affray and public order offences. Ordinarily bail would be denied, and you would be remanded until your trial. However, social reports inform us that you were a Royal Navy man of good standing until your discharge so on this occasion we are prepared to give you the benefit of the doubt. You will be released on bail pending your appearance at Ipswich Crown Court. Bail is conditional upon you surrendering your passport, reporting to Ipswich police station once a week, and appointing a legal representative.

'Thank you, Your Worships.' McLevy breathed an enormous sigh of relief as a crescendo of incredulity spread throughout the court. As he turned to go, the Chairwoman, had to raise her voice above the general hubbub of astonishment and disbelief as she reminded him,

'Representation, Mr Levy, you need representation.'

'Thank you, ma'am, and the name's McLevy, ma'am.'

'Of course, Mr McLevy.' Her smile was tainted with vinegar as she resumed chewing her wasp.

Patrick left the court and made straight for *The Black Horse*. After four pints which he downed in very quick succession he made his way to the railway station for a train to Liverpool Street, and from there to his newly acquired accommodation, the house in Fournier Street, Spitalfields.

***

'Wasn't it today that McLevy was in court? I wonder how he got on.'

'Knowing magistrates' courts, he probably got off!'

Cartwright and Armstrong were about to call on the proprietor of Berkshire Antiques with some photographs. The shutters were down and repeated knocking failed to elicit a response from within. It did, however, get the attention of Tommy Martin who emerged from the neighbouring Acme Discount Stores.

'What's all the f...? Ah, sorry, gents.' Tommy moderated his manners as he recognised the detectives he'd been introduced to a few days previously.

'You looking for ole Berkshire, I mean Mr 'unt? I 'ope you ain't come all the way from Suffolk special like, 'cos 'e ain't 'ere.'

'Mr Hunt? Who's Mr Hunt? We thought the proprietor would be named Berkshire.'

'Why on earth do you call him Berkshire?'

''Cos 'e is!' The Cockney humour fell on deaf ears.

'Any idea where Mr Hunt might have gone or when he'll be back?'

'Nah, sorry, pal. Sorry, I mean sir. I ain't 'is bleedin' keeper am I?'

'I guess not, who exactly are you?'

'I reckon you know the answer to that. Mr Willett will 'ave given you chapter an' verse?' Tommy went on the offensive. 'You sure yous are both coppers? Let's see some ID.' In response both detectives produced their warrant cards. Tommy studied them carefully. 'Says 'ere, Suffolk Constabulary. You's in London. You lost or summat?' he quipped in his best East End dialect.

'You know very well why we're here. We're investigating the theft of some antique furniture from a house in Suffolk and we're requesting the cooperation of all antique dealers in assisting with our enquiries,' explained Armstrong.

'Not only that, we believe this theft may be connected in some way to an abduction, rape, stolen jewellery, and a drug smuggling racket,' added Cartwright.

Tommy had gone into silent mode, his mind racing.

'Oh, nothing too serious then! I'll let 'im know you called, officers.' Tommy was about to return to his store, but Armstrong took hold of his arm.

'I don't suppose you've seen these pieces in Mr Hunt's shop?' Cartwright produced the copies of the insurance company photographs. Tommy made a pretence of studying them but knew that he didn't need to.

'Posh gear that ain't it? Nah, bit up market for ole Berkshire. 'E don't 'ave stuff like that, only old tat. Junk mainly, that's more 'is style.'

'Well thanks for your help anyway, and if you could ask him to give us call please?'

'Yes, ask him to give us a call as soon as it's possible.' Armstrong handed Tommy his business card.

Cartwright and Armstrong walked back to Victoria Park Square and met Lewis and Davies.

'Ready, sirs?' Lewis enquired. They got into the XJ12 and headed back towards Suffolk for the weekend, or more importantly for familiar territory and the regular Friday night gathering at *The Maybush*.

Tom threw the business card in the bin. He knew exactly where Gerry Hunt was, and he and Matt went directly to *The Blind Beggar* after work. Frankie and Gerry needed to be alerted to the recent *close call*.

'I reckon those Suffolk coppers 'ave ad a sniff. Of all the antique places in London why would they rock up at Berkshire's?' Frankie was working himself up to a state of agitation. Unusually, Tommy and Matt were in a bit of a state as well.

'What worries me is that they're connecting the antique blag to the smuggling, a kidnap and rape and they mentioned summat about stolen tom.'

'My dear boy, calm down, relax. All will be well, Francis. I merely need to conclude negotiations with Mr Hendriks and we can have the Suffolk pieces aboard *The Eamon de Valera* and off down the Thames. Thomas, you have organised the shipment with Mr O'Reilly?'

'Sort of, but 'e wants readies up front.'

'Ah, that could present us with a certain unnecessary and inexpedient complexity.'

'What's 'e say Tom?'

'Might be a bit of a bugger.'

'Oh.'

'However, I have no doubt that it is within one's influence to prevail over this minor inconvenience. Now, another small libation I think, gentlemen.' Matt looked quizzically at Tom again.

'Won't be a problem, an' what you 'avin'?' Drinks were ordered and the conversation reverted as per normal to football and the fortunes of West Ham United.

'We bin stuffed by them Suffolk swede bashers already this week. Bloody 3–1 'gainst Ipswich. We don't want them other nonces, them Suffolk coppers queerin' the pitch an' all.'

'Ah, no sweat. We got Leicester at 'ome tomorra. Should be a piece a piss.' It was Matt who noticed the latest arrival.

'Eh up, 'ere's Martini Susan.'

'I thought she drank *Cinzano*?'

'No mate, like the advert, *any time, any place, anywhere.*'

'I thought she'd packed that game up now she's working for the Old Bill.'

'Yes, an enormous shame. Susan had potential She could have been on my books and in demand. She could have gone a long way,' lamented Gerry.

'I 'eared she went all the way,' laughed Tom.

Susan ordered her *Cinzano* and lemonade and walked over to the table.

'Sorry to interrupt,' she simpered. 'Frankie, could we have a private word?' The ribald response was inevitable. She led Frankie to the opposite side of the room and whispered in conspiratorial tones.

'If I were to get my hands on some high-quality tom, would you be interested? Could you fence it for me? It's real quality stuff, expensive like.' Always receptive to *a nice little earner* Frankie was all ears and intrigued by what he was hearing.

'Where're you goin' to get 'old of a load a tom-foolery?'

'Best you don't ask.' But he didn't need to. What was Susan Robbins up to, and what did she know about jewellery? If there was any jewellery knocking about on the manor Frankie knew where it had come from. This was *his* she was referring to: the missing corn flake packet. So far, the special corn flakes packets and their contents had remained as intended, a private arrangement between Frankie, Liam, Jan de Klerk and Hendriks, peripheral to the main weed shipment. Susan finished her drink and with a 'I'll be in touch' gesture she left. Frankie went back to the table. This encounter had exacerbated his state of agitation and he was now in a flap.

'Now, Francis, were you at all tempted by whatever the delectable Miss Robbins was offering?' Frankie made no response.

'So, Frankie, we gettin' the coach or what tomorra?' Matt liked to have his social life organised.

'Sorry, what?'

'Tomorra, the game, away at Leicester.'

'Sorry, lads, I can't make it. Summat's just come up, urgent like. I got to deal wiv it.'

Without finishing his beer, Frankie left. The others had never seen him quite so distracted, particularly where travelling arrangements to a Hammers away fixture were under discussion.

Frankie went straight home and spent a fitful evening worrying about the jewellery. How was it possible that whatever Susan had been alluding to could be connected with the raid on *Juwelier Rijk* in Amsterdam's *Leidsestraat* and the theft of several thousand guilders worth of jewellery, precious stones and metals. Meticulously orchestrated by Jan de Klerk the burglary had taken place two years previously. Many of the diamonds had been recut by Pieter Hendriks. It was only now that de Klerk had determined that it was sufficiently safe for parts of the haul to resurface through reliable fences. Frankie Forsyth was deemed to be a reliable fence. What if Hendriks or de Klerk didn't believe the corn flake scam had been hijacked by the police? Would he be liable for the value? And all this on top of the law now on the trail of the Suffolk antiques blag.

He desperately needed to talk to Fergal Flaherty. Had Fergal managed to get the packages behind the linings in the van? When the modifications to Frankie's van had been made, the fitter's workmanship could not be faulted. It was intentional that the most discerning eyes would pick out the false panels. They were the decoy, the deception. Behind the false panels there were the factory fitted linings. But, behind those were steel moulded cavities, purpose-fabricated for the concealment of small packages, welded to the actual steel fabric of the van's bodywork. The intention had been that, whilst McLevy, Bosch and his daughters were being entertained on board the ship, Flaherty would extract the pouches from the marked corn flake packets and hide them. The Dutch girl, well she was extra cargo as a favour for Berkshire and merely had to be bundled into the very poorly fitted concealed compartment.

Frankie decided to go to the police station the next morning with the intention of insisting upon the return of his van.

Chapter 22 **Saturday**

'West End shows and fancy restaurants is what I've heard. It's simply not on, Cartwright. I daresay you were in a luxury hotel as well. Next thing, you'll be expecting me to sign off on your expenses claim.'

'With respect, sir...'

'Don't give me that. I've had Judge Bertrand giving me grief on a daily basis. The recovery of his antiques should now be your priority. I understand that the Dutch girl, the rape victim, has recovered with no signs of any long-lasting kind of traumatic stress. So, she can be moved down your agenda. As for the corn flakes, bloody corn flakes. I've never known such a fuss being made about corn flakes. Forget the corn flakes – and that's an order.' Chief Superintendent Gibbons was in full flight and judging by the manner in which the erubescence of his complexion was increasing, a stroke was imminent – or so Cartwright hoped.

'With respect, sir...'

'No, Cartwright! That's an order.'

Acting on Impulse Armstrong interrupted, 'We have very good reason to believe that we know the whereabouts of the Judge's antiques, sir.'

'Ah, you do? Well done, Armstrong. And on what is this belief based?'

'A gut feeling, sir, Instinct.'

'There you are, Cartwright. Instinct, copper's nous, a gut feeling. I expect your gut is too stuffed with posh restaurants, rich food and... and... bloody corn flakes... Cartwright get back in here!' Gibbons slumped back in his chair with his safety valve blown.

'If there's nothing else, sir?' Armstrong, not normally the obsequious type, made his escape too.

'Sorry, guv!' Back in Cartwright's office Armstrong was apologising. 'I thought it might at least buy us some time.'

'And it will, Doug. I just had to leave before I thumped him, pompous arsehole!' He reached for the bottom drawer of his desk and the comfort bottle. 'A little snifter and then we'll go and check on our petty officer, see how he got on yesterday.'

When they arrived at the Grafton Guesthouse, Mrs Arnold answered the door.

'Patrick? No. I haven't seen him for a few days now, I think he must be away.'

'Would you mind if we checked his room?'

'Don't you have to have a search warrant?'

'We can go and get one if you wish. It's a lot of unnecessary bother though.'

'Oh, OK then. While I'm not looking. Top of the stairs, second on the left. It's not locked. I looked in earlier.'

'Do you spy on all your guests?' Mrs Arnold dug her hands into the pockets of her apron and harrumphed a retreat into her own apartment.

***

'OK, Frankie, it's parked around the back. Wait here a second and I'll go and find the keys.' Frankie had, with some trepidation, gone to Victoria Park Square police station with the intention of reclaiming his van. He never imagined it would be quite so straightforward.

'Just one thing, Frankie, you initially reported your van as having been stolen, but now you're saying it wasn't stolen, but that it had been "lent" to someone, that someone "borrowed" it.' Willett put the inverted commas around the word *lent* and *borrowed* by a gesture with his fingers.

'Yes, sir, Mr Willett, sir. When it weren't there where I usually parks it, I assumed it 'ad been nicked. I forgot I lent it to a feller, name of McLevy, a Royal Navy bloke. It were a black bloke what came an' picked it up. Any road up, I got it back now, an' it ain't damaged, so no worries.'

'For the time being, Frankie, for the time being.'

***

While Suffolk's finest were on a wild goose pursuit, chasing Patrick McLevy, the man himself was enjoying all the home comforts that the house in Fournier Street had to offer, and they were considerable. As an anonymous international drug baron, Jacob Kahn trading as Mr Khan had done extremely well for himself. Patrick couldn't believe his luck, but then he had always maintained that one made one's own luck, be it good, bad or indifferent. Mr Khan had been toppled from the pinnacle of his empire. With diligent assiduity could he, Patrick McLevy, assume the position? He was the only person to know of Mr Khan's demise, therefore he could think of no reason why the empire could not remain intact and fully operational. Find a replacement for Rashid Khan and no one would be any the wiser. Whatever, all that could wait. McLevy would take the next few days off and make the most of what he now considered to be his inheritance, the pay-off. Lounging on a deep-button-back Chesterfield, with a box of *Montecristo* No.4 cigars and a bottle of *Macallan* 50-year-old anniversary malt on the side table was something he could get used to.

There were issues that he needed to deal with, however. He was the victim of some insidious dupery at the hand of a glib, congenial Irishman and his less than veracious brother-in-law. Vengeance would be wreaked. Never mind Nietzsche, Patrick was fully intent on monster status now. He spent the next hour in that no-man's land between asleep and awake fantasising on how he would exact revenge on the Irish fraudsmen and when the doorbell rang it was a full minute before the full realisation of where he was brought him back to reality. The ringing was fairly insistent. Should he answer the door, or would whoever just go away if he ignored it for long enough? He decided to answer the door.

'Oh, Patrick, it's you.' The caller was taken aback by the unexpected figure standing on the threshold. 'I was worried about Jacob. We normally play Bridge on a Friday, but he didn't show up yesterday and when I tried to phone him there was no answer.' Patrick recognised the caller but couldn't recall either from where or who he was. His blank expression prompted a reminder. 'It's me, Isaac, Isaac Goldmann. We met at the synagogue, remember?'

'Ah yes, of course, forgive me, Isaac. I couldn't place you for a moment. You're looking for Jacob? Well now, Jacob was called away on Wednesday evening, a problem with one of his business interests abroad. Pakistan apparently. From the way he explained it to me, he could be gone for quite a while, and he was a little worried about leaving the house unoccupied for any length of time so he asked me to house-sit for him.'

'Oh, I see, that's a pity, and very kind of you. I hope it's not putting you to any great inconvenience. I didn't know he had an enterprise based in Pakistan. I hope everything's alright.'

'I'm sure it will be.'

'You don't play Bridge, by any chance, Patrick?'

'No, Isaac, I'm afraid not.'

'Ah well. Sorry to have bothered you.' Isaac extended his hand in friendship. 'Maybe we'll see you at the synagogue today?'

'Maybe, goodbye.' Patrick closed the door rather abruptly leaving Isaac standing on the step. 'Don't hold your breath,' he thought with a wry smile.

It wasn't long after Isaac Goldmann's call that the doorbell rang again. 'Now what? Who the hell?' Patrick was getting annoyed. He opened the door and there stood an imposing figure dressed somewhat incongruously in a Bahawalpuri shalwar suit beneath a quilted gilet, with a Pakol cap which he doffed.

'Please pardon, sahib. I am Hashim Abidi, I look for Rashid Khan. He is missing. He is work with Mr Khan and me.'

'They have gone to Pakistan on a flight to Lahore. Give me your number and I'll get Mr Khan to call you when he returns.' This was the best McLevy could think of on the spur of the moment, but he could see how callers such as Hashim Abidi and Isaac Goldmann could become a nuisance at best and problematical at worst. He needed to give the entire situation some serious thought.

Chapter 23 **Sunday**

'I apologise for calling you on a Sunday morning, Your Honour, but I thought you would like to know that we have a lead on your missing furniture.' Cartwright had made the call to Judge Bertrand partly from the perspective of keeping him off his back and chiefly to prevent him from bothering Gibbons. If indeed a filling station receipt was a lead it was tenuous at best and a dead end at worst. Still, it warranted a search warrant, and Cartwright assumed that there would be no problem obtaining one through Judge Bertrand.

With Lewis at the wheel of the XJ12, Cartwright, Armstrong and Davies were back in Bethnal Green by midday. The shutters on the Berkshire Antiques arch had been raised and the lights were on in the showroom.

'And a very good day to you, gentlemen, or should I say detectives? How may I be of assistance?' Cartwright was about to flash the search warrant from his pocket in front of Berkshire, but he was pre-empted. 'Oh, you've gone to all that convoluted inconvenience of obtaining a warrant: the labours of Hercules, oh my goodness. Our policemen are wonderful.' Gerry Hunt examined the single sheet of paper. 'And from a court in Suffolk. Goodness gracious, Detectives. You have gone to inordinate lengths, completely considerate circumspection in circumstances I can't understand when I have absolutely nothing to hide. Your efforts have been wasted since everything in my showroom is legitimately acquired and you are most welcome to browse at your leisure. If anything inspires your interest do please let me know.' Whilst Cartwright was being subjected to the Berkshire brand of bullshit, Armstrong was already having a look around.

'Over here, guvnor. I'm no expert but this looks to me like a Jules Leleu Art Deco palisander and marquetry mother of pearl sideboard, oh and look here, surely a George IV Pugin table. Well fancy that!' Berkshire and Cartwright had crossed the showroom to join Armstrong.

'Oh, but, Detective, you are an expert. Your description of these pieces is perfectly precise.'

'Yes I know,' said Armstrong as he showed Gerry the insurance company photographs. 'Gerald Hunt, I am arresting you on suspicion of receiving and handling stolen goods. Anything you say will...'

'Oh spare me the caution please, I know it off by heart.' Gerry offered his wrists for handcuffing. 'I'm sure we won't need to go to those lengths will we now?' As he was escorted to the awaiting XJ12, Tom and Matt, attempting to appear anonymous but in a very conspicuous manner, stood watching amongst the small crowd of onlookers that the police car, an XJ12, not a regular Ford Anglia panda, and the suspect being led away had attracted. 'Lock up for me please, Tommy!' Gerry shouted as he was eased into the rear seat.

Gerry Hunt was driven to Victoria Park Square where he was formally charged and released on bail to attend Bethnal Green Magistrates Court the following morning.

'Bloody 'ell, Tom. You reckon the Ole' Bill 'as 'dentified that stuff we nicked from up country?'

'Well, Matt, it ain't the cupboard full of weed is it? It were those country coppers who was wanting to get into Berkshire's the other day. Remember? Best we get 'old of Frankie 'cos 'e's got a buyer for that gear.'

Later that evening at *The Carpenter's Arms*, Tom, Matt and Frankie were huddled around a table. Tom had the plan worked out in his mind.

'Now look. We know it's nicked 'cos we nicked it. The police knows it's nicked, the insurance company knows it's nicked 'cos we've seen their snaps, and Jimmy knows it's nicked but 'e's still happy to buy it. If it disappears out of Berkshire's shop tonight, who's the loser? Not the judge we nicked it off, 'e can claim on 'is insurance. Not Jimmy, 'e still gets what 'e's bought, not us, we still get our cut. It's the police what's the losers, my friends!' There were no conflicting arguments. 'So, soon as, we'll lift it again. You got your van back, Frank? Let's say early on in the morning. We can leave it in Frankie's van 'til we've sorted out the shippin' wi' that mercenary bloody tight-fisted Paddy.'

***

'Well, there's a result. What was it you said to Gibbons, Doug – copper's nous, gut feeling? More the diesel receipt that cracked it for us I reckon. Still, I'll give the Judge a ring and he can come and formally identify his stolen furniture.' Cartwright referred to his pocketbook, picked up the telephone handset and dialled the number.

'Melton Hall. His Honour Judge Bertrand's residence...'

After a few minutes conversation Cartwright explained to the others. 'The Judge is being driven down tomorrow to identify his property. When that's confirmed he'll hire a removals company to come and collect it. A good day's work, team. Let's go and get a drink. I've heard that *The Approach Tavern* is worth a visit.'

***

Meanwhile, in *The Carpenter's Arms*, Tom, Matt and Frankie had been joined by Gerry, released on bail. Tom went over the plan with Gerry.

'I know it'll make things a bit awkward for you, Berkshire, you know, when the Judge turns up to ID 'is furniture. But chances are you'll be in court when 'e gets 'ere...'

'...Or you might even be banged up by then,' chipped in Matt, unhelpfully.

'Thank you so much, Thomas, Matthew, your confidence is an enormous comfort to me. I am consoled beyond measure.'

'Sarky bastard!' observed Frankie.

'Look, give us your keys and we'll let 'im in when 'e gets 'ere. We'll 'ave 'im in an out quick as a flash. 'E'll be in out an' gone like a ferret down your trousers, an' as soon as 'e's gone we'll 'ave is gear away.'

'Be a first for me,' said Frankie in a lugubrious tone of voice.

'What's that then?' enquired Matt.

'Nickin' the same stuff twice.' The only one not laughing was Gerry Hunt.

***

Meanwhile, sitting in *The Camel*, only a couple of minutes from *The Approach*, Susan Robbins was nursing a *Cinzano* and lemonade waiting for Detective Constable Ray Davies. He made it just before last orders.

'Sorry I'm late. I had to have a drink with my guvnor then make an excuse to get away. I'm not sure he was convinced. Anyway, we had a good result this afternoon.' And, without giving a single thought to the implications or consequences, he gave Susan chapter and verse on Judge Bertrand's stolen furniture.

'Poor old Berkshire!' was the extent of her sympathetic response. After closing time, they left together and strolled arm in arm to Brick Lane where Davies was hoping he might be able to sneak Susan into his room in the guest house.

Chapter 24 **Monday**

Bandile Bosch picked up the brown manilla envelope that the postman had just dropped through his letterbox. He very rarely received any mail, and he had no idea who would be writing to him anyway. The previous week having seen the advertisement in the situations vacant column of the London Evening Standard he had taken the No.175 from Bethnal Green to the London Transport depot at Romford. More in hope than expectation he thought there might be a possibility of getting a job, training as a bus driver. With no qualifications, no UK driving licence, no experience, no National Insurance number he had no chance, but he'd clearly made an impression on someone because here was a letter from the London Transport Executive. The LTE had been formed out of the London Transport Board after it had taken over management of the London Underground from the Greater London Council a couple of years previously. The letter conveyed an invitation to Bandile to make an appointment with the station manager at Mile End Station with a view to a trial period as station assistant. This was almost as exciting as the morning he discovered the jewels in the corn flakes. A real prospect of a job, a wage, a foot on the bottom rung of the ladder. With Stellen and Kirsten having been offered situations with The Berkshire Escort Services Agency the Bosch's quality of life and standard of living were on the way up, he felt sure.

***

It was midmorning when the chauffeur driven Rolls Royce Silver Shadow pulled up outside the Pedley Street arches. The liveried chauffeur got out of the car and rattled the shutters of Berkshire Antiques.

'That'll be 'is 'onour then,' observed Matt from the window of the Acme Discount Stores. 'Best you go an' let 'im in.'

Tom ambled over. 'You'll be wanting Mr 'unt but 'e sends 'is 'pologies on 'count of 'im bein' 'disposed. 'E's asked me to let you in.' With a gesture almost resembling a bow, Tom unlocked the service door, went inside and raised the shutter. The chauffeur had returned to the car and opened the rear door for his passenger.

The sartorially and elegantly dressed figure of an immaculate Richard Bertrand emerged from the red leather interior, and in a posturing sort of manner brushed a non-existent piece of fluff from the lapel of his morning suit jacket. Tom thought for a second that it might have been a few crumbs from the bacon roll he'd had for his breakfast, but instantly discarded the thought as highly unlikely.

'This way if you please, Your 'onour.' That bow again. The Judge was led to the rear of the showroom and immediately his expression bore the affirmation of recognition as he approached his furniture.

'You may confirm to Mr Hunt that these pieces are indeed my property, and I shall arrange for their collection as soon as possible. Now I understand that Mr Hunt's indisposition this morning is due to his appearance in the local magistrates' court on a charge of handling and receiving stolen property. In my not inconsiderable experience, guilty of such a charge rarely receives a custodial sentence and, I assume he will plead guilty albeit maybe with mitigating circumstances. I would therefore expect him to be handed down a fine in the region of perhaps £50.00.' Tom merely stood there taking it all in, somewhat in awe of being in closer proximity to such a higher authority than ever before.

'You might care to pass on some words of advice to Mr Hunt since you are clearly an associate of his. He should in future satisfy himself with regard to the source and provenance of any property he buys in...' The Judge paused mid-sentence as his attention was drawn to the mid-seventeenth-century Swedish Rococo cabinet.

'I say, I do like this. Do you suppose Mr Hunt would be disposed to part with it?'

'You mean you want to buy it?'

'Exactly. I should think it has a value in the region of £400 would you say?'

'Search me, squire... sorry, your 'onour. But you's clearly knowledgeable 'bout these things, and a gent. I'm sure 400 quid'll do nicely. Cash of course!'

Judge Bertrand withdrew his wallet from an inside pocket, and, giving Tom a quizzical yet knowing smile, proceeded to count out twenty £20 notes into his hand. 'Kindly ask Mr Hunt to put the documentation and receipt in one of the cabinet drawers. I'll have it collected tomorrow along with my other pieces. Oh, and have everything carefully wrapped for transportation. We wouldn't want it damaged now would we?' The Judge left the showroom with just a brief glance at the Whistler forgery. The chauffeur opened the door for him, and he got back into the Rolls Royce which silently glided away. Matt appeared as if out of nowhere.

'Bloody 'ell, Tommy. 'E 'ad me shittin' bricks there. I thought 'e was goin' to open one of them cabinet doors for a minute. Still, what a motor. I'll 'ave one of them one day. A

Roller, Silver Shadow. Did you know that when Mr Rolls, or it might 'ave been Mr Royce, first come up with this model they was goin' to call it Silver Mist?'

'No, Matt, I didn't know that. You got some crap in your brain.'

'Exactly! That's what it means. Mist in German means crap, an' they decided Silver Crap didn't have the right ring to it so they comes up with Shadow. Still, whatever they call it, it's a beauty. Six litre V8 engine – pull some crumpet in that!'

Around lunchtime Gerry Hunt appeared at his showroom, just as Tom was about to lock up.

'Yeah, Berkshire me ole cock. 'Ow'd you get on? I see they let you out. Now I got some bad news, and I got some good news – well even the bad news is good news really.'

'OK, Thomas, if it's quintessentially imperative that you inflict either on me now. I've had a very tiresome morning. You are aware? Fined! Fined I was. Can you believe it? £50.'

'That just what the Judge said it'd be. But don't worry. The gear, you know that sideboard and the table, is 'is. But we knew that anyway, and we're goin' to nick it again anyhow. And...' Tom paused for effect, as he produced a wedge of £20 notes. 'I sold 'im that swede cabinet – for cash.' Tom handed Gerry £300.

'Oh, Thomas! I shall never cease to marvel at what a marvel you are!'

'So, c'mon, Berkshire, you're £250 up on the day – it must be your round!'

**

The first thing after breakfast, Bandile Bosch left the Bacon Street apartment and went straight to the telephone box on the corner of Sclater Street. He carefully dialled the number and inserted a fistful of copper when the line answered. A few minutes later he was running back to the apartment wearing a grin from ear to ear. The girls hadn't even started washing up the breakfast things or made the bed and were surprised to see him. Bandile was out of breath.

'I must get changed, Sunday best, interview in an hour,' he panted. The girls were almost as excited as he was and when he emerged from the bedroom wearing his navy blue suit with his only clean shirt, they fussed over him, helped him with his tie, and, brushing the dust from his shoulders, wished him luck and watched him disappear in the direction of Bethnal Green Tube Station.

Mile End Station was only one stop east-bound, and he could have walked it but chose to ride preferring to be half an hour early rather than a single minute late. The interview went well. It was a fairly menial position that he was offered but the offer came with an assurance that promotion for someone of his intelligence would follow before too long, with the usual provisos of course. It was a job. A proper job. He would have a uniform, a National Insurance number and, most importantly, a weekly wage. He couldn't wait to get back and deliver his news. When he did get back to Bacon Street, such was the euphoria in the apartment that the Bosch family felt completely justified in a small celebratory drink at *The Carpenter's Arms*.

It being a Monday lunchtime, the pub was sparsely patronised although the few who were propping up the bar also seemed to have something to celebrate.

'Well, if it ain't me ole mate.' Frankie had instantly recognised Bandile. 'Sorry about that business with me van, but, well, you know, these things happen and I knows you were only the driver.' Stellen and Kirsten were now the centre of Matt, Tom and Gerry's attention. 'Listen up,' said Frankie attempting to make an introduction, 'this is, this is, I'm sorry I forgot your...'

'Bandile, Bandile Bosch.'

'This is Bandile Bosch. 'E was the driver on that caper, week or so back. You know the pick-up from Liam's boat?' With everyone introduced to everyone else, Gerry bought drinks and they all sat together.

'If ever you're wantin' work, Bandy, you don't mind if I call you Bandy?'

'Well yes I do actually.'

'Oh you do, do you?' In that instant there was tension in the air. Just a few words exchanged, and Bosch and his daughters were immediately transported back to the all too familiar confrontations with white men in apartheid Cape Town.

'Well, I am sorry, Mr Bosch, but I was about to offer you a drivin' job for tonight. But if it ain't good enough for you, if we ain't good enough...'

Bosch interrupted and tried to restore calm. 'It's not that, Frankie. I've got a regular full-time job now. I'm a station assistant at Mile End,' he announced proudly. 'It's not that I'm not grateful for the offer, I am, but I've not been paid for the last job yet, and it got us arrested didn't it, girls?' The Pedley Street mafia listened intently as Bosch described the ill-fated excursion to the River Deben from his perspective.

'Well, we din't know any of that did we, lads? An' you ain't bin paid neither?'

'Are you out of pocket, dear boy? I'm sure you must be, what with these alluring darlings to take care of. Let me compensate you for your time, trouble and inconvenience. I've been fortunate enough to have had a visitation from Lady Luck this morning and besides which we'll extract it from Mr McLevy next time he deigns to put in an appearance won't we, gentlemen?' Before Bosch could decline, Gerry had handed each of the girls a twenty-pound note. Seeing the expression on his daughters' faces Bosch just didn't have the heart to instruct them to give the money back, as much as his conscience nagged him to do so.

'That's extremely generous of you, Mr Hunt...'

'Oh, dear boy, please. Call me Gerry, or Berkshire if you must.'

'Berkshire? Why Berkshire?'

'Because he is!' came the familiar response in unison from Matt, Frankie and Tom, followed by much profane ridicule and more drinks. After much longer than he had initially intended, Bosch disappeared to the gents and Stellen and Kirsten got up from the table and, putting on their coats, prepared to leave. Friendships had been made. Always the gentleman, Gerry also stood and taking Kirsten's hand, raised it to his lips.

'If you and your charming sister would care to call into my store I'm sure we can finalise the details of your contracts – you are going to accept my offer I hope? I can assure you both that there is a potential for very high earnings – more than your father could dream of.' The invitation was overheard by the others resulting in a ribald reaction.

***

It was late. Susan Robbins was in the post room finishing off typing up DS Willett's report on the trip to Theydon Bois: the report she'd volunteered to type. Most of the detectives typed their own reports but Susan was always prepared to show willing in the belief that her conscientious attitude would stand her in good stead. This particular piece of work, over and above her usual duties, was very much in her own interests. As far as Mick Willett was concerned Susan could do no wrong. In common with many of his colleagues, he fancied her and when his fertile imagination ran out of control he very often felt a stirring in his loins that needed Susan's attention which she was always happy to give. Included with the report was an amended inventory of the jewellery. With the typing finished she dialled the CID room extension. It was Ray Davies who answered, as she knew it would be.

'Ray, it's done. I'll meet you in the basement.' Mick had asked Susan to attach his report when it was finished to the original inventory which she had previously faxed to the Interpol offices. She now knew the inventory was with the jewellery in the safe in the evidence room. Although there was one slight flaw in the plot, the ruse that she and Ray had contrived should, if it all went to plan, present the opportunity to lift some of the uncut diamonds, and by substituting the report with an amended but accurate inventory of what was actually in the safe, no one would be any the wiser. Subject to any response from Lyons, The Hague or Wiesbaden it could be months before the discrepancy in the inventories would be discovered. Ray's part was the actual thieving, Susan's part was to distract the evidence room's duty PC and that would be just too easy.

After a few minutes, and with the duty PC rezipping his fly, the pouch of diamonds was in Ray's pocket and the safe was relocked.

'Goodnight, and thank you!'

'No, thank you!'

Chapter 25 **Tuesday**

It was still a good couple of hours before dawn when Liam O'Reilly positioned himself in Horseferry Road. From his vantage point he could see his boat quite clearly. It all appeared to be OK apart from the police van parked in Goodhart Place alongside *The Eamon de Valera* and the two armed policemen. One of them was pouring tea or coffee from a vacuum flask into the two mugs standing on the wall between the quay and the road. Liam had agreed with Frankie to ship a return load of stolen goods to Amsterdam, and he was anxious to get it loaded and get away from London and the UK in general. It was bad enough that the last trip hadn't gone according to plan, and he regarded the involvement of the police now as an unwelcome intrusion into his business. Why was his ship still impounded? The police had been over it; they'd removed whatever they thought they needed to, including his logbook. Whatever else were they expecting to discover?

Annoyed and frustrated, Liam decided he would go for the full-frontal confrontation. He would march into the police station and demand that his ship be released. Surely to detain either his ship or himself without charge represented an unlawful restraint of trade.

The public reception area of the Victoria Park Square police station was dimly lit.

'Be with you in a minute.' The demeanour of the duty constable behind the reception counter left much to be desired in Liam's opinion. The lack of courtesy bordered on rudeness.

'Ah well, what's another minute?' Liam thought to himself. He stood at the counter waiting for the minute to elapse then began tapping his fingers on the counter. He forced a cough.

'Constable, I've made a note of your number and I shall be having a word with your superior, so I will. Now, your attention please if you could possibly bear to tear yourself away from whatever's so bloody important and acknowledge my presence.'

'Be right with you in a minute,' the constable repeated as he adjusted the Anglepoise lamp on the counter.

'No, you'll be right with me now!' Liam thumped the counter with his clenched fist and, as a result, the bulb in the Anglepoise fizzed and went out.

Completely unfazed by Liam's outburst the constable looked up from the paperwork on the counter and in a laconic style which he had obviously perfected over the years said, 'Where's the fire?'

'There's no fire right now but I'll light one under your arse if you don't get the man in charge of the corn flake caper down here right now.'

'Your name?'

'Liam O'Reilly, I'm the owner of the ship you're unlawfully detaining in Limehouse Dock without just cause.'

The desk officer picked up a telephone, dialled an extension and spoke in hushed tones.

'Detective Sergeant Armstrong will be down in a moment.'

***

Since recovering his van Frankie had *garaged* it in the vacant arch in Pedley Street. As subtle as a bull in a china shop, Gerry Hunt tiptoed stage-like into the arch and as the wind caught the door in the main shutter it slammed shut alerting all those who hadn't otherwise noticed the fact that Berkshire seemed to have annexed the vacant arch next to his own.

'Bloody 'ell Berkshire, you want to tell the coppers what we're about?'

'Terribly sorry, Francis my dear fellow. Anyway, here we are. *The game's afoot; follow your spirit, and upon this charge cry God for Berkshire, England and St Gerald.*'

'I ain't got a clue what you're blethering on about. What time's Matt and Tom bringing the stuff in?'

'Imminently, dear boy, imminently.'

'An' what time's the Judge's removals van s'posed to be coming?'

'Imminently, old chap.'

'Is that the same in-a-minutely as the other?'

'Well, soon then.'

'What's that, before noon then?'

Interrupting the chronology question and answer session's descent into the realms of ridiculousness, Matt and Tom struggled through the shutter with the Jules Leleu Art Deco palisander and mother of pearl marquetry sideboard which the four of them managed to load into the back of the Transit.

'OK, c'mon, Matt let's get the rest before it gets proper light.' A few minutes later, the George IV Pugin table had also been loaded, the vacant arch secured and everyone back in Berkshire's Store.

'I s'pose it might be some consolation to the Judge that 'e's still got that cupboard 'e bought.'

'Would be if we left all that weed in it.' Tom, Matt and Frankie laughed. Gerry didn't.

'Gentlemen you have just planted the seed of a most beautiful notion which is germinating in my mind as we speak.'

'What's he say?' asked Matt.

'Gerry's got a plan.'

'What say you we leave the weed in the cabinet?'

'What, all that weed in the posh cabinet?' Matt was incensed. 'No way, it's worth thousands.' Tommy was ahead of Gerry's idea.

'What, an' let plod know the Judge's doin' a bit of weed dealin'?'

Frankie was getting the drift as well.

'Yeah, 'cos I knows for a fact that Anna likes a spliff now an' again.'

'Oh, I get it.'

'Well done, Matt. Try an' get with it.'

'Bloody brilliant!'

'Yeah, but not all of it eh? Just enough to convince the fuzz he's dealin'.'

'I can see the headline now – Judge accused of conspiracy to supply.' They all started giggling which gradually developed into guffawing. Matt set about removing half of the packages and concealing the rest in a manner to suggest they were purposefully hidden. The cabinet was then wrapped in plastic sheeting and bound with parcel tape.

'There we are then, not quite like Mother Hubbard's cupboard,' proclaimed Matt.

'What about the rest of it then?'

'Good question Frankie. I can generally fence most stuff, but drugs ain't really my scene, an' technic'ly the whole stash is mine.' Frankie's question was sympathetically received and considered. After a moment or two it was Matt that made a suggestion.

''Ow about we let Rancid know that we 'eard about Mr Khan's missing deliv'ry and after we'd made a few 'quiries we found it. P'raps 'e'd offer a reward.'

'Now that's the most sensible thing I've ever heard you come up with, Matthew.'

'Ah, thanks, Gerry.'

'Anyone seen 'im recently? 'E ain't bin about for a few days now,' mentioned Tom.

'Anybody 'ere' seen Rancid?' Matt started singing.

'Let's worry about that in a bit, after the van's bin for the Judge's stuff, what's left of it. C'mon let's go an' get some breakfast.'

To all intents and purposes four blokes sitting around a table in Sid's Cafe in Kerbela Street, with their bacon sandwiches and cups of tea gave the appearance of any other ordinary group of workers having breakfast. However, the conversation between this particular group was anything but ordinary everyday banter.

'When the Judge's removals van arrives and finds that the stuff they come to remove 'as already been removed, the shit'll 'it the fan and we'll have the Bill all over the place.' Frankie was becoming a real worrier.

'Gentlemen, do you think for one second that it might be just a tad more convincing if we say my store's been burgled?'

'Bloody selective burglars, they'd 'ave to be, just nicking the Judge's gear. Too much of a convenient coincidence, that,' suggested Frankie.

'Yes, now I think about it, Francis, you are absolutely correct. Perhaps we could get rid of a few other bits from my bargain basement selection, you know the cheap nasty stuff, make it look like a proper robbery.'

'No, Berkshire, now listen up all of you, this is what's happened when the coppers get 'ere. Early this morning, like, about now, a removals van pulled up outside, and I let 'em into Berkshire's shop assumin' they were the firm that the Judge had booked to come an' collect 'is stuff.' Tommy acted out the scenario. ''Ow was I to know they was bogus? 'Onest, occifer, I thought they was genuine removals men, you know wearin' them proper aprons an' gloves. They 'ad them proper blankets and straps an' everything. What's that, occifer, can I describe 'em?' The other three were delighting in the way Tom was outlining the plan.

'My word, Thomas, it's genius. Inspired, and off the rozzers will go on a wild removals van chase for a phantom removals van that doesn't exist. Brilliant!'

'So 'ow long's my van goin' to be tied up in 'ere then?'

'Well, that all depends on O'Reilly and his ship. As soon as the fuzz are no longer interested in it and keepin' it under guard, we can drive down to Limehouse, he can load up an' get underway.'

'I'll need to meet your purchaser, Francis, old boy, we haven't finalised our negotiations on the price yet.'

'Don't worry about 'im, 'e's safer than the Old Lady. What's more 'e's currently in the Country visiting friends in the country.' Matt was confused.

'Yeah, you said that, Frank, in the country. No need to repeat everythin', we're not stupid. An' what's your old lady got to do wi' it, 'sides, you got a bit on the side now?'

'Not my old lady, dumbass, The Old Lady of Threadneedle Street!' Frankie explained harking back to the James Gillray cartoon.

'We've also got to do somethin' about the weed. If Matt's plan doesn't come off for whatever reason 'as anyone got any alternative ideas?' Blank expressions greeted Tom's question.

'OK *Carpenter's* tonight. Frankie, can you get O'Reilly there? We could do wi' that Navy geezer as well. If anyone knows 'ow to get 'old of Mr Khan or Rancid, it's 'im, McLevy – and 'e owes the Bosch bloke'. Back in Pedley Street it was business as usual for both the unusual businesses that traded there.

***

In an interview room at Victoria Park Square, Liam O'Reilly sat across the table from DS Armstrong and DS Willett.

'We're glad you've come in, Liam. You've been the missing piece in this particular jigsaw right from the beginning.'

'I'm not sure about that, sir. I was just wanting my ship back.'

'Well, if we're satisfied with the answers to our questions, that's a distinct possibility. Now, when you left *Jan van Riebeeckhaven* in Amsterdam back in January, what was your destination – and be careful with your answer if you want your ship back, we've got your logbook.'

'Ah, well now, if you've got my logbook you know the answer.'

'Yes, but we'd still like to hear it from you.'

'I was chartered by a London syndicate to collect and deliver a consignment of *Connolly's Corn Flakes*.'

'Just corn flakes, nothing else? No passengers, no immigrants?'

'Just corn flakes, sir.'

'And did you deliver them?'

'That I did, sir. To a small quay called Methersgate on the River Deben in Suffolk. First time I've been there and I'm in no rush to go back in that ditch either.' O'Reilly was banking on the detectives not knowing where either the river or the quay was, ignorant of the fact that Armstrong often sailed his Wayfarer dinghy down the river from Woodbridge and passed the quay on his way down to Waldringfield. Armstrong had also spent many happy hours in *Ironside*, a houseboat moored on a mud-berth at Woodbridge.

'And who took delivery of these corn flakes?'

'All the cartons of corn flakes were loaded into a van.'

'All of them?'

'Ah it's a fair cop – you have me there, sir. I kept one packet for the ship's stores.'

'Yes I know. Would it surprise you to learn that hidden in that packet was a quantity of precious jewellery?'

'No, sir, I mean, no, really? Yes it would surprise me.'

'So, of all the corn flakes on board, the one packet you kept contained jewellery! What a coincidence!'

'Ah yes, sir, a coincidence for sure and that's no mistake.'

'Do you know a Dutch girl, Lotte van Dijkstra?'

'No, sir.'

'Would it surprise you to know that Miss van Dijkstra claims to have been brought to this country on your ship?'

'Then she'd have been a stowaway. I don't carry passengers.'

'She also claims she was bundled into a van along with cartons of corn flakes.'

'I know nothing of that, sir.'

'After you'd made your delivery your ship was tracked by Thames Coastguard to the Roughs Tower and then to the River Crouch and Paglesham Creek where you had some work completed at Shuttlewood's Boatyard.'

'That I did, sir. It's all in the logbook.'

'Why did you have the name of the boat changed?'

'Ah well, sir, we'd had a little problem, by we, I mean *The Michael Collins*. You see, sir, the South Wales miners took exception to our deliveries of Irish coal. They said we was scabs, crossing their picket lines an' all, bloody Druids. After I'd been beaten up I thought it might be prudent for the safety of my ship and myself to change the name.'

'Yes, Mr O'Reilly, prudent indeed – and a likely story.'

'Ah, well now, you can be checking the hospital where I stayed after I was beaten up and you can check with the Mercantile Marine Office in Dublin for confirmation.'

'We know, we already did.'

'Then why the feck are you asking me again?'

'Now, when you arrived at Limehouse, what were you unloading when we turned up?'

'Unloading, sir, oh no, sir, you have that all wrong. I had nothing to unload.'

'But we saw the van, a stolen van as it happens, a maroon-coloured Commer.'

'Ah yes, sir, that's right. I didn't know the van was stolen – nasty colour too. How could I know the van was stolen?'

'So, you weren't delivering a cargo?'

'Well now, here's a thing, sometimes Major Bates at the Tower has a delivery for me to make, but not on this occasion. We were about to load, not unloading, but you scared them off.'

'And what were you about to load?'

'Ah, well you see, I'll never know. Your lot scared them off so I'm guessing it might have been something illegal. So, as the Holy Mother is my witness, I must thank you, sir. By scaring them off you prevented me from getting involved with handling stolen goods or whatever it might have been. But now, I really do need my ship, to find a cargo and earn some money. I am a sailor and I get claustrophobia if I'm on land for too long.'

'Who is your crew?'

'Like it says in the logbook, Fergal Flaherty. He's my brother-in-law. He can be a bit fiery sometimes, especially when he's had a few. But he's not too bad a deckhand.'

'And where is he now?'

'Well now, I hope he's on his way back here. He went to see his dying grandmother in Liverpool. You see, I'm an optimist and I believe in the luck of the Irish. I was hoping to get my ship back today or this week, so I rang Fergal and told him to return to London. I hope we'll be allowed to live on board at least. Paying for bed and breakfast is crippling me, sir.'

'Just bear with us a moment please.' Armstrong and Willett left the room.

'What do you think?' asked Armstrong.

'It'll do no harm for them to live on board, but I think we'll need to clear it with the DCI before we let them set sail.'

'Yes I agree. At least everything he's told us tallies with his logbook, but there's a lot of blarney in what he says; something's not quite ringing true.' They re-entered the interview room.

'OK, Liam, you may return to your ship and live aboard, but the vessel is still impounded until you get official clearance from Detective Chief Inspector Cartwright.'

'Oh, and one last thing, Liam,' asked Willett, 'do you know Patrick McLevy?'

'Indeed, I do, sir. He was my contact for the corn flake delivery. We had a slight disagreement over his agent's commission, I'm afraid. A Navy man I think he was, to be sure.'

'OK, Liam, we'll be in touch. Don't leave the country!'

'Oh yes, sir, very amusing that, sir. What a sense of humour you have!' O'Reilly disappeared down the stairs and out through reception, without giving the desk constable a second glance, onto the street and off towards Limehouse.

Armstrong looked back through the notes he'd made.

'When we first encountered McLevy, as I recall although I'd had a few, there was no love lost between him and O'Reilly. I'm sure when the corn flakes were getting strewn across the pavement he called him a "rotten, lousy, crooked Irish bastard", or words to that effect. Something definitely not quite right. Even so, I think I'd take O'Reilly's word before McLevy's.'

'Me too!' said Cartwright who had re-entered the room.

***

It was on the crack of opening time that Patrick McLevy arrived at *The Carpenter's Arms*. After the visit from Hashim

Abidi, Patrick had done some serious thinking and in the knowledge that a few if not all the players in the corn flake fiasco used *The Carpenter's*, he wanted to make his peace with them since, in common with all the local criminals, he too had devised a plan, the execution of which would require an accomplice or three and make them all rich.

In *The Approach*, at more or less the same time, Willett and Armstrong were relating their cross-examination of O'Reilly to Andy Lewis.

'Did we do the right thing, giving him permission to return to his boat?'

'Look, Doug, you're senior to me. It's the guvnor you should be asking not me.'

'But, which of them would you believe, O'Reilly or McLevy?'

'Well.' Lewis paused for consideration. 'Seeing how McLevy's tried to sell us a crock of shite already, I'll go with O'Reilly, but with a pinch of salt.'

'Go on,' urged Willett.

'According to Bertrand Russell, people's opinions are mainly designed to make them feel comfortable; truth for most people is a secondary consideration.'

'So does your opinion on this subject make you feel comfortable?'

'I'm not most people!'

'Who's Bertrand Russell?' enquired Willett.

'Oh, he'll be some bloody philosopher yawping on and making no sense. Andy's always got his nose in some tome of intellectual clap-trap or other.'

'Look, you invited my opinion, my opinion, because you're concerned you might have exceeded your authority giving O'Reilly leave to return to his boat. Well, Doug, Mick, I'm not going to sit here and ease your consciences if you're going to take the piss out of the fact that I want to get on in the job by improving my own intellect and mental capacity reading the works of some of the world's greatest thinkers.' Armstrong could see his remarks had caused offence. Lewis was a bit touchy this evening.

'Andy, I'm sorry. I didn't mean to upset you, and you're right. I'm having second thoughts.' Willett added his apology.

'Yeah, sorry, Andy. Shows how thick I am. Didn't even know who Richard Bertrand was.'

'Richard Bertrand is the judge with the stolen antiques, or should that be without the stolen antiques? I'm quoting from Bertrand Russell, one of the most influential mathematicians, logicians and philosophers of the twentieth century. I'm surprised you haven't heard of him. He only died three or four years ago. Well here's another nugget from Bertrand, might make you feel better, Doug. In a nutshell he says the problem with the world is that idiots are always so sure of themselves and wise people so full of doubts. Seeing how you're having second thoughts, you're a wiser person than most in my book.'

'Thanks, Andy. Let me get you another pint.'

As they sat chatting, about the thirst for knowledge, the power of reasoning and intellectual thought and philosophical things in general, cerebral perceptions deteriorated in direct correlation with each round of drinks. It was now a thirst for pints.

'Why don't we go down *The Carpenter's* right now and round up the whole bunch? Bet your life they're all in there laughing at our expense because they're getting away with whatever it is they're getting away with.' Armstrong and Lewis both looked at Willett in such a way that Mick wasn't sure whether he'd said something eminently sensible or completely stupid.

'The minute you set foot in *The Carpenter's* they'll all leg it faster than Valeriy Borzov.'

'Who's he, Andy, another philosopher?'

'No, Mick. Valeriy Borzov won gold in the 100 metres at the Munich Olympics.'

'Yes, Andy's right, Mick. You're known in there. On the other hand, we're not, well, not as well as you. I've been in there a couple of times, how about you, Andy? Do you think you'll be recognised? Might be worth popping in, see who's there, ears and eyes open. What do you think?'

After a few moments' thought Lewis responded, 'Yeah, OK, let's do it.'

After the brisk twenty-minute walk from Approach Road to Cheshire Street, DS Armstrong was breathing quite hard. But for Lewis, on the other hand, being younger and fitter, it had been no more than a gentle stroll in the park. Lewis removed his tie and attempted to make himself look a little less like a policeman. Villains have a nose for coppers. Armstrong, who it had been agreed was only back-up, went and loitered on the corner of St Matthew's Row as inconspicuously as he knew how.

Lewis entered the public bar and was quite taken aback by the size of the gathering already there: not just the number, but almost the entire cast-list of the current caper under investigation. Head and shoulders above the rest was Patrick McLevy deep in conversation with Liam O'Reilly. 'I wasn't expecting that,' Lewis thought to himself. Over towards the one-armed-bandit there was Frankie *the Fence* with a ginger-haired chap, average build, ruddy complexion, and a tattoo on his neck. 'What's his name?' Lewis racked his brain but couldn't remember. He would need to get a closer look at that tattoo. Matt Taylor and Tommy Martin were talking to the antique dealer and then emerging from the ladies' toilet, 'Is that what's-her-name, the girl that worked in the post room at Victoria Park Square?' Lewis beat a hasty retreat. If it was the post girl she would surely recognise him. He made for the door without even ordering a drink. He brushed past Frankie on purpose to get a good look at ginger's tattoo.

'Excuse me, gents.'

'Nay bother, pal.' It was ginger who responded to the apology. Irish. Definitely an Irish accent and the tattoo, Gaelic? *Tiocfaidh ar la.* He ran into St Matthew's Row where Armstrong was waiting, his heart racing.

'It's him!' panted Lewis, now feeling the effects of adrenalin rather than exertion.

'Who?'

'Him! The Irish rapist. The bloke she described, with the ginger hair and the tattoo on his neck. Lotte van Dijkstra's rapist, crew on O'Reilly's boat. In the pub! They're all in there!'

'Calm down, calm down before you blow a gasket,' urged Armstrong. 'You're sure?'

'Absolutely, a hundred per cent certain.' They're all in there. It'd be my guess they're hatching something. Even the antique toff and the two likely lads. McLevy's in there as well talking to O'Reilly. Now that's weird isn't it? And you won't believe this...'

'Try me...'

'The girl that works in the post room at the nick, mixing with suspected criminals.'

'Maybe Mick's suggestion wasn't so stupid after all. Do you reckon they'll be in there for a while?'

'Hard to say, but they'd all got fairly full glasses.'

'OK, here's what we'll do. You leg it back towards Victoria Park nick, stop at the first phone box and ring for some urgent back-up and a van. We'll bust them all if we can. I'll hang on here, should be able to spot anyone leaving.' Lewis was on his way even before Armstrong had finished speaking.

There was a phone box on the corner of Dunbridge Street and Vallance Road. Dead. Vandalised. He ran up Vallance Road to the junction with Bethnal Green Road. Another phone box. Occupied. A woman on the phone. Lewis took out his warrant card and tapped on the window and opened the door.

'Sorry, madam, it's a police emergency!' Her initial expression of indignance rapidly turned to one of understanding and she handed Lewis the receiver as she stood aside.

Armstrong had sauntered past the front door of the pub from his vantage point in St Matthew's Row and into Hertford Street, taking a surreptitious glance through the windows as he did. The pub still appeared to be crowded. He waited on the corner of Hertford Street looking back down Cheshire Street. Then he posed the question 'Is that Ray Davies?' to himself but almost out loud, such was his disbelief. It was Ray Davies, no doubt about it. He was about to call him over when the pub door opened and out stepped Susan Robbins. She and Davies embraced and walked off arm in arm in the direction of Brick Lane.

'Oh bugger me, no. Not you, Ray, surely not?' Disappointed beyond measure he barely noticed the black paddy wagon pull up almost silently. DCI Cartwright and DS Lewis were sitting up front with the driver. The rear doors opened, and six uniformed constables got out, two of whom went around to the back door. With a variety of slamming, crashing, clattering and uproar mixed with the sounds of breaking glass, all the suspects were handcuffed behind their backs and marched out of the pub, each one escorted by a policeman into the waiting paddy wagon.

With the round-up successfully accomplished, the suspects

were ushered into the reception area at Victoria Park Square nick and booked in. Lewis walked through the area and the ginger Irishman glared at him with a look full of hate that said 'you're a dead man'.

'Now look here, Detective Chief Inspector,' Berkshire was remonstrating with Cartwright. 'I really must protest in the most vociferous of terms. My colleagues and I were merely enjoying each other's company, a reunion if you will, over a drink in our local hostelry. This is police harassment. I demand that we're released forthwith. What are the charges? What heinous crime am I and my colleagues alleged to have committed?' Gerry was really getting hot under the collar and being urged on in his protestations by the others.

'I'll think of something, Mr Berkshire.'

'The name is Hunt, not Berkshire, you, you... Detective person.' Gerry was becoming increasingly incensed. 'That is Gerald Hunt, sir to you! You may anticipate hearing from my solicitor, so may the chief constable, and the fucking commissioner if necessary.' Gerry had lost his customary cool.

Willett and Andy Lewis had brought Fergal Flaherty to the front of the group. Hunt and the others fell silent. 'Fergal Flaherty, you are under arrest on suspicion of the abduction of a woman in Amsterdam with the purpose of bringing her to London to engage in prostitution. Also for subjecting her to serious sexual assault and grievous bodily harm. You do not have to say anything, but it may harm your defence if you do not mention when questioned something you later rely on in court. Anything you do say may be used in evidence. Do you understand?'

'Ah, feck you!' And he spat on the ground as he was led away. The remainder of the fraternity stood looking at each other, somewhat dumbfounded not really knowing what to say or how to react. Gerry Hunt, normally very verbose, had gone very quiet. O'Reilly adopted a shrugged shoulders, outstretched arms, nothing to do with me pose. Cartwright took Lewis, Willett and Armstrong to one side.

'Give them all an hour in the cells and then release them. I can't see that legitimately we've actually got anything to hold them on or charge them with, yet!' His last word was loaded with promise.

'I will just have a word with McLevy though.'

'Patrick, I don't know what you're doing down here mixing with the East End Mafia, but you're very close to finding yourself in breach of your bail conditions.'

'Merely having a drink in the wrong pub at the wrong time, Mr Cartwright. Will this count as my reporting to a police station once a week?' He grinned.

'No it bloody well will not, as well you know. You're to report in Ipswich so we can keep tabs on you. Now go and get on the first train out of Liverpool Street and back to East Anglia.'

That may have been sound advice from the DCI, but not at all what McLevy wanted to hear, or had any intention of taking. Ipswich and his bedsit in Felixstowe were now part of his past if all went according to what had been agreed only a couple of hours earlier in *The Carpenter's*.

Chapter 26 **Wednesday**

Ray Davies had been mightily relieved to hand the uncut diamonds over to Susan after he had purloined them. She had given him chapter and verse of what she intended next, and he assumed it had happened. Poor, silly, Susan! Totally naive. There was a part of Ray that felt sorry for her. Why did such an attractive young woman have to resort to obliging men with sexual favours? But then her practised art had opened doors for her in the past. Is that how she got the job at Victoria Park Square? She really believed that the small velvet pouch and its contents represented her ticket to wealth and happiness. She would discover just how misguided she was when she came to sell them to Frankie *the Fence*.

Susan and Frankie met as prearranged the previous evening, and at 9.00am the stones were spread onto the green baize of the furthest table from the door in the Mile End Snooker Club. Susan was anxious to do a deal before she had to be at work at 10.00. She recognised that not turning up for work, or a late arrival, could be misinterpreted, especially by the unfortunate PC in the evidence room.

The snooker club was quiet, just a few unemployed or retired ne'er-do-wells having a cup of tea. Frankie looked at the stones and took a jewellers' loupe from his pocket. He always liked to look the part even though he wasn't.

'But these ain't bin cut! Ain't worth much 'til they've bin cut an' polished.'

'Oh c'mon, Frankie, stop teasing.'

'I ain't teasing, 'onest, Susan. They're what we in the business call raw. They don't get valuable 'til they've been cut an' polished. Ask any jeweller.' Susan looked crestfallen.

'So how much'll you give me for them?' Frankie rolled the stones around on the green baize mentally counting as he did so.

'I'll give you 250 quid cash in your hand right now. That's a fiver a stone.'

'I'm sure I can get a lot more than that.'

'I'm sure you prob'ly can – along with a load of questions like where'd you get 'em from, an' jewellers checking their lists of knockoffs an' the like. Now I ain't asked you a single thing about where'd they come from 'ave I?'

'Tell me truthfully, Frankie, what would you do if you were me?'

'Well, I'd try an' make contact with a cutter, someone who's an expert in cuttin' and polishin', but someone who don't mind doin' a dodgy deal with a thief. You be 'onest wi' me Susan. You've 'ad these away from somewhere ain't you? They ain't been left to you by your recently dearly departed granny that's for sure. If you could find someone like that, a top cutter, you could be looking at two grand an' a monkey; and that'd just be your share. I reckon a good cutter would want at least a 60:40 split.'

'And where would I find such a bent, expert cutter?'

'Doubtful you would in this country, but, as it 'appens, an acquaintance an' a very good Dutch friend of mine from the Netherlands is in the country at the moment. 'E's 'ere buying some antiques off of Berkshire an' I'm due to meet 'im tonight to finalise the deal. Would you like to meet 'im, 'e's a real nice gent?'

'Well what do you think?'

'Alright then, be at Berkshire's tonight. Of course, I'll need a consideration for introducin' you though.' Frankie's obscene gesture was sufficient to suggest what he had in mind.

'I'm sure I can oblige on that score.' Susan's day had just got better all of a sudden and off she went to work.

***

After *The Carpenter's Arms* bust everyone was aware that time was now of the essence. Goods needed shifting; buyers needed finding. There had been a new profit-sharing partnership agreed in the pub. Had the police arrived ten minutes earlier, they'd have witnessed the shareholders shaking hands and drinking a toast to their new collective association. There was some honour in this den of thieves, this fraternity of villains, some honour but very little if any trust. Patrick McLevy had been briefed to make contact with Mr Khan through his man Rashid Khan and act as the negotiator in the sale of 450lbs of herbal cannabis, cannabis that Mr Khan had already bought, and paid for, not that he, or his man were in a position any longer to be interested or concerned about it. Patrick did consider letting the others in on the grisly detail of the Blake Hall massacre but quite wisely decided against it. He stuck to the same story with which he'd palmed off Isaac Goldmann. The group readily agreed that Patrick could strike a deal with Hashim Abidi who had already had his name ridiculed. Within the group he was now *A Bidet*.

The newly established syndicate were meeting behind closed shutters at Berkshire's Antiques. As an absolute priority was the loading of Judge Bertrand's antiques, the Pugin table, and the Jules Leleu Art Deco palisander. Able's the specialist antique removal company were coming to collect by midday Thursday. Little did they know that there would only be the Swedish Rococo cabinet to pick up.

Shipping had been arranged with Liam O'Reilly. There were just two potential meddlesome impediments: Liam's crewman being banged up being one, and the prospect of the ship being re-impounded as a result of the coppers' visit to *The Carpenter's* the other. Matt was dispatched on a reconnoitring expedition on his Lambretta.

Frankie hadn't volunteered any involvement beyond introducing Pieter Hendriks. The antiques were just what Pieter wanted, and he paid well over the odds for the purchase and the delivery. Once that transaction had been concluded Frankie was about to disappear when everyone adopted a *freeze frame* stance as someone outside was rattling the shutter. Berkshire crept to his inner sanctum, picked up his gun and switched off the lights. After a moment's silence there was more rattling.

'Frankie, are you in there? Berkshire, it's me Susan, Susan Robbins.'

'Goodness gracious me, Susan darling, you almost gave me apoplexy,' he called out. 'It's OK, chaps it's only Berkshire's Bicycle.' He went to turn on the lights and the others chuckled at the crude reference. 'Now then, Susan, you dear sweet thing, what can you possibly want?' The overhead lamps were re-illuminated.

'Is Frankie there? He promised to introduce me to a gentleman from Holland.'

All eyes turned and focused first on Frankie and then on Pieter. 'Oh well, I suppose you had better come in then.' As she appeared through the door in the shutter, Pieter's expression said it all as a rosy-fingered glow bloomed in his cheeks. Susan had made an effort and was certainly dressed to impress if not more.

'It's a private matter, chaps, no need for you to get involved. I advised Susan that Pieter might be able to 'elp 'er out,' said Frankie.

'Help her out of her knickers, more likely, for sure!'

'We'll have none of that coarseness in here thank you.'

'Ah, sorry there, Berkshire, a little Irish humour. I would!'

Gerry attempted to restore a degree of propriety to the room. 'Let's leave Susan to do whatever business she has with our very important foreign visitor. We have equally important matters we must attend to. We're all loaded and ready to go. When can we deliver these fine pieces of antiquity to the docks?'

'Soon as Matt gets back with the "all clear".'

'Good, that's a start. Are you happy with that, Pieter?' Hendriks was still deep in conversation with Susan.

Chapter 27 **Thursday**

With Fergal Flaherty in custody at Victoria Park Square, Cartwright was keen to get the case to court. In his mind, and based on Lotte van Dijkstra's evidence, the balance of probabilities didn't enter into any determination of a trial outcome. There was absolutely no doubt that Flaherty, the man in custody, was guilty. It was true that there had been cases where evidence involving identification by distinguishing features had been disputed. In this case the tattoo *Tiocfaidh ar la* was more than distinguishing. There couldn't possibly be a jury in the land that would be persuaded there was an element of doubt as to Flaherty being the perpetrator of the abhorrent crimes of which Lotte was the victim, and he knew it. Cartwright rang Chief Superintendent Gibbons for an opinion.

'Has the girl made a positive identification of the suspect?' Gibbons asked.

'How positive does it need to be? The rapist had a tattoo on his neck. A tattoo in Gaelic. *Tiocfaidh ar la*. Lotte has this motto indelibly inscribed in her memory. Surely that is positive enough, sir?'

'Has she picked him out of a line-up?'

'For goodness' sake, sir, how can I put together a line-up of ginger-haired men with the identical Gaelic tattoo on their necks?'

'Yes, I see your point, but...'

Cartwright interrupted before Gibbons could continue. 'I'm not prepared to put this girl through an ordeal where she's obliged to confront the man who abducted her, subjected her to physical violent assault, inflicting GBH and sexual assault which culminated in rape.' Cartwright was beginning to become exasperated by Gibbons' dogmatic, obdurate blindness. 'If you are not prepared to sanction this case going to court without further delay I shall, with respect, sir, go over your head to the commissioner or even the Director of Public Prosecutions if necessary. I will stake my career, my pension, on the outcome of this trial. This man, Flaherty is...'

Gibbons had heard enough. 'Alright, Cartwright, you're clearly confident of the outcome. Incidentally, how does the Gaelic translate?'

'Our day will come!'

'Well let's hope it does.'

'Oh it will, sir, it will.'

Lotte had returned to her father's home in Amsterdam a week previously having been discharged from hospital. Cartwright wanted to give her the news in person and telephoned Willem van Dijkstra. Lotte, he explained, was back at university and had moved back to the apartment she shared with her best friend, Linde. So, Cartwright outlined how Lotte's written statement should be sufficient to gain a guilty verdict in which case there would be no need for her to attend the trial. However, she should be prepared to attend court and testify if Flaherty decided to plead not guilty.

On the day of the preliminary hearing the outcome was a foregone conclusion. Flaherty appeared under tight security at Old Street Magistrates Court. His common sense prevailed. Or was it that he realised the determination of his position was inevitable? He pleaded guilty and was committed for sentencing at The Old Bailey. The following week, the Right Honourable Steven Melford sentenced him to a minimum of fifteen years' imprisonment. Willem van Dijkstra had made the journey from Amsterdam for the sentencing and broke down when Mr Justice Melford made his pronouncement.

'*Gerechtigheid wordt gediend!*' he pronounced through his tears. 'Justice is served!' Cartwright and Armstrong were jubilant although not to the extent that they had lost sight of the greater corn flakes picture. Liam O'Reilly was amongst those sitting in the public gallery. 'Fecking eejit! What'll I do for a crew now?' he asked himself.

***

Whilst Flaherty's future was being determined for him, a Seddon Luton van bearing the inscription *Able's Removals & Storage* had arrived at the Pedley Street arches. Gerry, Tommy and Matt were there on the side of the road and a heated discussion with the driver and his mate was in progress. Tom was on the offensive.

'Look, pal, they've gone, left, which part don't you get? Departed, shoved off over an hour ago. They must be about there by now.'

'But it says here on our docket...'

'I don't give a monkey's what it says... the pieces 'ave already bin collected. You blokes thick, or just stupid? Which bit of that don't you understand? Let me explain again. There was a furniture van 'ere, what, an hour-an'-arf ago? Two blokes, loaded the Judge's bits and left. Not our fault is it? You should 'ave got up earlier!' The Able's men were clearly irritated not only by what they thought was a wasted journey, but by Tommy's hostile attitude. Gerry attempted to dissipate the tension.

'Gentlemen, gentlemen, please. There really is no need for this dissension. Quite clearly there has been some confusion with the removals company, or maybe the booking has been duplicated. However, and whatever. Despite this anomalous muddle, you gentlemen' – Gerry smiled as he looked directly at the Able's employees – 'have saved the day.'

'How do you work that out?' enquired the driver, still clearly very irritated.

'The previous van only collected two pieces. They neglected to collect the third. I'm sure the Judge will be more than grateful for your conscientiousness and attention to detail when you deliver the missing piece. Please, walk this way.' Gerry led the removals men into his store.

'If they could walk that way they wouldn't need the talcum powder!' quipped Matt.

Inside the store Gerry indicated the Swedish Rococo cabinet, carefully wrapped in plastic sheeting and bound with adhesive tape. The driver looked at it.

'OK, Arthur, blanket, straps and the barrow, mate.' Arthur went out to the van and returned with the accessories of the removals trade. Twenty minutes later the Rococo cabinet and its contents were on their way to Melton Hall. Tom, Matt and Gerry could hardly contain themselves.

'I do believe, gentlemen, that a small tincture would be in order. What say you?'

'Thought you'd never ask!'

In the pub, Gerry enquired on the situation at Limehouse after Matt's reconnoitre the previous evening.

'Well, I 'ad a drive by on me scooter last night as you know. Looked to me like there was still a couple of coppers keepin' the boat under observation.'

'Oh what a wretched nuisance.'

'We goin' to leave the stuff in the van in the arch then?'

'Yes, Matt. Best we leave the stuff in the van in the arch then.'

In the *London Evening Standard* a report of Flaherty's trial occupied a couple of column inches on the front page. Much more prominence was given to the £350,000 transfer fee paid for Birmingham City's centre forward, Bob Latchford, and his move to Everton: the highest transfer fee ever. Liam O'Reilly was sitting by himself nursing a pint of Guinness in *The Old Salt Quay* pub in Rotherhithe Street on the south side of the river, but close enough to take an occasional look with his binoculars at his ship in Limehouse Basin opposite. Despite the police allowing him back on board they were still maintaining their surveillance of it, and him, or that's how it felt. And now, things had regressed from bad to worse with his brother-in-law and crewman being locked up for fifteen years. He hadn't been too surprised by the *Standard*'s piece. It was after all a factual report. He had been there in court. He was still very much of the opinion, however, that the duration of the sentence was way over the top. But then Fergal only had himself to blame. He, Liam, had not been implicated, he had not been accused of, or charged with, complicity or involvement in any way. Whilst he had agreed to deliver a girl from Amsterdam at Gerry Hunt's request, he was expecting her to be a willing passenger, an exile from the Red Light District taking a chance by joining the Bethnal Green International Escort Services Agency. He most certainly wasn't expecting Fergal to kidnap, beat up and rape a university student. 'Feckin' eejit!' He took a long draught from his pint and returned to the *Evening Standard*. More reports of bombings in London by the IRA. Perhaps this was the reason the police still had his ship as good as impounded. Maybe they suspected him of gun-running for the IRA. Thoughts of the *Troubles* cast his mind back to his homeland, his friends, his relatives. Perhaps, he pondered, we, the Irish, Republicans and Loyalists have lost sight of the fact that our ideal Ireland, the Ireland we dream of should be home to a unified people. People who without any concern for different beliefs value material wealth only as a basis for decent living, satisfied with frugal comfort. 'Feckin' eejit!' Would another pint of Guinness help to ward off the waves of despondency which were beginning to engulf him? Well, it couldn't do any harm.

***

Susan Robbins had proved to be an enormous hit with Pieter Hendriks. He was flattered by the attention he was receiving from this pretty young woman. The feelings and urges he was experiencing were those of a man 50 years younger. Of course he would be delighted to cut the diamonds for her. He wasn't interested in where they'd come from nor the consequences of getting involved in a project the veracity of which was questionable. An amorous infatuation had given rise to a weakening of his intellect and the tantalising notion of a relationship in prospect had caused him to give leave of his senses.

At their meeting in Berkshire's Antiques the previous evening Pieter and Susan arranged a tryst somewhere out of the way, in the West End perhaps, where they could both remain anonymous. Pieter pledged to get tickets for a show that they might 'make a night of it'. He did, and they did. They met in *Brown's* in St Martin's Lane for an early dinner and to the casual observer here were a father and daughter possibly celebrating a birthday. After their meal *The Coach & Horses* in Old Compton Street was the next stop for pre-show cocktails from where they went on to the Palace Theatre on Shaftesbury Avenue and the production of *Jesus Christ Superstar*. Presumptuously, and possibly more in hope than expectation, Pieter had booked a room at *The Bonnington* on

Southampton Row. As they left the theatre, neither spoke. She took his arm as if it was the most natural thing to do. They kissed and Pieter hailed a cab. At the hotel Susan went directly to the ladies' room while Pieter checked in as Mr & Mrs Hendriks. The remainder of the evening and the early hours of the morning were spent in the sort of carnal pursuits which were *de rigueur* and completely familiar to Susan but quite the opposite to Pieter. His expectations had exceeded his hopes by at least a country mile. He was knackered.

The following morning at breakfast Susan readily agreed to the suggestion that she should accompany Pieter back to Amsterdam where she would stay as his houseguest on *Keisersgracht*. He would cut and polish the diamonds in his workshop and, when completed, they would be sold at auction after which Susan would be a wealthy lady. Even as her impossible dream of great wealth was beginning to look distinctly possible her background was never far away in the recesses of her mind. She was a thief and a prostitute. If the discrepancy between the jewellery inventories was ever to be discovered, she would be the prime suspect and probably end up in Holloway. This she realised. But then living abroad, perhaps she could better herself, perhaps she could learn to speak Dutch. Perhaps she could start a new life, a life beyond the reach of even The Metropolitan Police, *misschien!* Perhaps!

Chapter 28 **Friday**

Just as the political pundits and commentators had been predicting PM Edward Heath failed to convince the Liberals to enter a coalition with the Tories and he resigned. This left the door open for Harold Wilson to step up as Prime Minister for the second time and form a minority government. Within a matter of days, a revised pay offer had been made to the miners and a settlement reached. The strike was over, and the lights were back on.

It didn't happen very often, talk of Politics, but on the drive back to Ipswich this latest news was the hot topic. On the other hand, small 'p' politics, the politics of the police force were often under scrutiny and top of the agenda. Inevitably, when they got back to Kesgrave Chief Superintendent Gibbons would be waiting and demanding, with menaces no doubt, a full report on this, that and the other. Cartwright informed the others how Gibbons had attempted to interfere with the Flaherty case, interference which could well have jeopardised the case.

'Why doesn't he just sit behind his desk and get on with administration, counting paperclips, ordering light bulbs or toilet paper? Be better at that than police work. Isn't that what he's supposed to do anyway?'

It was intended as a rhetorical question but Armstrong

provided an answer. 'Don't go getting yourself worked up, guv. Let's get in there and pre-empt him. We've got two great results this week. The Judge's antiques have been returned, and Flaherty's inside for fifteen years. Gibbo's got nothing to complain about. Just remember that in the police force, just like in many other walks of life, the job can be likened to an enormous cesspit where it's the biggest turds that rise to the top. There you are, Andy, a piece of homespun detective sergeant philosophy for you.'

'I'll have to remember that one, Sarge.'

Ray Davies had remained silent throughout the entire trip and when Lewis parked the car he disappeared without a word.

'What's eating him?'

'I've got half an idea,' responded Armstrong. 'I'll try and have a word if he'll listen. He needs someone to straighten him out if I'm any judge.'

***

It was the last thing in the world he wanted to do, but he knew it had to be done. DCI Cartwright tentatively tapped on CS Gibbons' door. Maybe he'd gone for the day. No chance.

'Enter!' came the order from within. Not 'would you like to come in?' Or even a straightforward 'come in'. Cartwright hesitated, like the errant schoolboy at the headmaster's door.

'Enter!' came the repeated instruction at twice the volume.

'Ah, Cartwright, I was wondering if and when you'd deign to put in an appearance.'

Taking Doug Armstrong's advice he went on the attack.

'Just like I said, sir, "Our day will come". It did. Flaherty, the rapist, got fifteen years.'

'Yes I heard. Tickner phoned me...'

The DCI hit him again, 'And we recovered Judge Bertrand's antiques which have now been returned to him.'

'No you bloody well have not, nor have they been returned!'

'But...'

'I don't want to hear your futile excuses, Cartwright. A removals van turned up at Melton Hall, apparently, and some kind of old foreign cupboard was unloaded. That's all. No antique sideboard or expensive table. According to the driver, from Able's Removal & Storage Company, the company engaged by the Judge, a different firm had previously removed the antiques except they neglected to pick up the cupboard which he'd bought. Perhaps you'd care to explain to me what the bloody hell is going on, Detective Chief Inspector?' Cartwright was dumbstruck. 'Well, I'm waiting.'

'As far as I was aware, the Judge positively identified his antiques and arranged for a van to collect them. I spoke to the proprietor at Berkshire's Antiques, who incidentally has been charged with receiving, and he assures me that the Judge's property was collected. I didn't realise I was supposed to provide a police escort for the van, or perhaps you would have preferred me to ride shotgun in the van.' The last remark incensed Gibbons. He raised his portly stature to the fullest extent of its five feet six inches, leaned forward on his desk and thumped it repeatedly as his complexion turned the colour of water in which beetroot has just been boiled and with the steam still rising.

'You, sir,' the cynicism in his tone would have turned milk sour. He repeated, 'You... you and your team of remedial incompetent boy scouts will deliver a personal apology to Judge Bertrand. You will then return to Bethnal Green, and you will bloody well get this matter sorted out. Top priority! Forget the rapist, forget the breakfast cereal, forget the smuggling racket. What's more, if you fail to sort it out, you can forget your pension as well. Now get out!'

Cartwright turned, deliberately, slowly.

'I said get out.' Gibbons was now fired up to the point of spontaneous combustion.

'I heard you perfectly well, sir.' Cartwright remained calm and collected and in a protracted fashion took his time across the carpet and gently closed the door, in the certain knowledge that this would infuriate Gibbons even more.

He had intended to go straight home to Pin Mill and spend the evening with Helen, his wife who he'd not seen for more than a few moments for over two weeks now. However, Gibbons' aggressive pugnacity had left such a bitter taste that Cartwright really felt the need for a drink.

Many of the regular Friday night crowd were in *The Maybush* when he arrived. Looking disconsolate and sitting by himself was Ray Davies. Cartwright chose to go and sit with him.

'Something on your mind, Ray? You want to talk about it?'

'Not really, guv, but unless I do it's going to do my head in.'

'I'm listening.'

'I've been incredibly stupid. No, worse than that, I've been self-delusional, naive, and just downright foolish. Such was the extent to which I was infatuated I believed every word she said.' Cartwright immediately jumped to the wrong conclusion.

'Ah there's a woman involved. You'll get over her whoever she is or was. Plenty more available for a personable, eligible young bloke like you.'

'No, sir, it's worse than that. It's not just that I've been dumped it's... it's...'

'Look, Ray, we've all been in similar situations. Have a few pints, a good night's sleep and all will be OK in the morning.'

'No, sir, you don't understand, I've...' Ray was on the point of confessing his crime when Doug Armstrong came over and interrupted.

'How did it go with Gibbo?'

'Let's get another one in and I'll tell you all about it. Another one for you, Ray?'

'No thanks, guv.' By the time the DS and the DCI returned to the table with fresh pints, the DC had gone.

'Is he alright?' enquired Armstrong.

'Woman trouble!'

Chapter 29 **Saturday**

Patrick McLevy had taken the earliest train from Liverpool Street Station to Ipswich. He walked the short distance to the police station in Civic Drive and reported his presence in compliance with the terms of his bail. The sergeant on duty at the front desk recorded the fact in the register.

'Ah, I see here there's a note about your hearing at the Crown Court. Friday 1st March at 10.00am. You should have received the summons at your Felixstowe address.'

'Yes, sir. It's in my diary. Thank you. See you next week.'

Walking back to the railway station Patrick determined to himself that he would not be reporting in next week or ever again. Nor did he have the slightest of intentions of being in court at 10.00am on 1st March. He'd been scouring the local London papers on a daily basis for reports of the Blake Hall massacre having been discovered. So far there had been none. It could only be a matter of time and when that time came he wanted to be as far away as he possibly could be. By midday, he was back in his recently adopted residence in Fournier Street. After a cup of coffee, he decided that for the sake of keeping up appearances he would show his face at the synagogue.

Since adopting the late Jacob Kahn's residence and all that went with it, McLevy, with the help of Isaac Goldmann, had located the lock the second Yale key fitted. Opening the door of the lock-up garage in Lamb Street, behind Spitalfields Market, revealed a white Range Rover, an almost new one by the look of it. Not having driven for a few years McLevy was a little hesitant about getting behind the wheel but it made sense from the convenience aspect. Public transport especially to outer London destinations was complex. Later that afternoon and stepping up to the part he had been assigned at the meeting at Berkshire's the previous Wednesday he eased the Range Rover out of the garage and set forth to an address in the heart of the Azad Kashmiri community in the outer London Borough of Waltham Forest: the address he'd been given by Hashim Abidi. After a precarious start, travelling east on Cheshire Street, he turned into Cambridge Heath Road and his confidence grew. By the time he reached Clapton Road, the left turn into Lea Bridge Road was almost second nature. The automatic gearbox certainly helped. He found the address fairly readily and picked up Hashim Abidi. McLevy then retraced his route to Lea Bridge Road, and they stopped at *The Hare & Hounds*.

Over a pint of lager and a glass of lemonade, Patrick listened whilst Hashim (whom Patrick had decided was a neurotic worrier) expressed his grave concerns for the welfare of Mr Khan and Rashid Khan. Since his early Navy days Patrick had developed the ability to come up with a convincing line of bullshit and Hashim fell for it. Mr Khan, assisted by Rashid were back in the Khyber Pakhtunkhwa Province engaged in extremely delicate negotiations for supplies of future imports with dealers from across the border in Afghanistan. From the mystified expression on Hashim's face it was easy to see that he knew little if anything of the geography of Asia, but, as Patrick discovered, he had never been there. He was British: of Pakistani immigrant parents. Hashim was completely taken in by Patrick's convincing explanation. There was more bullshit to come.

'Now, Hashim, I'm not sure how much you understand, so I'll presume you know nothing. You are now Mr Khan's top man in London.'

'Oh, Mr Patrick, I'm thanking you very much.'

'Yeah, never mind all that. I have a consignment for you. Marijuana is the most popular recreational drug in the world. It has been used for centuries as a recreational and medicinal drug. The cost depends on the quality. What I have for you is high-grade, so it is a little more expensive. But one ounce is enough for about fifteen joints, so on a price per-joint basis it's quite cheap. Are you with me? Do you understand?'

'Oh yes, sahib Mr Patrick. I am clearly understanding.' In fact, Hashim knew more about cannabis than Patrick ever would. What it cost, where it came from, who and where most of the European dealers were. Hashim had a pedigree as a drug runner.

'What is price please?'

'Well, I have 450 pounds which is 7200 ounces. I can let you have it all for £5 per ounce, but you have to take it all. Any less, and it's more expensive.' Hashim had done the multiplication before McLevy could add anything further to his sales pitch.

'That is £36,000. I pay no more than £26,000.' McLevy realised Hashim was brighter than he'd originally thought.

'£34,000.'

'Too many. £28,000.'

'You collect and it's yours for £30,000.'

Hashim frowned. He stroked his furrowed brow for a few seconds, sipped his lemonade then offered his hand. 'We have deal, Mr Patrick.'

Driving back to Spitalfields Patrick pondered over the deal he had concluded with Hashim, and he could hardly believe just how remunerative the weed racket was. Thinking back to how he first became involved, it was all a little confusing and he went through the various transactions out loud to himself. 'Frankie had originally bought the weed, 500lbs of it, from Jimmy Hendriks for 30000 guilders, which as far as I know was not much more than £15000. Liam had concluded that sale for Frankie and no doubt taken a slice for himself. I then made two grand out of Mr Khan's twenty by paying Liam £18000. So, the weed, which technically belongs to Frankie, has now been sold to Hashim for £30000. That's 15 grand's profit on the original price and Frankie's recovered his cost. Between five of us that's... £3,000 apiece. Bloody hell, rock and roll!' He hadn't noticed the red light at the Clapton Road junction until the last second and had to stand on the brake pedal to avoid running into the car in front. 'Bloody hell,' he repeated. 'And I haven't even seen the bloody stuff! It's win–win all round.'

Patrick was thinking of driving straight to *The Carpenter's* but thought better of it when it occurred to him that he might have to explain where he'd got such a prestige motor from. So, with the Range Rover back in the Lamb Street lock-up, he walked up Brick Lane towards the pub where he fully expected to receive a hero's welcome when he imparted the news.

***

With tedium and frustration in equal measure, Liam O'Reilly's lonely vigil in *The Old Salt Quay* was beginning to get him down. *The Eamon de Valera*, just across the river, still appeared to be under guard by at least the two policemen he could see. There would be absolutely no point in trying to make a run for it. Even if it was remotely possible, and it wasn't, for him to creep through the open lock at high tide and take the ebb all the way down the Thames, he would never outrun *The Patrick Colquhoun*, the Met's Marine Police launch. There was no alternative. He had to sit it out and wait. He went to the toilet and ordered himself another pint of Guinness as he returned. He lost count of how many pints he'd had. Maybe he'd developed an immunity to the brew's normal *feel-good* ingredient. He picked up his drink from the bar and returned to his observation position. There was something different. Where were the police? Had they gone? He took his binoculars outside and stood on the pavement scouring the roads around the Limehouse Basin. The police had gone.

He'd had more than several pints and downing the pint he'd just bought in one was not an option, neither was leaving it. He eventually walked westwards on Rotherhithe Street and boarded an East London Line train, two stops to Shadwell. He walked from Shadwell to Limehouse, and the police were conspicuous by their absence. He boarded his boat and started the Listers. They hadn't been run in two weeks or so and the batteries would need charging as well. The sound of the engines firing up attracted the duty lockkeeper and he walked around to the quay where *The Eamon de Valera* was berthed. Liam was by now leaning back against the rail on the afterdeck, grinning from ear to ear and, in the manner of an orchestral maestro, conducting his Listers in a monotonous diesel duet.

'Would you be listening to that now. The sweetest music I've heard in many a day, for sure it is!'

'Oh it's yourself then, Liam. Just wondered who'd started her up. The police came by earlier as they were packing up. You're free to leave whenever you like, but I expect you've been told.'

'Well actually I haven't but never mind. As much as I love bein' here in London,' he lied, 'I'll be leaving just as soon as I can get loaded. I've a small cargo booked. I just need to find a crew and get victualed up.'

'OK, Liam, safe trip.'

He ran the Listers for about an hour and then took a cab to Cheshire Street hoping to find Frankie or Berkshire or Tommy and Matt. In the event he found them all, celebrating by the look of them. *The Carpenter's Arms* was busy, but it was Saturday night after all. It was Tommy that spotted him first.

'Liam, mate, what you 'avin', *Guinness*?'

'Ah, no, sir thank you. I'm all Guinnessed up. *Jameson's* or *Bushmill's* would be nice.'

Tommy fought his way to the bar. Gerry caught sight of Liam.

'My dear boy, what a pleasure it is to see you. May I buy you a drink?'

'Ah, that you may, sir. *Jameson's* or *Bushmill's* if you please.' Gerry made his way over to the bar. Away from the bar Liam noticed Frankie talking to Patrick. He made his way over to them, excusing himself through drinkers.

'Well now, 'ere's Liam. The gang's all 'ere.' Tommy and Gerry rejoined the group, and both handed Liam a whiskey. He decanted the one into the other. 'What are we celebrating then?' Liam enquired.

'West Ham beat Chelsea three nil!'

'Patrick has secured a most favourable, even unbelievable, deal on the herbs.'

Liam looked blank for a minute. 'Ah, the herbs. With you now. Well, I can give us a third cause for celebration.' He took a long, slow sip of his Irish. The others, now including Matt who been gambling on the bandit, looked on in anticipation. '*The Eamon de Valera* is good to go just as soon as we're loaded.' A table became free as a crowd bedecked in claret and sky blue favours staggered out. The Berkshire Syndicate sat down.

'Well, that's even better news. How fortuitous. Thomas, can we get Frankie's van down to Limehouse early tomorrow?

It being the Sabbath there shouldn't be too many people about. Does that sit comfortably with you, Francis?' All were in accord. Patrick indicated he wished to speak – the Navy meeting protocol well drilled into him.

'Yes, Patrick, you have a contribution to make.'

'Thank you, Gerry. Hashim Abidi should arrive tomorrow to collect his purchase and pay for it. It won't be until after midday. Will we be done loading the ship by then?'

'If we all pitch in, we'll 'ave plenty of time. What's 'e payin' again? I just want to 'ear it.'

'After Frankie's been repaid his initial investment, we all get an equal share amounting to £3k.' Glasses were banged on the table, there was applause and a general celebratory pandemonium.

'We'll need to dust off the custard powder!'

'Right then,' said Frankie, 'it's all comin' together at last. One last round for the frog an' toad? We've got an early start tomorra.'

***

After his night of unbridled passion, Pieter Hendriks decided they should stay at *The Bonnington* Hotel until they were ready to leave for Holland. After breakfast Susan went directly to Victoria Park Square and her desk in the post room where she typed out her letter of resignation. Not being quite sure who her immediate superior was, she decided to leave the letter on Mick Willett's desk. He was sympathetic, he would understand. In the letter she apologised for not giving the two weeks' notice she was contractually obliged to do, but, in truth, she didn't care. Sure, there was a month's salary owing but she was more than content to write that off. Pieter would take care of her. She left the police station and hoped she hadn't been seen. She went home to her small apartment and packed as much of her wardrobe as would fit into a well-travelled holdall. She collected her passport, Post Office savings book and a few personal effects, put them in her handbag and went straight back to *The Bonnington*.

After returning to bed for an hour followed by the luxury of a shower which they took together, Pieter rang for room service: coffee and biscuits for two and a bottle of distilled water. They sat together on the bed and Pieter emptied the contents of the little pouch onto a clean facecloth.

'I want you to understand a little of what we have here. Sometimes, we think we have raw diamonds, but sometimes they're *nep*, you say fake. Now are these real, or have they been manufactured in a laboratory?'

'How can you tell?' Susan's curiosity was genuine enough but there was a hint of anxiety in her question.

'Don't worry. *Jij bent kostbaarder* than these little rocks. You are more precious to me. I explain *ja*?'

'Oh *ja*. Yes please.'

'Genuine diamond deposits are deep in the ground and are brought up through volcanic eruptions over millions and millions of years. Just imagine, maybe 250 tons of earth and rock has been moved just to discover one of these tiny little rocks. None of them look pretty until they're cut and polished. They are nothing more or less than crystallised carbon atoms, but they are the most expensive carbon atoms you will ever come across.'

'Isn't the lead in a pencil made of carbon?'

'Graphite, yes, my dear, but it's the arrangement of its atoms that distinguishes it from a diamond, one is grey and soft, the other hard and colourless: all to do with the atomic structure. When I cut these, they will lose perhaps 50% of their weight and from your little collection here, I might be able to cut perhaps a half of them. The others are too small. Diamonds are weighed in carats and a carat is about 200 milligrams which is, I don't know, only just a tiny fraction of an ounce. A one carat diamond will fetch perhaps 3000 guilders.'

'How much is that?'

'Let me see, nearly £1000.' Susan let out a little whoop of excitement. 'We would need 150 of these little stones to weigh one ounce. One on its own is no heavier than a hair from your pretty head.' Susan smiled and kissed him.

'Now a simple test. Please pass me that glass.' He filled the glass three quarters full from the distilled water bottle, and, one by one, he dropped in the stones.

'The specific gravity of a real diamond is greater than a fake one or any other gemstone and it will sink.'

'I see.'

They all sank.

'I think we have a little more than one ounce of genuine raw diamonds.' Susan giggled and began to stroke his inner thigh.

Chapter 30 **Sunday**

At the same time as the Berkshire Syndicate were on manoeuvres, Bandile Bosch was on his way to work. For all that he hadn't been in the job very long, he had made an impression on his bosses, a very favourable impression. When he arrived at Mile End Station he passed the time of day with the train dispatcher and walked the entire length of the platform, picking up litter, discarded cigarette packets and the general detritus of the 1970s commuter, he took the lift to street level, straightened the advertising boards on the pavement, and followed the routine he had established in such a short time for ensuring that the station was neat, tidy and as presentable as possible. The station manager called him into the office in the ticket hall.

'Bandy, I say, Bandy, leave that for a second please.' He didn't like it, but he'd now accepted the inevitability of his forename being corrupted. So, what did the station manager want? He wasn't quite sure of what to expect.

'Yes, sir, is something wrong?'

'On the contrary. We have received so many complimentary remarks from passengers and your colleagues since you started work here. People have remarked how your smile, your cheerful disposition, brightens their day, and how much the tidiness of the station in general has improved. If only all our employees were the same! Anyway, we'd like to make your position full-time. If that's OK with you, you're no longer a station cleaner, you're Station Passenger Liaison Officer Bosch? There will of course be a small increase in wages to go with your new role. What do you think? Yes?'

Bosch was momentarily speechless, but he managed a nod.

***

In East Anglia, Cartwright and his wife Helen were taking advantage of a rare, clear and sunny morning with a walk along the River Orwell foreshore, and a pub lunch at *The Butt & Oyster*. Doug Armstrong was also taking advantage of the east coast weather and the low tide to give his houseboat *Ironside* a coat of antifoul paint to the hull. He'd recently bought the houseboat, permanently berthed on the quay at Woodbridge, after the previous owner moved away when her fiancé died. The weather in Amsterdam was also almost spring-like and Willem van Dijkstra was making the most of some quality time with his daughter Lotte, strolling around *Bloemenmarkt*. In Bloomsbury, Pieter Hendriks and Susan Robbins were still in bed, the *do not disturb* sign hanging on the door of their room at *The Bonnington*. They were oblivious to the overcast skies and drizzle in the capital. When the Berkshire Syndicate began their day, morning had barely broken and on the one hand, the weather was helping, people not wanting to venture out in the wet, yet on the other, it was making the removal of antiques something of a mission. Getting the Pugin table aboard *The Eamon de Valera* had been fairly easy compared to the much heavier and cumbersome Art Deco palisander sideboard. At one stage it seemed that the marquetry sideboard would have to remain on deck, and it would have done had it not been for Gerry's insistence that such a valuable piece could not be put at risk from the elements, no matter how well it was covered and secured. With the ship loaded the team returned to Pedley Street to package up the marijuana consignment and await the arrival of Hashim Abidi.

Matt rummaged amongst the discarded cartons and boxes at the back of the discount store and managed to find several boxes which remained in a serviceable state. Previously, according to the labelling, these cartons would have contained twelve bottles of *Stolichnaya*, a popular Russian vodka. Most of the plastic bags, about the size of a sandwich bag, contained about an ounce of weed. The vodka cartons each held 60 bags.

'We'll need more boxes, Matt, and not bloody corn flakes.' Laughter.

'Best we don't seal 'em up, in case the Bidet bloke wants to inspect what 'e's buying.'

'That is very astute forward-thinking, Thomas.'

It wasn't very long after midday that a dark blue Volkswagen Transporter pulled up outside the Acme arch. Two men got out. From behind the closed shutters, Tommy had heard the van arrive.

'I reckon that'll be our man.' He opened the shutter, and the five men inside stood staring at the two men outside wearing the traditional shalwar kameez beneath anoraks that looked like they'd come from Millets.

'Are you Mr Bidet?' asked Frankie.

Patrick shushed him and extended his hand which the younger looking of the pair shook. 'Hello, Mr Patrick.' He continued by addressing the others, 'I am Abidi – Hashim Abidi – pleasing to meet. This man my cousin. No speak.'

Patrick introduced his colleagues and invited Hashim to inspect his purchase. Hashim picked up one bag and opened it. Then in an almost ritualistic manner he held the open bag to his nose and inhaled deeply. He passed the bag to his cousin who did likewise. They looked at each other, nodded and smiled. The cousin removed a single leaf and rubbed it between his thumb and two forefingers. He licked his fingers. He smiled and nodded a second time. Throughout the inspection, whilst the product's quality was under scrutiny, the syndicate members stood silently spectating. It was Patrick who broke the silence.

'We trust everything is to your satisfaction. Good quality weed, yes?'

'Yes quality very good please.' Hashim reached into his anorak and withdrew several envelopes which he handed to Patrick who in turn passed them to Frankie, with a gesture that suggested 'count the money'. The cousin picked up the first two of the boxes and made a move towards the door.

Patrick stood in his way. 'What do you think, OK, Frankie?'

'Looks like it's all 'ere, OK, Pat,' came the response.

The cousin opened the back of the van which revealed racks of traditional Pakistani garments, on hangers in cellophane covers. He slid the hangers to one side and pushed the first two boxes to the far front of the van. Everyone else, with the exception of Frankie who was still counting, had formed a chain and the boxes, a total of 120 purporting to contain vodka, lime juice cordial, teabags and digestive biscuits were all loaded. Several of the garments were used to cover the heap of boxes. The remainder, including burqas, churidars, sherwanis, shalwar kameez, achkans, plus extra Punjabi patiyala, kaftans and pahani kurta which had been on the front seat were hung tightly together on the fitted rails. To all intents and purposes, a cursory inspection of the van's contents would suggest a couple of Pakistani blokes, trading in traditional clothing, off to a street market.

'Thank you and many please, men. Thank you, Mr Patrick. We go now Ramsgate for ship.'

'So, where do we suppose our Islamic Republican colleagues are off to? I find it curious in the extreme that they should be boarding a ship. As bizarre as the bazaar in the back of their van.'

'Well, Gerry, your guess is as good as mine. My guess would be that he's got a buyer abroad, but quite frankly, my dear, I don't give a damn. All I care about is that the weed is gone, and we've all had nice little earner. What say you all?' There was a concordant euphoria amongst them all and the road to *The Carpenter's* might well have been strewn with roses.

With the ill-gotten gains shared out, Liam announced that he would be off just as soon as he'd refuelled the ship and loaded provisions aboard for the trip back to the Netherlands. Completely out of the blue, unpremeditated and impulsive, Patrick, thinking on his feet, heard himself speak. Much to the surprise of the others they also heard, 'Liam, you'll be needing a crew, what with Fergal out of commission.'

'Ah, well now, there's an offer I can't refuse, and from an ex-Navy man as well. Patrick, it'll be a pleasure to have you aboard to be sure.'

***

On the quay in Ramsgate lay *The Olau Vig*. A roll-on-roll-off daily freight service for vans and lorries bound for Vlissingen in the Dutch province of Walcheren. A dark blue Volkswagen Transporter had taken its place in the queue of vehicles waiting to drive on. When it came to the VW's turn, the driver proffered documentation to the officer in charge of loading. He merely gave Hashim and his cousin a cursory glance, opened and closed the rear doors and waved them on. A member of the crew directed Hashim to park behind an articulated lorry from the Van Opijnen BV freight company. Hashim locked the VW and he and his cousin made their way up to the drivers' cafeteria.

***

By midmorning, Pieter Hendriks and Susan Robbins had surfaced, checked out of the hotel and caught the train to Sheerness from Victoria. On arrival at the Isle of Sheppey port, they boarded *Basto V*. The ship's master welcomed them on board and escorted them to the officers' mess. All things being equal they should be in Amsterdam by the evening.

***

Liam and Patrick left the pub quite early, Liam to start preparing *The Eamon de Valera*, Patrick to collect his few possessions, plus a good many which weren't, from Fournier Street. With their departure, several for the road and an equal number of 'bon voyages', the previously convivial and elated gathering became somewhat deflated as Frankie took the others into his confidence.

'I'm tellin' you, guys, 'cos you're my oldest mates an' I didn't want to say owt in front of the others.'

'We are all ears, Francis,' said Gerry earnestly as he, Matt and Tom leaned in closer, the better to hear what Frankie wanted to get off his chest.

'When I first put this caper together, the weed, you know, it were a deal 'tween me an' my Dutch mate, Jimmy Hendriks. But, on top of that were a private 'rrangement. A load of stolen tom 'e wanted me to fence for 'im in London. All O'Reilly knew was that there was three packets of corn flakes 'ad to be kept sep'rate, see, an 'e' were gettin' an extra bung for lookin' after 'em. I know the coppers 'ad one packet...'

'Are you certain, Francis, how can you be sure?'

'I knows 'cos Martini Susan 'as 'ad some of em away out the police safe at the nick.' This statement brought a mass reaction of incredulity. Matt's jaw fell open, Tom was struck dumb and Gerry spilled his gin.

'My dear boy, I have never heard anything so implausible. Are you absolutely sure? How can you be so positive?'

'Cos she told me, an' she shewd me some of 'em. Raw diamonds. She was goin' to ask Hendriks to cut 'em for 'er. Can't imagine what 'e'll say when 'e sees 'em 'cos it were 'im what nicked 'em in the first place from a jeweller in 'olland. You must 'ave see'd em the other night, thick as thieves...'

'Yes, well they both are after all,' observed Gerry.

'Anyway, that ain' the point. It's the other packet. Where's the other packet?'

'You're not thinkin' what I think you're thinkin' are you?' asked Tom.

'Well, if you're thinkin' you think you know what I'm thinkin' then yes I am.'

'Not still on the ship?' asked Matt in disbelief.

'Yeah. I reckon that lyin', thievin' Irishman as 'idden 'em up for 'imself.'

'Oh dear, oh dear, oh dear. Is there no honour amongst us anymore? What has happened to moral principles, to loyalty, our ethological investment? Oh dear, oh dear.' Gerry's expression had *grief stricken* written all over it. 'This really is too bad!'

'Right, lads! C'mon!' Matt had downed his pint and grabbed his coat. 'We're goin' down Limehouse before 'e shoves off.' Matt's assertiveness left no room for doubt. 'Frankie, where's your van?'

'Still in Berkshire's Arch.'

'Right, come on, no time to lose!'

Frankie parked the van in Goodhart Place. *The Eamon Valera* was still alongside the quay. There was a light on in the wheelhouse and a wisp of smoke was rising from the flue. Gerry positioned himself on the quay, Matt and Tom climbed on board. Matt climbed on to the coach-roof. Tom knocked on the wheelhouse door. No answer. Tom knocked again.

'Who the feck is it?'

'Liam it's me, Tom, we forgot something and didn't want you to leave 'til we got it sorted.' Liam appeared in the wheelhouse and opened the door. Immediately, Matt leaped down and grappled one of Liam's arms up behind his back.

Frankie appeared out of the shadows on the quay.

'O'Reilly you thievin' git. Thought you could get away with it eh?'

'I have no idea what you're on about.'

'I think you do. Where's my packet of corn flakes?'

'The Garda took it, the police have it, your man Armstrong, the detective.'

'Not that one the other one.'

'There is no other one.' O'Reilly was quite adamant despite Matt thrusting his arm even further up his back.

'Look, come aboard, search my ship. I'm tellin' you, there is not another one.'

Gerry appeared from the shadows.

'Mr O'Reilly, in this country, we have a code, a code of honour. It is incumbent upon those of us who follow our nefarious profession to observe and uphold our ethical philosophy.' From his Crombie, Gerry produced a Colt .38 pistol, cocked it and pointed it directly at O'Reilly's chest at a distance of six feet. Matt let his arm go and moved to the side. The appearance of a gun invoked a rerun of the reaction of incredulity from the others.

Liam O'Reilly put his hands in the air. 'OK, OK, it's a fair cop. I didn't think you'd miss it.'

'Where is it?' demanded Tom.

'There's a secret locker under the floorboards under the helmsman's seat.' Tom disappeared into the wheelhouse and after a few moments reappeared with a slightly crushed corn flake packet wrapped in a bin-liner. He handed it to Frankie. Frankie thrust a determined hand into the packet, and a smile slowly spread across his face. Gerry uncocked the pistol and replaced it in his overcoat pocket.

'A word of advice, Mr O'Reilly. The arm of our syndicate is longer than that of the law. Should it be brought to our attention in the future that you have attempted a duplicitous *tour de force* such as this again we will turn you over to the Welsh miners.'

Leaving O'Reilly to heed his guilty conscience, Frankie's van was back on its way to the Arches.

'Bloody 'ell, Berkshire, don't you ever pull a stunt like that again. I very nearly soiled my undergarment.' Matt's impersonation of Gerry had them all laughing. *The Carpenter's* was closed when they got there so they convened in the Acme Discount Stores. Tom found four glasses and produced the bottle of 1932 *Casterade* Vintage Bas Armagnac that they'd liberated from Melton Hall.

Chapter 31 **Monday**

DCI Cartwright, DS Armstrong and Sgt Lewis were roaring down the A12 once again and there's nothing better at clearing a path through traffic than a marked Jaguar XJ12 doing what it does best. Cartwright was complying with Gibbons' strict orders despite his resentment and his enmity for his superior.

'Has Tickner been told we're coming?'

'Yes, guv.'

'OK, we're going to hit Berkshire's Antiques and take it apart. That bastard Hunt is behind this, I'll stake my pension on it.' Cartwright quite regularly staked his pension on something or other.

'Have we got a warrant, guv?'

'No, but I'm sure Bertrand will grant us one retrospectively if need be.'

The Jaguar pulled up in Pedley Street, attracting a great deal of attention as it did so. The shutter was halfway up, or was it halfway down? Neither up nor down, either way. Lewis was attempting to see if there was any life inside with Cartwright and Armstrong sitting in the warmth of the car watching him on his hands and knees.

'You lookin' for summat, copper?' Lewis turned to see an

unkempt lad, about twelve or thirteen years old, presumably bunking off school. Before Lewis could respond, the boy had provided crucial intelligence. 'They'll be in Sid's, the cafe in Kerbela Street. They alus go there for breakfast.' Lewis put his hand in his pocket and was about to hand the boy a 20p piece.

'Stuff it up your arse, I ain't no copper's nark.' With which he ran off. Lewis got back in the car.

'See you made a friend,' joked Armstrong.

'They're all in a cafe around the corner.'

Sid's Cafe was always fairly busy between 7.00 and 10.00am. This particular morning was no exception until the Jaguar XJ12 pulled up outside. All of a sudden there was a mass exodus with half-eaten fry-ups left on tables, but with one exception.

'Cool, guys, stay calm. We got our story straight an' they got nowt on us. Eh up again, Mr Cartwright. You got a trans-fer down 'ere or what?' Tom greeted the policemen cheerfully and took the initiative. 'Let me guess – there were a problem, a cock-up with them antiques I bet.'

'Well, you might call it a problem or cock-up. I might call it something else, like a theft or burglary for instance.'

'Aw, c'mon, Mr Cartwright, 'ow were we s'posed to know if the first mob weren't for real. Look this removals van turns up, two blokes, got the aprons on an' everything, looked the business to us didn't they lads?' There were nods of agreement from Matt and Gerry. 'An' they knew what they were doin' alright, carried the stuff proper professional-like. If Gerry 'ere is guilty of owt it's that 'e forgot that there cabinet thingy. Ain't that right, Gerry? Any road up, a while later another van turns up an' the driver's a bit miffed. Still, 'e takes the cabinet thingy...'

Gerry interrupted, 'You mean the seventeenth-century Swedish Rococo cabinet *thingy*, as you call it. Please excuse my colleague, Detective Chief Inspector. He is a little… a little… sorry it's not often I'm lost for words. He's a Cockney you know.' As if that explained anything.

There wasn't a great deal Cartwright could do and for once he too was momentarily lost for words. It was Armstrong that came to his assistance.

'We shall need a statement from each of you. A description of the van, a description of the men, every last detail. You'll present yourselves at Victoria Park Square police station at 11.00am this morning to help us with our enquiries. If you fail to turn up you'll be arrested under suspicion of burglary, in the first instance, that is to say we have reason to believe you broke into Melton Hall and stole the antiques in the first place, and secondly under suspicion of aiding and abetting a theft from Berkshire's Antiques.'

'Why don't we just arrest them now?' asked Lewis.

'Good question, Sergeant,' stated the DCI. 'Do it. Read them their rights.'

'Now, now, Mr Cartwright, let's not squander each other's time. We will happily give you a statement without you resorting to this unnecessary heavy-handedness. And besides you have no evidence of burglary or theft.'

'But I think you're mistaken, we do,' affirmed Lewis who went out to the Jaguar and returned with an empty bottle, the previous contents of which, according to the label were 1932 *Casterade* Vintage Bas Armagnac. 'How do you explain this, in the bin outside your store? What a coincidence that your taste in brandy should be exactly the same as Judge Bertrand's. Did you know that such a bottle was stolen from the Judge's home at the same time as his antique furniture?'

'Well done, Lewis – but you know how I hate coincidences! Now, gentlemen, are we going to need handcuffs?'

'Chief Inspector, it may surprise you to know but the coincidence is that the Judge should share my taste. I drink the *Casterade* all the time. Anyway it seems you're intent on making an arrest despite our having nothing to hide. However, you will kindly permit me to settle our account with Sidney for our breakfast before we are to be incarcerated, or you'll be charging us with stealing by non-payment as well.'

'Very well, get on with it.'

Gerry Hunt approached the counter at the back of the cafe and surreptitiously handed ten £20 notes to Sid who then made pretence of putting them in the till whilst Gerry hastily scribbled on the order pad which had been left on the counter, *Urgent, buy a bottle of 1932 Casterade Bas Armagnac and bring it to the nick at 11.00am.*

'Right then, Doug, you go with Lewis and take these reprobates to Victoria Park Square. There's not room in the car for all of us so I'll stay here and have some breakfast. Come and collect me in half an hour, Andy. Sid is it? Yes please, egg, two rashers, sausage...'

'All right for some,' muttered Lewis.

The suspects were interviewed individually by Cartwright and Armstrong and their respective statements hardly varied. With the interviews concluded the detectives were comparing their interpretations.

'These blasted scallywags have been well rehearsed. They're almost word perfect and reciting from the same script. I really don't see that we've got enough to charge them. I reckon Gibbo'll have apoplexy. All we can do is circulate the details and photographs and hope these bloody pieces of furniture turn up somewhere. Personally, looking at the pictures, I wouldn't give them houseroom.'

'Excuse me for intruding, Detective Chief Inspector.' Gerry Hunt had returned to the interview room. 'As a gesture of goodwill would you be so kind as to pass this on to His Honour from my own personal cellar. Clearly he is a man of impeccable taste and I trust he will accept this as a token of our commiseration for his loss in what must be an absolutely frightful experience for him. I have no doubt that you will apprehend the perpetrators before too long.'

Cartwright sat looking at the bottle of vintage Armagnac, barely able to believe what had just occurred.

'In the whole of my career I can honestly say without fear of refutation that I have never encountered such an ingratiating yet audacious arrogance. Talk about having a nerve!'

'Taking the piss, I'd call it.'

'You're not wrong, Doug, but you know, I quite like him.'

***

Frankie had driven to Dover having prebooked a single ticket to Calais on board the SNCF/British Rail *Seaspeed* Hovercraft service. From Calais he caught the SNCF train to Paris Gare du Nord from where he took a taxi to *Rue du Faubourg Saint-Honoré* to keep an appointment with a jeweller of unscrupulous renown. The jewellery which originated in the Netherlands had found its way into Frankie's hands through his Dutch contact Pieter Hendriks. For all that Francis Forsyth was merely Frankie *the Fence* in the East End there was much more to him than his friends were aware. For a start he had a reputation as an international *trader* and artful negotiator, and it was in that capacity that Hendriks had entrusted him to sell the proceeds of the robbery which had taken place several years earlier. The traceability of the stolen gems had been impeded by the involvement of many well-disposed collaborators and the circuitous route around Europe which the loot had taken over a prolonged period. Hendriks, the mastermind, had now deemed the time to be right for the final sale. The penultimate leg of the jewellery's journey had been courtesy of Liam O'Reilly on his ship *The*

Michael Collins. There had been a certain amount of *wastage* on its travels but the bulk of it was still all in one place despite the police and Susan Robbins. That one place was the sports-bag with the false bottom carried by a man looking uncomfortable in an ill-fitting grey suit. He had round shoulders and was stooped forward as he walked. He looked older than his 60 years. The false pencil moustache and grey felt Fedora did little for him by way of a disguise.

Lucas Toussaint was waiting in the lobby of the *Hotel Costes* on *Rue du Faubourg-Honoré.* He was extremely elegantly dressed in a style that only Frenchmen seemed to manage. He'd been furnished with a description of Frankie and, notwithstanding his incognito effort, Toussaint recognised him the moment he crossed the threshold. Together they went to the bar. Toussaint ordered *pastis a deux* and they took their drinks to a private room, the use of which had been booked previously by the Frenchman. Necklaces, bracelets, brooches, gold and silver chains, cut and raw diamonds, earrings were all laid out on a blue baize cloth which Toussaint had produced from his shoulder-bag. Selecting certain pieces from the table he used his loupe for a minute inspection. The cut diamonds were of particular interest and especially those set in hallmarked gold or silver mounts. The costume jewellery and the raw diamonds were largely pushed to one side. He took a small writing pad and pen from his jacket pocket and made notes with columns of figures, laying some items to one side as he did so. After an hour during which very little was spoken, perhaps due to language difficulties, perhaps not, Toussaint spoke. *Je paierai deux cent un mille francs.* 'I will pay 201000 francs.' He took a *Disque Bleu* from a silver cigarette case, lit it with a gold Dunhill lighter and sat back while Frankie did some calculations of his own. He too had a pad and a pencil. He took a packet of ten *Players No.6* from his pocket and lit one with a Swan Vesta.

'Make it another 600 francs an' you've got a deal.' Toussaint offered his hand which Frankie readily shook. He watched carefully as the agreed sale price was counted out in 500-, 200- and 100-franc notes. He put the cash in an envelope and the envelope in his sports-bag. Toussaint put the loose diamonds into a velvet pouch and wrapped the rest in the blue baize cloth, the pouch and the cloth went into a leather bag, inside a chic satchel, very chic compared to Frankie's holdall. They shook hands once again and went their separate ways.

Frankie was going over the arithmetic in his head. 'According to the Bureau de Change the exchange rate was eleven point something to the pound, so that's – blimey, that's somewhere near on eighteen grand. He agreed the extra 600 a bit quick. P'raps I was too cheap? Anyway, I really weren't expecting even that much.' The stoop had gone and there was a spring in his step. He looked and felt ten years younger.

Back at Gare du Nord he booked a ticket to Amsterdam. He had a meeting with Pieter Hendriks to get to followed by a tryst with Chantal, he hoped.

Chapter 32 **Tuesday**

It was very early. Patrick had spent his last night in Spitalfields. He packed his old Navy bag with a few clothes, personal possessions, a selection of bottles from Mr Khan's booze cupboard and a box of *Montecristos*. He hastily scribbled a note and put it in an envelope with the Fournier Street house keys. He would post them through the letterbox at Berkshire Antiques on his way to Limehouse. 'Bound to be something in the house that Gerry can knock out,' he thought. He pulled the door closed behind him and walked up a deserted Brick Lane towards Pedley Street.

When he arrived at Limehouse, he climbed aboard *The Eamon de Valera*. The Listers were already purring away, and Liam was making ready to leave. Patrick familiarised himself with the ship's layout, went on deck and with a practised art, courtesy of the Royal Navy, expertly flicked the eyes of the mooring lines from the bollards as Liam eased the vessel away from the quay towards the lock-gates which were obligingly open. The skipper pushed the morse controls forward and the Listers responded. There was still an hour before the ebb tide would set in, but what was left of the flood didn't impede progress around the Isle of Dogs and into Greenwich Reach. Patrick looked back across Rotherhithe and Bermondsey knowing that his mind was made up. He was never intending to come back to London.

***

A high-level discussion was taking place in the Superintendent's office between Cartwright, Armstrong, Willett and Tickner following the previous day's aborted attempt to charge someone for something in connection with Judge Bertrand's missing antiques. The telephone rang. Tickner picked up the receiver and when he heard who the caller was he switched to speakerphone.

'Robin, this is Chief Superintendent Nigel Gibbons, Suffolk Constabulary, here. Just an enquiry, one of my DCs hasn't turned up for work for a second day now. Davies. He's not answering his phone either. Then it occurred to me he might be down there with Cartwright's idiot squad.' Tickner looked at Cartwright with a broad grin. Cartwright shook his head and returned the smile.

'No, Nigel, he's not here with us. Would you like to speak to Cartwright, he's right here with me?'

'I don't think so unless he's got something positive to report. Has he said anything to you?'

'I've not heard anything,' he lied.

'Ah well, could you tell him to call me. I'll need to have something to tell the Judge.'

'Yes I will, of course. Bye for now, Nigel.' Tickner replaced the receiver.

Cartwright was slightly worried. 'Strange? Ray not turning up for work. Very conscientious, high-flyer. Should go far.'

'He seemed a bit distant when we drove back last weekend,' commented Armstrong.

'Yes, I know, I had a word with him in *The Maybush* on Friday night. Some kind of woman trouble from what I could gather. Most unlike him.'

'He'll turn up. There'll be a perfectly good reason for his absence. He's not one to go skiving off.'

'Yes you're right. Now, what about these bloody antiques, and we still haven't got to the bottom of the corn flake caper either.'

***

As was his wont, Gerry Hunt very often took a constitutional stroll after breakfast at Sid's. His regular route would take him down Vallance Road into Stepney Way and Stepney Green where, if the weather was clement, he would sit for a while and do a spot of people watching. This particular morning the weather wasn't exactly spring-like but comfortable enough. As usual there were a variety of dog-walkers and pram-pushers in, on and around the green. However, an additional attraction caught his eye, two young women, jogging. As they got closer he could make out who they were.

'Stellen, Kirsten, over here, girls!' he called. Bosch's daughters altered their course and ran towards the bench where Gerry was sitting. He stood, as only a true gentleman would, and raised his hat.

'Good morning, girls, and I must say it has just improved beyond measure. How lovely to see you both.' His greeting was both friendly and genuine. The girls looked at each other and appeared to be a little apprehensive.

'It's OK, it's me, Gerry Hunt, you know, Berkshire's Antiques and the Bethnal Green International Escort Services and Model Agency.' He extended the title of his call-girl business in the certain knowledge that they would be captivated by the last two words. 'Perhaps you may recall that we were introduced and spoke briefly in *The Carpenter's Arms* a week or so ago. You were with your father.'

'Oh yes, I remember,' said Kirsten, smiling.

'Of course, how silly. I'm sorry if you thought we were being rude, but girls like us can't be too careful,' added Stellen.

'You are absolutely right,' affirmed Gerry. 'Now, if my memory serves me well, you're both hoping to be discovered by a modelling agency. Am I correct?' The girls nodded enthusiastically, and he was encouraged to develop his line of flimflam. After ten minutes of meretricious misrepresentation, the Bosch girls were totally taken in by his disingenuous Machiavellian bullshit. The smooth-talking Mr Gerry *Berkshire* Hunt could have provided a hog-roast for a Jewish wedding breakfast! 'Whilst I can't actually guarantee it, I will get you both an interview within a week.' Sold!

'Call by my shop this afternoon and we'll deal with the paperwork.' Excitedly the girls jogged off. 'Don't tire yourselves out!' he called after them.

When Gerry got back to his Arch he telephoned a friend, also in the pimping racket.

'Dai, this is Gerald. I've just landed two beauties but they're going to require a little nurturing. Could you take a couple of snaps, you know what I mean, oh and some model-type poses? ... You could, oh you wonderful man. I owe you.'

Chapter 33 **Wednesday**

When Robin Tickner arrived at his office he found a fax on his desk from Nigel Gibbons. It was a facsimile of a piece in that morning's local newspaper, the *East Anglian Daily Times*.

Early last evening police were called to an address in Rushmere St Andrew, Ipswich, after being alerted by a neighbour to a white Triumph Dolomite which had been parked on the drive of a semi-detached house with the engine running for over two hours. On arrival the police found a deceased white male in the driver's seat. A hose had been connected to the exhaust pipe of the vehicle and into the car through a rear window. A note was discovered on the dashboard addressed to Chief Superintendent Nigel Gibbons at Suffolk Police Headquarters.

On investigation, the deceased was identified as Raymond Hanford Davies (32), the registered owner of the vehicle, and the householder. Mr Davies had been a serving police officer with the Suffolk force, a detective constable. Chief Superintendent Gibbons described him as an affable young man with a promising career in the police force ahead of him. The Ipswich Coroner has been informed although a verdict of suicide is anticipated.

Tickner rang down to the front desk and spoke to the duty sergeant.

'John, do we know where DCI Cartwright is right now?'

'He was here earlier, sir. He said something about going to interview a couple of suspects, the guys that run the Acme Discount Stores, Martin and Taylor. I assume his DS and driver are with him as well.'

'OK, good. Do we have a number for Acme, or failing that have we got a spare PC with a bike we can send down there? I've got some urgent news and the DCI should return here immediately.'

'Leave it with me, sir.'

Some twenty minutes later the Jaguar XJ12 pulled into the yard at the rear of the police station. Cartwright and Armstrong went straight up to the Superintendent's office.

'You'd better sit down, both of you.' Tickner passed Cartwright the fax. After he had read it, Cartwright passed it to Armstrong. No one spoke. After a few moments, Doug Armstrong could contain himself no longer and the tears began to run down his cheeks. Cartwright leaned across and placed a comforting arm around his shoulders. Tickner rang through to his secretary. 'Could you rustle up three teas please, Deirdre? Quick as you can please.'

'This is one hell of a shock. I knew something was troubling him, but... but...' Even Cartwright had to take a few deep breaths. Armstrong had managed to compose himself.

'When we left here last Friday, Ray didn't say a word during the whole trip back. I knew something was eating him, but I never would have imagined...' Armstrong lost control again.

'I went and sat with him in *The Maybush*. He said something was doing his head in, incredibly stupid, I think he used the phrases, self-delusional, downright foolish, but he wasn't specific about anything. I assumed there was a woman involved.'

'There was.' Armstrong, drying his eyes with his handkerchief told of how, when he'd had *The Carpenter's Arms* under surveillance over a week previously, he had observed Ray Davies pick up Susan Robbins and walk off, arm in arm with her. Tickner was about to speak when Deirdre arrived with the tea.

'Susan Robbins? You mean the girl we'd hired for a probationary period as the post room clerk?'

'The same. They seemed very "friendly" – if you know what I mean.'

'Well, here's a coincidence then...'

'I don't like coincidences!' Cartwright spluttered.

'Mick Willett was sort of overseeing Susan's work. I think he seemed satisfied with it.' Tickner called Deirdre again. 'Deirdre could you ask Mick to join us please, straight away.' Mick knocked and entered a few seconds later.

'Yes, sir?'

'Susan Robbins.'

'Ah yes, sir. I meant to tell you. She's left.'

'What'd you mean left?'

'Left, gone, resigned. She left a note on my desk on Saturday, I think it was dated, Saturday. I think it was. Just a couple of lines tendering her resignation and not to worry about the salary she was owed. Sorry, sir, I should have mentioned it sooner. Is there a problem?'

Willett was put in the picture. He too found the news of Davies' suicide upsetting. Cartwright asked whether Gibbons had called or just sent the fax.

'Just the fax.'

'Doesn't surprise me. After all, I think he regarded Ray as one of my "idiot squad". Wouldn't expect any condolences or sympathy from good old Gibbo! I suppose I'd better call him.'

'Are you going to go back to Ipswich today?' Tickner enquired.

'No, sir, I have to complete the enquiries we're making here. We'll be back for the funeral when we know the date.'

'Right. In the meantime, Mick, find Susan Robbins. We need to have a word.'

***

Bandile Bosch had been happy to hear his daughters' news and couldn't help but smile when they were up early and off jogging again. 'We models have to keep in shape, Papa.' He was on the afternoon shift but with nothing better to do he decided to explore the Central Line a little further than Mile End. He had only ever seen names such as Newbury Park, Hainault, Chigwell on indicator boards and the front of trains and being the conscientious Underground Passenger Liaison Officer that he had now become, he felt it was his duty to know something of such places. When the train emerged from the tunnel at Leyton, daylight came as something of a surprise to Bosch since he had always understood that the underground was, well, underground. So, sitting taking in the scenery, suburbia and the countryside was a real treat, and the real bonus, all for free as an employee.

When the train came to a stop at Blake Hall a woman got on and seeing Bosch in his uniform she approached him. 'You ought to go an' find out what's going on over there.' She nodded in the direction of the station building, the original Blake Hall. 'There ain't 'arf a pen an' ink chucking up, an' I seen rats.' Bosch just squeezed through the doors as they were closing and walked up the platform to the building. There was, as she had described, a pretty awful stench which seemed to be emanating from the building. A small deputation of people was gathered on the platform, some with scarves or handkerchiefs over their mouths and noses. When they saw the uniform, there were a few mutterings along the lines of 'about time too'. Bosch was aware of the Central Line rumour of several stations on the line being considered for closure and recognised this as one of them. The door appeared to be secured with a padlock. Bosch gave it a sharp tug, a technique he had been shown by a colleague at Mile End. The sliding shackle lifted out of the lock and Bosch tentatively opened the door. The onlookers all backed away as several rats ran out and the fetid, foul fumes inside drifted out. Bosch covered his own nose and mouth and very cautiously, one step at a time, entered the building. The scene that greeted him was horrific. Perhaps the most horrendous sight he'd ever had. His mind tore back to a distant memory when, what seemed like a lifetime ago, as a boy, he had come across the rotting, putrid remains of a half-eaten okapi in the bush. There were flies everywhere. Bosch felt nauseous. The bile was rising in his throat. He hurried out of the building and vomited onto the track. He managed to speak to the woman standing apart from the group.

'Get someone to call the police, and then stop the next train and tell the driver to radio the control-room. There is a serious incident here and we need urgent assistance.' The woman seemed to understand from the way she stood nodding, nervously. 'Some air freshener would be welcome as well!' His attempt to lighten the mood did little to ease the woman's anxiety.

Bosch returned to the building and the noxious smell of death. The quarry tiles around the corpses were black with dried blood. Two corpses in an advanced state of decomposition. One much bigger than the other. Not just big but massive. An image of a wrestler he'd seen on TV flashed up in his mind's eye: Giant Haystacks, that was it. This man was similarly built but this man had no face. There was a great mass of hair and beard all matted together with what Bosch knew would be dried blood. There was movement in the eye sockets, and the opening which used to be his mouth: maggots. The body had fallen and spread into a haphazard heap, almost sitting or squatting but slumped. One arm protruded awk-wardly from the heap. Bone was visible where it had snapped and penetrated the skin. The wound through the flesh which was now blackened was also alive with maggots. There was a gun in his hand. An enormous hand in which the gun looked so small. From his apparel he was Muslim. The other man was of a much slighter build and conventionally dressed. His Harrington jacket was stained with dried blood from a bullet hole. He'd been wearing half-moon glasses. These were lying on the floor, one lens broken. As far as Bosch could sur-mise, the smaller man, a Jew, had been shot by the big man, a Muslim. The Muslim had then shot himself. The combina-tion of the sights, sounds and smells was the most repulsive experience of Bosch's existence.

He had seen enough. He retreated to the platform, to the waiting group of onlookers which had multiplied. He pulled the door closed and slipped the padlock back through the staple but didn't snap it shut. Being amongst the living was somehow comforting compared to the carnage, the slaugh-ter on the other side of the door. A southbound train was at the platform, doors closed, passengers gazing out of the windows. Bosch walked over and spoke to the guard. After a few moments two police cars arrived. A Jaguar XJ12, and a 1.8 Morris Marina. Four uniformed officers got out of the Marina, three constables and a sergeant. From the Jaguar emerged Cartwright, Armstrong, Willett and Lewis. Willett and Armstrong went over to speak to Bosch, who gave a brief, but nonetheless detailed, resume of the discovery. The detec-tive sergeants gave each other a look of realisation. Two of the uniformed PCs were deployed in controlling the ever-in-creasing crowd, the sergeant and the other constable were cordoning off the area with tape whilst the detectives entered the building. Their initial reaction was all but identical to Bosch's. A very pale looking Willett came out of the building and from the Jaguar radioed Victoria Park Square for a forensic team and transport to the mortuary at Poplar. He also retrieved his camera.

The detectives were later considering a variety of tragic situations which might have led to the crime scenario. There was one name common to all their theories, Patrick McLevy.

***

The Basto V had arrived in Vlissingen on Zeeland from where Pieter and Susan had taken the train which necessitated a change at Rotterdam. After the picturesque journey to Amsterdam, Susan was beside herself with excitement and could hardly believe she was in one of the most beautiful and romantic cities in the whole of Europe. From the magnificent Central Station they walked hand in hand passed the *Oude Kerk* and through the Red Light District. Susan was captivated. Prostitution organised in such a fashion as to be almost respectable. They passed the Rembrandt Museum from where it was a pleasant stroll alongside the *Reguliersgracht* to the junction with the *Keisersgracht*. Pieter explained that the Kaiser's Canal had been named after the Emperor Maximillian of Austria although he suspected she wasn't listening, her mind on other things.

Other recent arrivals had included Frankie Forsyth. He left the Central Station by following the same route as the man he was due to meet, through the Red Light District, hoping to catch a glimpse of Chantal, but her curtains were closed. Somewhat distracted he took a wrong turn and found himself in *Rosemarijusteeg*. Parked by the side of the road outside *Kadinsky's Coffee Shop* was a vehicle he was certain he'd seen before. He stopped, lit a No.6 and paused for a few moments. When he saw what was being unloaded he had total recall. It was the same dark blue VW Transporter. It was Hashim

Abidi and his cousin, and they were delivering cartons of vodka, lime juice cordial, teabags and digestive biscuits to the coffee shop. Not for the first time, he thought, 'This is bizarre.' He continued on his walk and when he found himself at the *Waldorf Astoria Hotel*, he decided to check in. Expensive? Yes, but he was currently loaded. He knew that Pieter Hendriks' house was only a short distance from the hotel, so there was time to take advantage of a freshen up and the mini bar.

Five minutes before the appointed time, Frankie rang the doorbell at Pieter Hendriks' house and his housekeeper answered the door.

'Meneer Hendriks verwacht u. Kom binnen alsjeblieft.' Frankie followed the housekeeper up a flight of stairs and into an extremely elegant sitting room furnished with all manner of expensive antiques. He immediately stood stock still. There was Susan Robbins. The chair was a Tisbury high-backed Chesterfield chair with Howard arms, covered in Zefferino emerald floral fabric. He recognised it as one he'd previously acquired for Pieter during the early days of their friendship. Susan was sitting in it and for all the world looked to be as comfortable and at home as the lady of the house would be.

'Wotcha, Frankie! Pieter said he was expecting you.'

'Susan, seein' you 'ere! Crikey, you coulda knocked me down with a feather.'

Pieter was seated at a mahogany escritoire engrossed in some paperwork, smoking his pipe. 'Ah, Francis *mijn vriend*. Welcome! Good to see you in Amsterdam again. You know Susan, of course?' Pieter rang a little bell that he took from a vintage Edwardian oval inlaid mahogany two-tier occasional table. Almost immediately the housekeeper reappeared.

'Meike, *breng alsjeblieft een fles Jenever en drie glazen mee.* I assume you like a drop of our Dutch equivalent to your London gin?' The bottle and three glasses duly arrived and Meike set the tray down on the table. Pieter poured generous measures.

'So how did it go with Toussaint in Paris?'

'Like a dream, mate. Like a dream. No hassle, an' I 'ope you'll be 'appy with the result.' He took two envelopes from an inside pocket on both sides of his suit jacket and handed them to Hendriks. 'Sorry it's in francs. I thought you'd know a place for the best exchange rate. Anyway, look there's 201600 French in there.'

Pieter put his pipe down and took the envelopes.

'*Goed, heel goed inderdaad!* Very good indeed, Francis, you have done well.' He removed a painting of a girl with a pearl earring from the wall to reveal a safe into which he placed both envelopes, closed the door and spun the dials. As he replaced the painting he announced, 'It's not the genuine Vermeer unfortunately.' They all laughed, although Susan wasn't entirely sure what he was referring to.

The next hour or so was spent in small-talk and how, after their introduction in Pedley Street, arranged by Frankie, Susan and Pieter had become such good friends. Frankie was given a tour of the house, all four floors. Of special interest was the workshop in an attic room. There on the workbench were the tools of Pieter's former trade as a lapidary. Susan became animated and gabbled on a bit as the prospect of cutting and polishing her raw stones was spoken of. No mention was made, however, of where they had come from or how she came by them. The evening wore on.

'I expect you are tired, Francis. I hope you'll be staying for a few days to see my Art Deco palisander and Pugin table installed. I do hope they're having a safe crossing. I will arrange for us to have dinner with Jan de Klerk amongst others in a few days' time. I hope that's OK with you?'

'I shall look forward to it. Thanks for the gin. I'm off to see my Chantal now!' The men shook hands and Susan gave Frankie a peck on the cheek.

***

Having detected as much as there was to detect at the Blake Hall crime scene, Cartwright, Armstrong, Willett and Lewis left as soon as the forensic investigators arrived. Back at Victoria Park Square nick Superintendent Tickner was being treated to a vivid description.

'I'm glad you're here, Cartwright. We're currently without a DI. Sure we have DS Willett, for all that Mick's a good man, he doesn't have your experience. I've telephoned CS Gibbons and he's quite happy for you three to stay here for a while, in fact I'd say more than happy.'

'Right-ho. Quite how we'll identify either of the corpses I'm not sure. The Muslim fellow especially. I'm not even sure they'll get him to the mortuary in one piece. The little bloke we'll assume to be Jewish from his skull cap. Doug, you and Mick do a trawl of local synagogues, see if there's anyone who might be prepared to take a look – see if we can get a positive identification. Andy, yours is a longer shot. Have a go at the local mosques. Somebody somewhere will know the big guy. Shame we've not got Davies here to give you a hand.' Everyone was momentarily subdued.

Chapter 34 **Thursday**

For the most part the trip across the North Sea had been fairly uneventful. It proved to be an enormous relief to Liam O'Reilly to have Patrick, an experienced, competent seaman, on board. *The Eamon de Valera* hadn't got far down the Thames before it became apparent to Liam that Patrick was a far better hand than Fergal, his liability of a brother-in-law. Daylight was fading as they approached the Oaze Deep. Off to starboard, the chilling distant silhouettes of the Red Sand Towers were a stark reminder of WWII. Intended to protect London and the Thames Estuary from German attacks from air and sea they weren't actually built until after the Blitz. However, these nautical bastions, along with the Shivering Sands Forts some four miles further eastwards, shot down 22 aircraft and 30 V1 flying bombs and no doubt saved many, many lives. The ship followed a north-easterly course up the Knock Deep Channel and after three hours, the quick flashing light characteristic of the Long Sand Head buoy came into view. Off to port they could see the Sunk Light Vessel and Patrick plotted the course change for the Noord Hinder Light Vessel. Alternating a watch of two hours, the skipper was on the helm as dawn was breaking. There was a considerable amount of shipping coming and going, in and out of the deep-water route to and from Hoek van Holland and

246

Rotterdam but nothing to concern *The Eamon de Valera* which would pass to the north. Patrick had made breakfast and he joined Liam in the wheelhouse. The chimneys of the IJmuiden steelworks were now visible and the entrance to the *Noordzeekanaal* beckoned. It was well into the afternoon when they finally tied up in the *Jan van Riebeeckhaven* and both men went ashore to find a bar and a telephone.

Some time later, a dark blue VW Transporter pulled up on the quay alongside *The Eamon de Valera*. After a few seconds a black Porsche 911 drew up behind the van. From out of the van the familiar figures of Hashim Abidi and his cousin appeared. From the Porsche emerged Pieter Hendriks, Susan Robbins and, just managing to extricate himself from the rear seat, Frankie *the Fence* Forsyth.

'Bloody hell! What's this, a fucking reunion? A right bleeding reception committee!'

'Steady on there, Patrick, there's a lady present,' suggested Frankie.

'Excuse my Dutch,' apologised Patrick. This amused Pieter.

'Forgive my curiosity, Pieter, but when you said you'd arranged transport...'

'Ah, Francis, you mean my friend Hashim. Hashim has moved all manner of things for me in the past. Twice, I think he carried cannabis to England for me. But now, by road is too dangerous, *te riskant*, how you say, risky? So, I choose you and Liam's ship. Now he will move my palisander sideboard and my table. No damage I hope, Liam?'

'Oh no, sir, all safe and sound.'

'OK, Hashim, if you will...' The cousin had opened the rear doors and Frankie's curiosity was redoubled. The van was completely empty.

Two days later and having had their fill of the Red Light District, coffee shops and *Amstel*, Liam O'Reilly and Patrick McLevy boarded *The Eamon de Valera* and slipped away via the *Noordzeekanaal*, the North Sea and the English Channel on a course to Ireland. They were never seen again.

***

Following his horrific discovery at Blake Hall, his manager at London Transport gave Bandile Bosch the rest of the day off. The apartment in Bacon Street was empty. Stellen and Kirsten had both gone to Soho and the *Imagery Photo Studio* in Brewer Street. They were welcomed by a young woman chewing gum and wearing denim dungarees and precious little else. She introduced herself as Ali.

'Dai's with another client at the moment but he shouldn't be long now.' And he wasn't.

'Hello, ladies, let me guess, you'll be Gerry's girls right?' He offered his hand and Kirsten wasn't sure from his mannerisms whether she was supposed to shake it or kiss it. In the event she did neither. They were led upstairs and along a dimly lit corridor with peeling wallpaper to a sparsely furnished room with one wall covered in tinfoil. On a couple of stands there were what appeared to be umbrellas, and on another a large floodlight. On a sofa there was a white sheepskin rug.

'Now then, don't be shy, just be natural. I'll take a couple of you together, just as you are, if you'd like to take off your jackets. You'd be amazed how many people like to get it on with twins.' Ali positioned the girls in front of a white screen and switched on the floodlight. 'OK, babes, just be natural, look at the camera, try and look coy, you know, tip of the tongue just between the lips... that's it, lovely, and another one.' The camera was clicking away. 'OK, now the nude shots, one at a time I think.'

Stellen and Kirsten looked at each other with apprehensive misgivings bordering on trepidation.

'Mr Hunt never said anything about posing naked.'

'Now look, love, don't waste my time. If you want the work, people want to see what they're paying for. Now get your kit off or leave.'

With a hesitant nervousness, they undressed.

'You can put your clothes over here.' Ali pointed at a chair.

'OK, who's first, Kirsten is it? Right you are, babe, lounging on the sofa, I think. Mmm, nice, oh yes, lovely!' The camera whirred away and then it was Stellen's turn.

'You sure you've not done this before? You're natural, both of you.' Sheepishly, the girls walked off the set to recover their clothes.

'I'll get the prints to Gerry in a couple of days, and I'll be seeing you two in the mags before long I reckon.' Dai blew kisses in their direction as they were getting dressed. Ali showed them out.

'Not quite what I was expecting,' remarked Kirsten.

'Me neither,' replied Stellen, 'but if, like he said, we might be in magazines...'

When they got home, Bandile was preparing a meal.

'How'd it go then, girls?' Their responses were fairly non-committal. Neither of them made any reference to the seedier side of the experience.

***

When the seventeenth-century Swedish cabinet was delivered to Melton Hall, Anna had carefully removed the protective coverings and began to give it a good dusting and polish. She could not believe her luck when she discovered several packets of herbal cannabis concealed in some the cabinet's inner compartments. 'What should I do?' went through her mind. 'Surely the Judge doesn't know that he's bought a cupboard full of weed – or does he? Maybe he likes a spliff now and again.' Anna took the bags and, upon consideration, decided that a man in the Judge's position would not be a user. It would be for her use, and she secreted it away back in the cabinet's inner compartments.

***

Doug Armstrong and Mick Willett initially identified four synagogues from somewhere in the region of 40 in the East End. Between them, they decided that taking two each would prove to be a far more productive use of their time than doubling up. Hoping to get lucky and not have to check any others, Mick took the East London Synagogue in Nelson Street in the Whitechapel area which left Doug Sandy's Row and Bevis Marks near Spitalfields Market. Doug was curious.

'How come there are so many Jews, so many synagogues in East London?'

'Tenement buildings, cheap living, markets, there always were a lot of Jews in East London and then a great many more arrived to escape persecution in Eastern Europe and Russia. Probably about a quarter of a million now. That synagogue on your list, Bevis Marks, is reckoned to be the oldest in London. Worth a look inside.'

'And we're trying to identify one man out of so many – bloody needle in a haystack already, my boy.'

The detectives went their separate ways agreeing to meet back at *The Brick Lane Tap Room* to compare notes. By lunchtime, neither Armstrong nor Willett had enjoyed even the remotest sniff of a clue and sat in the bar somewhat dejectedly thinking about how their afternoon would have to be spent. Police work at its most arduous.

'Is that Andy over there?' Willett had spotted Lewis through the window on the opposite side of the road. He went outside and called him over.

'We've drawn a blank. How'd you get on then?'

'Result!' boasted Andy. 'I was talking to the Imam just down the road at East London Mosque in Commercial Road' – he referred to his notes – 'Hazrat bin Khattab. When I described our corpse, all 50 stone or more maybe, the mass of black hair and a beard, he reckoned he knew him... a Rashid Kahn Baba, named after some legendary Pakistani geezer. Bit of a rum bloke by all accounts, Pakistani, wrestler. Did a bit of fetching and carrying for a drug baron named only as Mr Khan.'

'Well done. It's a start I suppose, and if drugs are involved, might give us a motive.'

Together the three of them walked back in the direction of Bethnal Green.

'Have you tried the synagogue down Cheshire Street, the United Working Men's?'

'Might be worth a look since we're passing.'

'Good afternoon, gentlemen, I am Rabbi Levi Metzenbaum. How may I help?' Doug Armstrong introduced himself and colleagues and gave a resume of the information they were seeking. The description of the smaller of the corpses was sketchy at best and the Rabbi wasn't being very helpful.

'Ah, the police. You in trouble again, Rabbi?'

'Isaac, maybe you can help. Do we have a slightly built man, sixties, half-moon spectacles, in our community? Seems he was wearing maroon-coloured corduroy trousers and moccasin-type shoes, collarless shirt with a sleeveless pullover, a Harrington style jacket... Sorry, Sergeant, this is one of our regulars, Isaac Goldmann.'

'Sounds like Jacob. Jacob Kahn. He always wore those

maroon trousers, and the glasses. Could be Jacob for sure – and I've not seen him in a while. I went to collect him – we play Bridge you know – but he wasn't in. The man staying at his house told me that he'd gone to sort out a problem with one of his business interests and could be away for a few days.'

'There was a man staying at his house?'

'Yes, a friend I guess. I brought him here, Rabbi, remember, Patrick McLevy?'

'Mr Goldmann, thank you so much. You've been more help than you'll ever know. I'm sorry to have to tell you that Jacob Kahn is dead, we believe he may have been murdered.' Both the Rabbi and Isaac began a unison recital of something in Hebrew. Armstrong waited a few moments out of respect and then took down Isaac Goldmann's contact details and Jacob Kahn's address. He also ascertained that, if necessary, he would be available for identification purposes.

The three sergeants left the synagogue in a hurry, on a mission, direct to the address in Fournier Street. No answer. Lewis found a telephone box and rang Victoria Park Square nick and gave Cartwright a full report on their findings.

'Brilliant! That bastard McLevy again. I reckon we've got him this time. Wait there, don't break in until I get there. I'm on the way.'

Cartwright arrived in a marked 1.8 Marina along with two PCs, one with a ram which made pretty short work of opening the door. Apart from a few cushions in a heap and a pile of bed linen and blankets any furniture that there might have been had gone. In the kitchen there was cutlery and crockery, pots and pans, and in the refrigerator a half pint of milk which had turned sour.

'So, it seems our bird has flown – again! Any thoughts anyone?'

'It has to be him!' Mick was emphatic. 'We were on the

same tube. We were going to Theydon Bois, he got off at Blake Hall.'

'And gave us the finger,' Doug reminded everyone.

'At every damn turn since we first encountered those bloody corn flakes, the name McLevy crops up. We'll issue a warrant for his arrest and circulate a wanted notice.'

'Might not have to, guv, if he turns up for his court appearance in the morning.'

Chapter 35 **Friday**

On the pavement below his bedroom window the dawn chorus of old men coughing as they queued for their *Daily Mirror* and packet of *Park Drive* from the newsagent next door woke Lewis. He packed his weekend bag the previous evening and was up and out within ten minutes. The Jaguar was in the yard at Victoria Park Square and the brisk walk from his Brick Lane bedsit took a little under another ten minutes. He collected Cartwright and Armstrong from their hotel and they were now on their way through Ilford and Dagenham, homeward bound on the A12. There was no time to lose, given that McLevy's hearing was scheduled at the Ipswich Crown Court for 10.00am. Cartwright was expecting to be called to give evidence. First, they all needed to get home for a change of clothes. After court was Ray Davies' funeral.

Potential jurors were waiting in the jury room. His Honour Judge Richard Bertrand was waiting in his robing room. 10.00am came and went, and neither judge nor jury were called. The defendant had failed to appear.

'Well there's a surprise! We could have had him bang to rights this morning. Did you notice from your interviews with Isaac Goldmann and the Imam that our corpses are Kahn and Khan: one a Jew, English but with Polish parents, and the other a Pakistani? When he was house-sitting in Fournier Street McLevy told Goldmann that Kahn, Jacob Kahn, the Jew that is, had gone to Pakistan. Surely, if anyone had gone to Pakistan it would have been Khan.'

'Didn't spot that, guv.'

'That's why I'm a DCI and you're still both DSs,' Cartwright joked. 'Anyway, it's all academic. They're both dead and McLevy's legged it somewhere.'

'Sir?' From the look on his face, Lewis had been thinking.

'Yes, Andy?'

'Down in Bethnal Green I've heard several mentions of a Mr Khan, a Mr Big drug baron by all accounts. You don't suppose Jacob Kahn or Rashid Khan could be him do you?'

'Crikey, Andy! Good point. That hadn't occurred to me.'

'And I'm only a sergeant, guv, not a DCI!'

***

Anna Cohen set about making soup for the Judge's supper. He had mentioned that he would be sitting in the Crown Court. 'Some ex-Navy chap, fellow of the name McLevy.' What random chapter of misfortune had befallen Anna's brother that he should be appearing before her employer?

His Honour always favoured home-made soup after a day in court. With the leeks and potatoes prepared, and ready to boil, Anna was overcome with a wave of delinquent devilry. She crushed several leaves from a cannabis plant and, with a sprinkle of mixed herbs, added them to the soup.

Later that evening after supper as Anna was clearing away, the Judge remarked that the soup was simply the best he'd enjoyed in a long time. Anna thanked him for the compliment. Her initial smile developed into a chuckle, a giggle, and by the time she got to the scullery a full-blown belly-laugh.

From that day forward soup-of-the-day always contained the extra herbal ingredient.

***

When they arrived at the crematorium in Cemetery Lane, Ipswich, the occupants of the Jaguar XJ12 were in sombre mood. There were already several cars in the car park including a few marked ones. Cartwright was aware that Davies had lost both his parents in a road traffic accident when he was a teenager, after which he had been brought up by his grandmother in the house she left to him when she died a few years ago. That was the extent of Ray's background of which Cartwright was aware.

'Did he have any family, Doug?'

'I think there's an older sister, lives up north somewhere. He never spoke about her. His mates were all coppers. The force was his life. That must have been something fairly catastrophic to have driven him to top himself.' Doug's eyes were welling up.

In the West Chapel there were more empty pews than occupied ones. A middle-aged woman with a teenaged girl and a man sat in the front pew on the left. Cartwright assumed these to be Ray's sister, brother-in-law, and niece. On the second row, there were several uniforms including Superintendent Tickner who had made the effort. Conspicuous by his absence was Chief Superintendent Gibbons who hadn't. Cartwright, Armstrong, Lewis, Rudd, Mennens and Randall sat in the front row on the right. Several members of the civilian staff at Kesgrave, mainly young secretarial assistants, sat a little further back as did the landlord and lady from *The Maybush*. In all, a total of 24 people. 'Not much of a send-off is it?' thought Cartwright.

A recording of Jimi Hendrix's 'The Wind Cries Mary'

announced the arrival of the cortege, with the plain wooden coffin borne on the shoulders of six uniformed constables. The small congregation stood. The coffin was placed on trestles at the front of the chapel and the pallbearers retired to the rear. Ray's sister placed a small floral tribute on the coffin. A clergyman intoned the opening words of the funeral service.

We brought nothing into this world, and it is certain we can carry nothing out. The Lord gave and the Lord hath taken away; blessed be the name of the Lord. I am the resurrection and the life sayeth the Lord: he that believeth in me, though he were dead, yet shall he live, and whosoever liveth and believeth in me shall never die.

'Never did understand much of this malarky,' whispered Armstrong.

'Don't worry, I won't be doing any God-bothering,' Cartwright whispered back.

After a few more minutes of sham piety it was obvious that the vicar knew nothing of the deceased in the coffin and was merely going through the motions. He announced Cartwright.

'Detective Chief Inspector Cartwright will now say a few words.' In truth the DCI had had neither the time nor the inclination to prepare a eulogy. Instead, he opted for a quote from Shakespeare's *King Lear*. He rose from the pew and stood at the lectern.

'The weight of this sad time we must obey,
Speak what we feel; not what we ought to say.
The oldest hath borne most: we that are young,
Shall never see so much, nor live so....'

And that was as far as he got before he decided he couldn't continue and left the chapel.

'Would you please stand for the committal.
  To everything there is a season and a time to every purpose on earth, a time to be born and a time to die...'
The strains of 'All Along the Watchtower' were faded in and ultimately drowned out the vicar. The congregation filed out of the chapel.

No wake as such had been organised but, it being a Friday, most of the Kesgrave complement would have been at *The Maybush* anyway, and it was in that general direction that a procession of police vehicles now proceeded. When the Jaguar arrived, Cartwright made his way into the pub and could not believe his eyes. Standing at the bar, in civilian clothes, a pint in hand, was Gibbons.

'I'm not one for funerals and I couldn't bring myself to attend, I hope you'll understand. Still, I'm sure we can put our differences aside for this evening, oh, and by the way, the bar tab tonight is on me.' Not only could Cartwright not believe his eyes, he was having trouble with his ears as well. Then to cap it all his wife walked in.

'Helen, what are you doing here?'

'Taking care of you. I thought you might be a bit fragile.'

'Yes I am, and it's going to get worse as the night wears on – and Gibbo's paying! Pints all round!'

Chapter 36 **Saturday**

Dai's photographs of Kirsten and Stellen had been processed and returned from the printer. Dai was mightily impressed. In colour and black and white these were without a doubt some of the best shots he'd ever taken. The subjects looked stunning, the prints were magnificent glossy 8 x10s. He was so thrilled with them he took a cab directly to Pedley Street.

'Just look at these, Berkshire, you'll go a long way to see anything better. Ravishing, oozing sex appeal yet retaining gracefulness, poise, what can you say? If ever there was a centrefold, these are it, both of them, dazzlers.'

'Dai, old love, you're not wrong. They are indeed amazing. Gorgeous. But then I told you they were beauties. Did they put up much resistance to stripping off?'

'Just a little hesitation that's all. I don't think there'll be any problem on that front. So, what's your plan?'

'These girls are just too divine. Just looking at them is an orgasmic experience. A career as an East End tart is not for them. No sir! No, I think I'll put them on display in a window in Amsterdam. Show them off to the high rollers. The more they make, the more I'll make. Speaking of which, what do I owe you?'

'Nowt. I've already taken the liberty. *Come Again* magazine have already taken them for next week's edition.'

That evening, Gerry called at the Bacon Street apartment where Kirsten and Stellen were watching television. Bandile was on a late shift.

'Get your coats, girls, we're celebrating.' They were soon settled in a quiet corner of *The Carpenter's* with a bottle of cheap champagne, not that the girls would have known *Spumante* from *Bollinger*. Gerry produced the prints from a manilla folder.

'Phwoar...' There was a roar right behind Stellen. It was Matt slobbering into his lager.

'Matthew, we enjoy your company, sometimes but not right now. I am advising these lovely girls on their vocational calling, something you would know less than nothing about. If you would like to study these portraits, then buy next week's *Come Again*. I don't wish to be rude, but just go away for now. Please!'

'*Come Again*? What, the girly magazine? Are we going to be in *Come Again*?'

'Well,' hesitated Gerry, 'yes.' He wasn't sure what sort of reaction to expect. 'How do you feel about that?' The girls looked at each other, shrieked and hugged each other.

'How exciting! Oh, Gerry, thank you, you fixed it for us.' Gerry sat there beaming, proud of what he'd *fixed* – which in truth was not a lot.

'Now, girls, calm down, it doesn't end there. You've both got an audition.'

'What, a show?'

'Well, sort of, but not exactly. You'll see when we get there.'

'Where?'

'Amsterdam. We're going to Amsterdam. I'll pick you up after lunch.'

Using Jacob Kahn's white Range Rover but with false number plates Gerry picked up his future starlets from their apartment in Bacon Street. Using some of his £3k commission, he'd bought British European Airways tickets from Gatwick Airport to Schiphol. He'd also prebooked one single and one double room at the Amsterdam Waldorf Astoria. The girls had bought themselves matching outfits and for all the world looked like Miss World contestants. Bosch's daughters had never known anything like it. The luxury of their room! Bath robes, shampoo, perfumed soap, soft towels, a hairdryer, a minibar: it was all a dream.

Downstairs in the lounge they were sitting on barstools taking it all in and drinking expensive Martinis rather too quickly.

'Girls, the Martini is known for its allure and sophistication. So should you be. Slow down please.'

'Sorry, Gerry. It's all so exciting. I could wet myself,' giggled Stellen.

'Keep drinking like that and you will,' responded Kirsten. Then, as if out of nowhere came a familiar voice.

'Well, I'll go to the foot of our stairs! Berkshire, 'ow's it 'angin'? What the fu... 'scuse me, ladies... what're you doin' 'ere? Sorry, 'ow rude. This is Chantal, my lady friend. Chantal this is Gerald, a business 'sociate from London. *Aangenaam kennis te maken*. Pleased to meet you.' The last person Gerry had expected to see was Frankie. But, thinking about it, he could turn this chance encounter to his advantage knowing that Chantal worked in the *industry*.

'Pleased to meet you too, Chantal. Allow me to introduce my two proteges, Kirsten and Stellen. I'm hoping I can get them into the business.' There was that discreet tapping the side of the nose gesture again.

'*Ik denk dat ik het begrijp*. I think I understand. Maybe I can help. *Hallo Meiden*.'

There seemed to be an instant bonding as the three girls held each other in a group hug.

More Martinis followed for the girls who were becoming bosom pals in more ways than one, whilst Frankie and Gerry chatted away over *Amstels* with *Jenever* chasers.

***

It hadn't been quite the same without Frankie on the terraces, but Matt and Tom couldn't get over the fact that West Ham had beaten Chelsea 3–0. Celebrations were well underway in *The Carpenter's*. It was noted that Gerry was also missing on parade. Still, never mind, their loss.

Before they'd left to go to *The Blind Beggar,* as per usual on a home game, they'd taken delivery at the Acme Discount Stores of a big box of refillable *Clipper* gas-lighters. The discerning purchaser upon looking a little more closely would have noticed that these were not actually *Clipper* but *Chipper* lighters. A second even bigger box containing butane cylinders were of an equally dubious provenance. Several of the cylinders were leaking.

***

Bandile Bosch was sitting at home, alone, studying the various pamphlets he'd been given by London Transport. He was enjoying his newly promoted position but always seeking ways in which to improve himself. He hadn't noticed it right away, but his daughters had left a note. They didn't want him worrying about their whereabouts.

Hello Papa, our modelling portraits have been printed and there's a chance of work in Amsterdam. We've gone for an audition. Gerry is with us acting as our agent and taking care of us. You wouldn't believe the hotel! It's fabulous. Love you Papa.

'Wow, Amsterdam eh?' he thought. Bandile had read about Amsterdam. It had always been one of the top five cities in the world he wanted to visit. In particular, the museums were what interested him, especially *the Rijksmuseum*, with its magnificent exhibit of some eight thousand works including those by Reubens, Rembrandt, and Vermeer. Maybe if his daughters got jobs there he could visit, a holiday, sightseeing. Meanwhile, he was back to his reading. Perhaps there was an opportunity for him to become a driver. Drivers were well paid.

***

Cartwright had spent the morning tidying the garden in an absent-minded sort of way. He couldn't help but think there was something he'd missed at Melton Hall. The way things were, there was precious little chance of recovering the stolen antiques, they were long gone. But his self-esteem demanded that he brought the perpetrators to justice. It was, after all, his professional obligation and Cartwright had always maintained a strong sense of duty. The oath he swore all those years ago when he attested amongst other things ... *to prevent all offences against people and property ... to the best of my skill and knowledge* was indelibly branded on his memory. He decided to visit Melton Hall again after lunch.

Anna Cohen answered the door and Cartwright introduced himself.

'DCI Cartwright, Suffolk police. I hope it's not inconvenient but...'

Mrs Cohen interrupted, 'If you've come to see the Judge, you've had a wasted trip. He's not here I'm afraid. He's gone shooting for the weekend.' The image of some flunky trotting dutifully behind His Honour carrying his Purdy shotgun, with himself in his plus-fours and a deerstalker only served to compound the DCI's low opinion of Judge Bertrand.

'No matter, Mrs Cohen. I came to talk to you as much as anyone and to have another look at the crime scene, so to speak.'

'Oh well, you better come in then. I'll make you a cup of tea.'

While Mrs Cohen was making tea, Cartwright carefully examined the suspected point of entry again. There were still traces of fingerprint dusting powder on the frame of the French windows. A key was in the lock. He unlocked the door and stepped out onto the patio. 'Nothing out of the ordinary,' he thought, 'although I would have thought the Judge would employ a gardener and not take too kindly to having rubbish left lying about.' There was an empty box, the flimsy sort that greengrocers use, propped up against the wall. Stencilled on the side of the box but very faded he could just make out *Webb's Sidcup*.

'Tea, Chief Inspector!' Cartwright stepped back inside carrying the box. 'Any idea where this might have come from, Mrs Cohen?'

'Yes, Gilbert picked it up in the drive a week or so back. Gilbert's the handyman cum gardener. He reckons the wind blew it into the grounds. He uses it for the weeds when he's, you know, weeding.'

'I see. Apologise to Gilbert, but I'm going to take it away. It might be an important piece of evidence. Oh, and there's the cabinet the Judge bought from Berkshire Antiques. Do you mind if I take a look?' Mrs Cohen was hesitant, but even before she answered Cartwright had opened one of the doors. The intensity of the smell hit him immediately and he took a step backwards, wrinkling his nose.

'I think the previous owner must have kept herbs and spices in there.' Mrs Cohen was trying to be helpful.

'Wouldn't surprise me if there were still some in here.' Cartwright opened one of the inner cupboards and pulled out a bag of cannabis.

'Oh dear, Mrs Cohen, what have we got here? Would you like to explain?' She burst into tears. 'It was in there when the cabinet was delivered, honest, Inspector. I use a little bit, the oil's good for my arthritis, it's my joints you know.'

'Yes I'm sure it is,' responded Cartwright with a hint of sarcasm. 'Does the Judge know about this?'

'No, but he has some in his soup. Helps him relax, so he says.'

'Now, Mrs Cohen, may I call you Anna? Anna, we know you've got previous for possession. I think it will help if you come clean now. I'm going to have to caution you I'm afraid. Tell me the truth now.'

'Oh dear,' she sobbed. After ten minutes Cartwright had the entire story, almost her life history. He found it incredible that it was only now he was finding out about Anna's relationship with Frankie Forsyth as her supplier, and beyond belief that her maiden name was McLevy, Patrick's sister. Why did he not know this?

'Have you told the Judge that the defendant who was due to appear before him on Friday was your brother?'

'No, sir.'

There was no doubt in Cartwright's mind that this latest revelation provided the link that involved all the elements of his recent workload. Smuggling, corn flakes, cannabis, stolen jewellery, stolen antiques, stolen vehicles, two dead bodies and, on the side for good measure, an abduction and rape. At least he could now identify the whole team. Gerry Hunt, Frankie Forsyth, Patrick McLevy, Liam O'Reilly, Fergal Flaherty, Tommy Martin, Matt Taylor. Problem was all but two of them had gone walkabout, disappeared. Abroad more likely than not. A call to Victoria Park Square with the instruction to arrest Taylor and Martin was the next step. What was that he'd said, 'Give me some proper policing to do.'

Chapter 37 **Sunday**

The sound of the explosion was heard as far away as Aldgate, Whitechapel, Liverpool Street, Shoreditch. Residents in the immediate Pedley Street locality were denied their Sunday morning lie-in. What was left of the Acme Discount Stores frontage didn't amount to much more than the *Road Runner* cartoon character and even he looked a bit shell-shocked. A spark from the shutter's electric motor ignited the butane which had been leaking from the unsound cigarette lighter cylinders for almost 24 hours. The force of the blast had thrown both Tommy and Matt across the street. Happily, they only suffered minor contusions. Not so happily, the contents of the arch were now ablaze, with further explosions from time to time. Next door, the shutter at Berkshire's Antiques was beginning to buckle from the heat and it was only a question of time before the contents of the showroom would go up in smoke as well. A crescendo of sirens from emergency service vehicles could be heard as they approached, and the area was soon cordoned off. Two appliances from the London Fire Brigade's Islington and Hackney Division arrived first, followed by a third from the Barking and Dagenham Division. A crowd of spectators had gathered, and vast clouds of smoke were billowing. In the early morning light, the scene was reminiscent of the Blitz.

'Did you take the cash tin home yesterday?'

'You know I did. You saw me pick it up before we went to *The Beggar*.'

'Just checking. There must be best part of three grand in it.'

'What we goin' to do?'

'Scarper!'

A squad of uniformed police from Victoria Park Square police station had arrived and were effectively managing to keep the onlookers under control, every one of whom was too engrossed in the spectacular inferno they were witnessing to notice Tom and Matt disappear in the direction of Bethnal Green Tube Station. At Mile End they decided to have breakfast and take stock of their situation. They got off the train and waited for the lift. When the lift doors opened they were greeted by the gleaming white smile of the Passenger Liaison Officer.

'Morning, Tommy, Matt, you're up early.'

Bosch was full of *joie de vivre* and excited by his daughters' news which he simply had to impart. '...and they're staying with Gerry in a posh hotel in Amsterdam. *The Waldorf Astoria*, no less.'

'What? Gerry's in Amsterdam? Well thank fuck for that.'

Back at the Pedley Street blaze, Mick Willett was mingling with the crowd looking for and enquiring after the respective proprietors of the Arches. In his pocket, three arrest warrants.

After several hours the Fire Brigade had the fire under control. The crowd was dwindling, and the police were not too worried about looters. The stock had been too hot to handle even before the fire, and besides which, there was nothing left worth looting now from either the Discount Stores or the Antiques Showroom. DS Willett would not want DCI Cartwright to hear the word *coincidence* even though it was.

An arrest warrant gets issued and their premises burn down. 'They'll all be gutted, the Arches, the proprietors and the guvnor,' he thought. 'And where are they? Tom, Matt, Gerry? Disappeared from the face of the planet. If that's not a coincidence, I don't know what is.'

Back at the apartment they shared, Matt and Tom were pillars of pragmatism.

'I guess we ought to try an' let Berkshire know.'

'Yeah, I reckon. Poor sod. I wonder 'ow much 'e'd got tied up in there? Don't s'pose for a minute 'e was insured.'

'What do you think?'

'Yeah, I know, stupid question.'

'So, your Aunty 'azel's then?'

'Yeah if she's got room.'

Tom's aunt ran a small guest house in Southend. She also had several commercial interests, an ice-cream kiosk, a doughnut stall, and a crazy golf course. She was always looking for preseason help to spruce things up, and then staff to run them through the summer. Matt and Tom would surely fall on their feet.

***

All the great and the good (and the not so good) were gathering at *de Silveren Spiegel* in the *Kattengat*: reputed to be one of the best restaurants in Amsterdam. At the invitation of Pieter Hendriks: Susan Robbins, Frankie Forsyth, accompanied by Chantal, Gerry Hunt, with Kirsten and Stellen, Jan de Klerk, the antique and jewellery dealer, Willem van Dijkstra, one of the curators at the *Rijksmuseum*, and Politie Commandant Ronald Gerritsen were seated at one long table with Pieter at the head. This was to be an experience the likes of which the Bosch girls, Susan and Frankie, had never ever had before.

The array of silver cutlery and the number of glasses in various shapes and sizes at every place setting was bewildering but nonetheless awesome. A wine waiter was working his way around the table, pouring a dry white port as an *aperitif.*

Pieter stood and gently tapped the side of the crystal port glass with a knife to bring everyone to order. The chatter was accordingly silenced.

'Friends, *vrienden*, thank you for your attendance this evening for this very special celebratory occasion, *een viering.* This evening marks the end of a very successful year for me, thanks to every one of you here. Successful in terms of profit and keeping clear of Ronald's attention.' This remark caused much hilarity, especially from Ronald. 'It also marks the beginning of my new life, together with a new love: Susan.'

Pieter raised his glass in the manner of a toast, and everyone followed suit: 'Susan.'

Pieter continued, 'After we have had our meal, I would like you all to join me at *Keisersgracht* for a nightcap and a special presentation. So for now, eat drink and be merry. *Omarm de dag en al zijn mogelijkheden!* Embrace the day and all its possibilities!'

The wine continued to flow, and the first of many courses was served. After something like an hour of gastronomic indulgence and near Bacchanalian imbibing, Gerry got to his feet.

'On behalf of my charming and absolutely beautiful escorts, I would like to take this opportunity to thank our host Pieter not only for his most generous hospitality but for the opportunities he and his friends have afforded us, your English associates and collaborators. I am delighted to announce that the sublime gorgeousness on my left and my right will, thanks to the beautiful Chantal and to Commandant Ronald for his endorsement, be joining the ranks of the City's most alluring tourist attractions. Furthermore, and not wishing to take up your time, I publicly acknowledge with the most humble and grateful thanks *Meneer* Jan de Klerk who has invited me to join him as a consultant at *Binenbaum* since my own enterprise in London has sadly ceased to exist. *Heel erg bedankt.*' A round of applause ensued as waiters began delivering the next course.

Three taxis took the dinner guests back to *Keisersgracht* where Meike, Pieter's housekeeper, was waiting to welcome everyone into the richly furnished luxury of the Hendriks' sitting room. When all had gathered Pieter rose from his chair and held his guests' undivided attention.

'I hope you have all had the opportunity to admire my latest acquisitions, the Jules Leleu Art Deco palisander with the exquisite mother of pearl marquetry, and the splendid table by Augustus Welby Pugin, originally commissioned for the English King George IV. I am deeply indebted to my friends Francis and Gerald without whom... well let's say no more.' Frankie and Gerry acknowledged the smattering of applause that followed.

'Francis was also instrumental in bringing the lovely Susan into my life, and to me this is worth so much more than my new furniture.' More applause (and a very embarrassed Susan). 'No, please, enough. So...' He moved over to the Vermeer copy on the wall and removed it to reveal the safe. He rotated the dial this way and that and the tumblers fell into place. From within he took three bundles of bank notes, each bundle in a different currency and secured with a broad elastic band. Frankie recognised the stack of French francs, an amount twice as much at least to that which he had delivered. Standing tall on the Pugin table was the bundle of guilders. The biggest pile, in terms of size and more than likely value, was in sterling.

'I have here a significant sum of money which is superfluous to my requirements, and I am donating the pounds and the francs to the *Rijksmuseum*.' The applause was sponta-neous and genuine.

'Willem, we hope your daughter has fully recovered from her horrific experience and I ask you please to accept not only this donation on behalf of the museum, but also the guilders which are to be put towards the cost of Lotte's education. Before anyone asks, it comes from a benefactor who wishes to remain anonymous. Most of this money has been raised through a shipment of...' he hesitated as if trying to find the right word '...a shipment of let's call it merchandise, which has travelled many miles, sometimes overland through Belgium and France and sometimes to England by land and sea. But *mijn vrienden*, it always returns, having earned much revenue, *winst*.'

Expressions of incomprehension passed from guest to guest until the entire room was staring at Hendriks with looks that demanded an explanation.

'Meike, please.' He gestured towards the double-doors of an adjoining room. Meike opened both doors wide. Everyone moved forward to see what the mystery merchandise was.

'Here, *dames en heren*, is the merchandise awaiting its next adventure.'

The revelation behind the double-doors did nothing in the slightest to enlighten the unknowing, with blank gazes from all but two of the company. They stood looking incompre-hensibly at a monument constructed from cardboard cartons. *Stolichnaya* vodka, lime juice cordial, teabags and digestive biscuits.

Coda **Monday**

Detective Chief Inspector Cartwright was sitting alone in his office idly browsing through the *East Anglian Daily Times*. A report caught his eye.

'Now here's a coincidence!'

Yesterday morning a police patrol stopped a Rolls Royce Silver Shadow which was being driven erratically and in excess of the speed limit on the A12 near Woodbridge. The driver, and owner of the vehicle, His Honour Judge Richard Bertrand, who sits in the High Court in Ipswich was suspected of driving whilst unfit through drink or drugs. He was arrested and taken to Police Headquarters in Kesgrave where he provided a blood sample which later tested positive. He will appear at Ipswich Magistrates Court this morning. When cautioned the Judge said, 'I've only had a bowl of soup.'

DS Armstrong gave a gentle tap on the door and came in.

'Anything new, guv?'

'No. We're no further forward. More like nine yards back with the fire at the Arches. Never mind. Some you win. Here read this and have a laugh.'

Cartwright pointed out the report in the *EADT*.

'Have you ever used that old cop trick of using a

familiar diminutive to denigrate a person's sense of self respect?' Armstrong gave his boss a quizzical look.

'Next time I see His Honour Judge Richard Bertrand I shall greet him with "Wotcha, Dickie old chap. Fancy skinnin' up?"'

***

In Southend Matt and Tom had also been to the newsagent's. They were sitting in the early spring sunshine outside the kiosk on the crazy golf course. Tom was polluting the sea air smoking a cigarette, Matt was studying form in the latest edition of the *Come Again* magazine. He'd flicked through the first half but was now having trouble getting beyond the centrefold with a garish banner headline, *Black Beauties*.